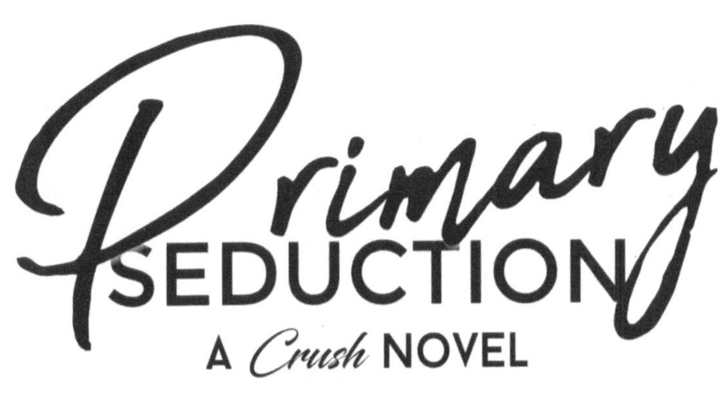

Primary SEDUCTION

A *Crush* NOVEL

ELOUISE EAST

CONTENTS

PRIMARY SEDUCTION

Analise, Bartender at Crush, Friends with Crush group

Asher, Childminder, Sean's boyfriend (Instant Desire)

Ava, Police officer, Trent's sister

Carter, Trent's brother

Catherine, Trent's mother

Charles, Trent's father

Charlie, Bartender at Crush, Josh's boyfriend (First Kiss)

Charlotte, Max's sister

Dane, Zak's son

Eric, Actor, Ethan's brother, Friends with Crush group

Ethan, Architect student, Eric's brother, Friends with Crush group

Frederick, Dom, Max's friend

Gemma, server at Crush

Ginny, Tom's girlfriend, Friends with Crush group

Harper, Trent's youngest daughter

Janie, Asher's niece
Jocelyn, Trent's eldest daughter
Josh, Charlie's boyfriend (First Kiss)
Karen, art gallery curator, Max's friend
Kieren, Dom, Max's friend
Logan, Detective Sergeant, Friends with Crush group
Mavis, Max's neighbour
Max, Interior designer, Siblings: Charlotte and Olivia (Livvy)
Olivia (Livvy), Max's sister
Owen, Gardener, Sean's friend
Rosalia, server at Romano's
Samuel, Lawyer, Trent's brother
Sean, Architect, Asher's boyfriend (Instant Desire)
Tom, Owner of Crush, Ginny's boyfriend
Trent, Teacher, Children: Jocelyn and Harper, Ex-wife: Trish, Siblings: Samuel, Carter, Luke and Ava, Parents: Charles and Catherine
Trish, Trent's ex-wife
Zak, Woodworker, Friends with Crush group

TRENT

Trent coughed into his hand as he parked his car on the driveway. He felt awful, which was why the school had sent him home early. He shouldn't have gone this morning to be honest, but he had arranged for the class to have a special visitor today and hadn't wanted to leave it in the hands of someone else. His class had enjoyed every minute of the firefighters' visit, but once they had gone, his teaching assistant had appeared with the principal. Adele—Mrs Barton—had taken one look at him and sent him packing, taking over his class herself.

He was so glad she had. He was getting worse by the minute; his throat felt like there was broken glass embedded in it, and his head pounded. All he needed was some paracetamol and his bed, in that order.

Trent climbed out of the car, remembering to take his bag with him, and weaved across the driveway to the front door. He knew Trish was at work and the kids were at school, so he didn't yell out that he was there. Dropping his bag to the floor, he stalked to the kitchen where they kept the medicine and filled a glass with water, popping two tablets and drinking the whole glass down. He rinsed the glass and set it on the draining board, frowning when he noticed two unclean mugs next to the sink; he didn't remember them from this morning, but then his memory today was not to be trusted.

He trudged up the stairs, sniffing and coughing along the way. As he reached the bedroom door, he heard noises inside and stopped. His heartbeat ratcheted up; it had never crossed his mind someone might be in the house. He opened the door, expecting to see Trish; maybe she was ill too.

Trent stalked towards the bathroom when he realised the room was empty, distantly noting the spray of clothes across the room. Upon entering, he spied a scene he probably should have been more annoyed by. Trish was in the shower, her back pressed against the tiles, legs wrapped around the waist of a naked guy as he pumped into her. They hadn't noticed Trent standing there.

He blew out a breath and retraced his steps, reaching into the wardrobe for a suitcase. Laying it on the rumpled bed, he turned to the dresser and emptied the contents into the case to the background noise of moans and groans. He rolled his eyes at the crescendo and continued to transfer his belongings. When the case was full, he reached for the empty backpack, placing the items from his bedside table: his charger, book and the photograph of Jocelyn and Harper from when they were on holiday in Spain two years ago.

He heard the shower turn off and conversation start up, but he didn't quicken his movements. His wife wandered into the bedroom just as he zipped up the main part of the bag. She stopped, eyes widening upon seeing Trent stood at the side of the bed.

"Trent, I…" Trish began then stopped when Trent held up his hand.

"No need for explanations, Trish. I'll be out of your hair in a few minutes. I just need a few things from the bathroom before I go." He coughed again, the pain making him wince.

Trish didn't reply as Trent brushed past her, seemingly frozen in place. He entered the bathroom to see the guy—whose face seemed familiar—wrapped in a towel and sat on the toilet seat. Trent glanced at him with his eyebrows raised, then picked up his toiletries before walking back into the bedroom. Packing those items in the side pockets, he placed the backpack on his shoulders and picked up the case, walking around Trish who was now in the process of getting dressed.

"Trent, wait…"

"What do you mean, wait? How many chances do you want? I told you the last time, one more fuck up and I'm gone! I've had it up to here," he said, flinging his hand above his head.

He walked down the steps and deposited his bags by

the front door near his school bag, coughing and sweating with the exertion. He stomped towards the study, grabbing a carrier bag to fill with his school documents. By the time he had finished that, Trish stood by the front door, hands on hips, lips pursed in what Trent knew was annoyance.

"You're overreacting, Trent," she said, dispassionately. "There's no reason for you to leave."

Trent stopped next to her. He cocked his head to the side as his gaze roamed her face. "Yes, there is. The kids are older now and don't need me around as much. You obviously don't need me, and probably never have. Your parents were the ones who wanted us married, remember. If it hadn't been for Jocelyn, you'd have probably been with Tom Clayford now." Tom Clayford was the son of her parents' friends, another wealthy family hoping to keep their status by marrying into good families. Trent had never lived up to her parents' expectations because he came from a lower-class area. They were more than happy to have him marry her when she got pregnant though—to save face with society. He picked up his bags and opened the front door. "I'll be in touch."

"Trent, don't be stupid. You're taking this too far yet again. You always do this when something doesn't go your way." She stomped her foot. "You're being an idiot. You don't have anywhere to go anyway."

Trent was used to Trish's tirades and turned away, ignoring her words. He did have somewhere to go, at least for now.

Trent knocked at the door, case at his feet and hoped his appearance didn't disturb Logan's sleep; he wasn't sure what shift he was on.

Logan's tousled demeanour made Trent apologise instantly. "I'm so sorry, man. I didn't want to wake you."

Logan's gaze dropped to the bags at his feet, then back to his face before he opened the door further, allowing Trent access. "I hope this means you've finally come to your senses?" His usually gravelly voice sounded even rougher from his sleep.

"Yeah." Trent hacked up a lung as he brought the bags into the hallway. Once he'd finished and had gotten his breath back, he turned to find Logan stood with a mug outstretched. Trent took it with a nod of thanks and drank deeply, feeling the soothing flavours of honey and lemon in warm water. Although his throat still felt like it was on fire, it wasn't as agony-ridden as before. "Thanks," he rasped.

"Guest room is already set up with clean sheets. Help yourself. Stay as long as you want." Logan yawned and clapped him on the shoulder. "I'm heading back to bed. I gotta be up in…" he checked the clock on the wall, "…three hours."

"Thanks, man. I appreciate it." Logan left him to it once he'd helped Trent to put his bags in the guest room and told him where the medicine cabinet was.

Trent stared around the room as he sat on the bed. This was his world for the next few days.

Trent had just moved into his newly rented apartment when Trish dropped by with the kids. Now he had a place of his own, the kids were able to stay overnight, and tonight was the first time they'd seen the place. It was also Jocelyn's fifteenth birthday and Trent had a surprise for them.

"This place is awesome, Dad!" Harper shouted as soon as she'd set her bag on the floor. She went walking through the place, looking at everything as she went before disappearing down the hall.

The apartment wasn't huge and came unfurnished, but it had two bedrooms and an open plan kitchen, dining room and living room. It was all he needed although he was sure the kids wouldn't approve of having to share a bedroom. He came up with a contingency plan of a sofa bed for the living area so he could sleep there if they really did kick up a fuss. He'd managed to get some furniture from friends and some from charity shops so at least he had the basics.

"Have you come to your senses yet, Trent?" Trish's disdain about her surroundings was evident on her face. "There is no need to take it *this* far." Trish didn't keep her voice low, yet again making it clear that his opinion wasn't valued, and she didn't care who knew it.

Trent had told the kids that their relationship wasn't working, and they had decided they would be better off apart. Trish hadn't acknowledged the separation at all to the kids, still talking as if Trent was just at work or away for a holiday. She didn't seem to understand that he wasn't going back. So Trent kept talking to the kids, reminding them that they loved them, and it wasn't their fault. Harper had taken it well so far; Jocelyn was a little more reticent about it all.

Trent answered her question quietly. "Trish, enough now, okay. I'm not coming back. You need to get over it." He'd been gone for two weeks, and he was finally finding his way back to being himself. He hadn't realised how much he'd been putting up with from Trish until she wasn't there every day. Now, he could think and figure out what his own thoughts were saying instead of having them interrupted by her voicing her own demands—which he usually caved to.

"You're making a big mistake." Trish pinned him with her gaze, and he saw fury blazing. She turned without a goodbye to the kids and slammed the door behind her, rattling the shelves next to it.

Trent blew out a breath and shook his head, catching Jocelyn looking in the direction of the door.

"Shall I show you around, kiddo?" He purposefully called her that, so she'd focus on that rather than her mother leaving.

"I'm not a kid, Dad," she said in exasperation. "Where's my room?"

Trent braced himself for the onslaught. "This way."

He took her through to their bedroom and, as he expected, when they realised, their voices rose dramatically.

"No way am I sharing with her!"

"Not a chance!"

"Let's go for some dinner, shall we? Romano's?" He said the magic word. They loved that place and didn't go very often because Trish hated it. He had organised a small cake for Jocelyn too. Hopefully that will delay the arguments until they got home later. "Come on."

As they left the apartment, Trent looked back surveying what he'd thought was an empty life until he saw Harper's bag, and then a smile grew across his face. He had done it. He was free.

Max scrolled through the search engine results, seeing nothing new. He rolled his head back on his shoulders, staring at the ceiling for a moment. He was fed up with the same places and people all the time. There had to be something new, *somewhere* new. There had to be. He had visited so many BDSM clubs in the last six months, nothing clicked with him. Nothing felt right.

He stared at the screen, deciding to change his search terms one more time. He blew out a breath, readying to scroll through the same websites and links as before. He got halfway down the first page when an advert on the right-hand side caught his eye.

A white 'A' and a red 'N' on a black filigree background stood out from the usual. There was nothing else there except that: no name, no description, nothing. He clicked it hoping it wasn't a virus, but he was at his wits end, there had to be something out there.

The logo expanded to fill his screen before fading into the top right corner, leaving behind a black background and the word 'Anonymity'. As he waited, a white button appeared beneath the word telling him to 'click for membership details.' He wasn't one hundred percent sure what this was and considered exiting, but something held him back.

He stared at it for a moment longer, then clicked. As he read the terms and conditions, he became more and more excited about it. He had to wait for his checks to come back, which they had warned could take several weeks, but everything seemed right. He completed the application form, paid the membership fee and submitted his details. Now all he had to do was wait.

Seven weeks later, he received his confirmation email containing his login details. He didn't postpone it, just logged in right there and then.

It turned out to be one of the best decisions he ever made.

TRENT

Trent drank heavily from his beer bottle, almost draining it. It was his third and they'd only been at Crush for an hour. He didn't usually drink so quickly, but Trish was wearing him out. She constantly asked for money for the kids—as if he wasn't already paying for the whole of the kids' university funds. She'd asked for money again today to pay for the extra uniform Harper needed, saying she had grown out of it already. He didn't know what happened to her own money, but he could only think it paid for the house that she'd decided to stay in after their break-up. It was a large house, and he'd been surprised when she said she could afford it on her own, but then she did have her parents to help her.

"What's wrong, Trent?" Asher asked when Logan went up to the bar for more drinks. Logan was just about matching Trent drink for drink when usually it was the other way around.

"Trish. Need I say more." He sighed. Trent didn't know what to do about finding the money, but he wasn't going to burden Asher or Logan with his problems more than he already did.

"She's a bloody nightmare. She was while you were married, and she still is now that you're divorced." Asher shook his head. "If it wasn't for your kids…" He left the rest of the sentence silent, but they both knew what he meant. Trent would do anything for those kids, and the problem was, Trish knew it.

Logan dropped down into the seat next to Trent with a round of shots as well as their usual drinks. "I thought we could use these." He placed the shots in front of them. "Ready, go." They slammed the drinks back, Asher coughing his way through it—he had never been able to stand them. When Logan finished his, he cleared his throat, took a drink of his beer and said, "Oh, and there's a woman at the bar who's interested in you, Trent."

Trent spat part of his beer across the table, the shot thankfully already swallowed, or it would've burned like hell coming back up. "What?" he croaked.

Logan smirked at him. He indicated over his shoulder to the bar. "There's a woman at the bar who asked if you were single, so I told her you were. She'll probably come over in a bit." He smiled at Trent. "You're welcome," he said sarcastically.

"Jesus Christ, Logan. I'm not interested, for god's

sake. What did you tell her that for?" Trent was not amused by Logan's proclamation. He had no interest in dating, especially after all the hassle Trish had been giving him. He'd stay a bachelor forever, thank you very much.

"I just answered her question, that's all." Logan drank more of his beer, shrugging.

"Fuck sake, Logan." Trent rubbed at his forehead, trying not to yell at him in the middle of the bar. He didn't have long to wait before the woman came sidling up to their table. Trent watched as she eyed the other two before settling her gaze on him.

"Hi. Your friend here says you're unattached. I'd like to get to know you a little better if you'll let me?" Her voice was soft and melodic, speech not too fast or too slow, words appearing measured; he couldn't figure out what her accent was. She had chocolate-coloured, chin-length hair with a small fringe and dark eyes. Her face was oval shaped, making her chin more prominent, although not large. Her features appeared dainty, almost elfin-like, and she wore tight jeans with rips and a plain black fitted t-shirt.

Trent became aware that she waited for an answer from him. "Um, thank you, but I'm not interested, sorry," he mumbled, glaring across at Logan. Glancing over at the woman again, he caught the frown and disappointment in her expression. "Sorry," he said again, shrugging slightly.

She nodded slowly. "Okay, well if you change your

mind…" She let the sentence taper off, getting her point across.

"Thanks."

Trent watched her walk back to the bar and sit down, raising her hand for the bartender's attention.

"Why didn't you do something about that?" Logan sounded exasperated. "She was perfect for you."

"Because I don't want anyone, Logan. I have enough shit to deal with. I don't want to bring anyone else into it." Trent drank heartily from his beer, ignoring the looks Logan and Asher exchanged. His gaze roamed the room to see if he knew anyone until he stopped on a figure wearing well-fitted black tailored trousers, a white shirt and a beige jacket sitting at the bar, elbows leaning backwards against the counter, flaunting their chest. Trent felt his heart begin to race and the blood heating his body. As Trent's gaze flowed up the figure, his cock rose. He arrived at their face and, even as he felt his arousal flooding his body, he stared in shock at the sight of the man's face. He was gorgeous. Trent frowned. He was a *guy*!

"Who have you seen to get that look in your eyes?" Asher's voice interrupted Trent's perusal. He snatched his gaze back to the beer in front of him, feeling out of sorts. He wasn't gay! Why was he looking at that guy? Trent frowned again, trying to make sense of his emotions. He shook his head, clearing the picture from it and turned back to the conversation.

"Huh?" he said when he realised they were both looking at him.

"Who've seen? You looked smitten," Asher said with a smile.

"Oh, nobody. Just looking around." Trent was *not* going there with them.

"Whatever. Who's up for food?" Logan said.

Logan was always in the mood for food, regardless of the time of day. But then, he did work long hours as a police officer.

"Yeah, I could eat," Trent replied, grabbing the menu. Even though he conversed with Logan and Asher, he couldn't get the vision of that guy out of his head.

By the time he'd gotten home, it was a different matter. He was so drunk that he passed out on his bed the minute his head hit the pillow, clothes and all.

MAX

Max had agreed to do this job because it was good money, and he'd believed he would have a certain amount of freedom to work with. He *had* until the woman had decided to hit on him. She knew he was gay because he'd told her, but she had tried repeatedly to flirt with him and touch him, regardless of his expression of disinterest.

He sat in her dining room, which was the final room he was working on for her. He'd been working with her for a week already and, so far, had completed the lounge, study and her bedroom—that was an experience he never wanted to have again. He couldn't wait for this job to be finished. Max looked at the laptop in front of him, studying the design he'd come up with. He thought it looked fresh, inviting and simplistic—exactly what she had asked for. Oh, and of course, elegant.

This woman had money to burn, apparently. She spared no cost for any of the items he'd purchased for the other rooms, which had made his life a little easier, truth be told. He stood up, grabbing the laptop and going to find out where the woman was. He found her in the lounge, thumbing through a magazine.

"Hi, um, I have the final design for the dining room. Would you like to have a look before I go ahead with it?" Max was a confident person in every aspect of his life, especially his design business, but this woman put him on edge.

"Oh, yes, great. Come sit by me, and you can show me." She pushed the magazine to the side and patted the seat next to her.

He hesitated for a split second, then went and sat where she'd indicated. He kept the laptop on his knee but turned it towards her. Even though he knew she could see, she pressed her breasts against his upper arm as she leaned forward to look. He winced but didn't pull away as much as he wanted to.

"Oh, these look wonderful. So stylish. Yes, it's perfect. Thank you, Max," she purred. There was no other word for it. She patted his chest, then smoothed her hand upwards towards his neck. He went to stand up, but her other hand gripped his thigh. She was surprisingly strong for such a petite-looking woman. "Thank you, Max. Let me show you how much I appreciate your help."

Max could see her face coming closer, and he knew she was going to kiss him unless he moved. He turned his head away and slid to the side, making her hand slip off his neck. He stood abruptly, and his laptop fell to the floor. He winced, hoping he hadn't broken it.

He looked back at the woman. "Look, I am flattered that you like me, but I'm gay, remember. I'm only into men, not women. Like at all. Sorry." Max didn't know why he apologised, but she just didn't seem to get the hint, no matter how many times he told her.

"Okay," she said. Max didn't trust the look in her eyes but chose to ignore it.

"Right. I'll get on with these designs." He picked up his laptop and retreated to the dining room again. He blew out a breath as he began ordering the supplies needed. If everything went to plan, he'd be finished within two days.

Of course, nothing went to plan because the woman was a bitch. Max didn't usually call women bitches but this one was, without a doubt. He was just very grateful she'd already paid for his services. He didn't think she would have given him the money otherwise.

Since their...altercation...she found fault with everything relating to the dining room, even though she had agreed the plans were good before it happened. First, the curtains were the wrong fabric, then the table wasn't solid pine like she wanted, then the pictures weren't famous enough. He was at the end of his tether with it all. Instead of the two days he had hoped for, it had taken him four days, and even then, she still wasn't happy with some things, but he was putting his foot down now.

"I'm sorry, but I can't change any more aspects now. I have another client starting tomorrow, and I've delayed as long as I can. It might be better if you find someone else to change the items you don't like." Max lied through his teeth, his next client wasn't booked in until Monday and it was only Wednesday now, but he'd had enough.

The woman huffed. "Well, it will have to do then, won't it. Even though it looks like a disaster. What will people think?" She huffed again. "Fine, finish what needs doing today. But don't think I'm going to recommend you to anyone." She walked out of the room to Max's relief.

He blew out a breath. Luckily, everything was done. Other than tidying his stuff away, he had already finished everything, she just hadn't realised it.

He called to her when he left two hours later but received no response. He let himself out of the house, ensuring the door was firmly shut behind him. He didn't want anything to come back and bite him about that.

Several hours later, he entered Crush. He was meeting a guy in about half an hour and wanted to get in a drink before then.

He wore his best tonight: perfectly tailored black trousers, which cost him a pretty penny; a crisp white shirt, ironed to perfection; and a beige suit jacket that he loved. He knew he was dressed too smartly for the "date" later, but he loved the feel of being comfortable, as well as sexy, in what he wore. He didn't have to look smart to feel comfortable, but sometimes he wanted to.

He ordered a beer from the bartender, and then turned on his stool and rested his elbows behind him. His gaze roamed the area, seeing regulars and strangers intermingled throughout. He caught a guy staring at him from a booth near the back but moved his gaze away. Although the guy was hot, Max didn't have the energy—or inclination—to flirt tonight, which was why he'd arranged a hook-up through AN.

Someone walked into his line of vision, and he peered at them. Mmm-mmm.

"Max?" the guy said, his voice deep.

Max nodded and smiled. This was going to be a good night.

CHAPTER ONE

MAX

PRESENT DAY

Max blew out a breath as he sat sprawled in his seat at Crush, gazing at the public display of affection before him. Out of the corner of his eye, he noticed Trent trying to adjust himself subtly. Interesting. He'd known Trent for just under a year now, having met initially at Asher's house one night, and then many times since when Sean and Asher's relationship took off. He knew Trent had an ex-wife and two daughters and, as far as he knew, was straight. He'd be surprised if Trent found that PDA hot. "Hey, Trent. Wanna get out of here? These two lovebirds are going to end up fucking on this table any minute now." He had a nice buzz going, the alcohol warming his body and his libido. He never drank in excess when he was around Sean—since his best friend's parents died in a drink drive accident, Sean was wary of alcohol and being drunk.

Sean broke away from the kiss and snapped, "Hey! I heard that!" garnering a chuckle from Asher, even as he pulled Sean closer.

Max noticed Sean's entire body relaxed as he leaned into Asher. "We all know that was just about to happen, and you know it too!" He tilted his beer bottle towards Sean, raising his eyebrows, daring him to disagree.

Sean's face flushed a deep red in answer.

Max laughed. "My point exactly." He turned to Trent, who had snorted his beer at Max's words. "Want to head out? I need some fresh air."

Trent stood unsteadily. "Yeah, sure. I won't be driving in this condition so may as well walk."

It was Max's turn to snort. "If you *can* walk." Max bumped shoulders with him as they called their good-byes to everyone. Max headed over to Tom to thank him for the free drinks. Tom was the manager of Crush and had worked closely with every member of the crew to ensure they had what they needed to make the Garden Bar happen. It had been great working with the whole team. He hadn't done as much compared to others, but his expertise had come in handy with the lighting aspects.

"No problem, Max. You've worked as hard on this extension as everyone else, and I'm grateful for it." They shook hands, then Max brought Tom into a hug.

"It will be a huge hit tomorrow, you'll see," said Max, releasing him.

"Let's hope so," replied Tom, looking away with a furrowed brow, then his face lit up. "Excuse me," he said as he made his way towards Ginny, Tom's girlfriend, who was cradling their baby to her breast as she sat talking to the people around her. As Tom approached, Max saw Ginny gaze up and smile at him, their love an almost tangible thing.

Max headed back to Trent. "Let's go, hotshot," he said, slapping his back. He turned towards the entrance and walked into the cool night air, instantly feeling some of the buzz recede. He hadn't drunk a lot but enough to feel his slowed thought process. Being outside woke him up a bit, which he was sure he would need for the following conversation.

Trent stumbled out the door behind him, catching himself before he fell flat on his face but cursing like a sailor.

"You okay there?" Max tried to hide his smile. "Need any assistance?"

"No, I bloody well do not," replied Trent snarkily. Max began walking slowly, allowing Trent time to catch up. He just picked a direction; he had no idea where he was going but was just happy to move his body after being sat for so long.

"How's the job going?" Max asked after the silence became uncomfortable.

Trent cleared his throat. "Um…yeah, okay. The kids are ready for the break. So am I, if I'm honest!" he said.

"Oh, are you on break now?"

"Not quite. Tomorrow is the last day, then we have a week off." Trent looked up into the sky and blew out a breath.

Max frowned. "Everything okay?" he asked quietly.

Trent glanced over at him, then to the ground. "Yeah, I just wish…"

Max kept quiet, waiting for Trent to finish. When it was clear he wasn't going to, Max asked, "What do you wish?"

"I wish I could see my kids more. They're older now and don't want much to do with me, especially since the divorce. I'd like to see them this week, but they're probably busy." He trailed off, looking uncomfortable.

"Why don't you call them and ask? The worst they could say is no." Max glanced around when Trent initiated crossing the road. He had no idea where they were going, but Trent obviously did.

Trent didn't say anything for a few minutes, they just kept drifting down the street.

"I don't know if I'm ready to hear no," Trent whispered.

Max barely heard him and realised that was the whole point. He could pretend he didn't hear, or he could answer. Max decided to answer. No point hiding from fears, it sometimes made them worse.

"They may surprise you and say yes. Don't let fear stop you from doing what you want. Nothing would ever get done if people stopped when they were scared. I know I wouldn't be where I am today if I hadn't faced my fears." Max frowned when he realised what he'd revealed. Trent glanced over at him, but Max tried to deflect potential questions. "Just ask them."

Trent made a non-committal noise, then stopped walking. Max looked around him, trying to figure out exactly where they were. He didn't see anything he recognised.

"Where are we?" he asked Trent.

Trent looked up at an apartment building and frowned as if he wasn't sure how he got where he was. "My place."

Max raised his eyebrows. He'd not known Trent long in the grand scheme of things, and this was the first time he had ever been to Trent's place. "Oh, okay. Nice." It was a small building compared to some around this area, but Max could see the security features: CCTV cameras were visible, and a security guard posted in the foyer.

"Thanks," Trent said slowly, still staring at the building, brows furrowed.

"Well, I best leave you to it then. Have a nice evening, Trent." Max held out his hand for Trent to shake. Trent looked at his hand and reached out to shake it, not immediately letting go. Max felt the familiar tingles running along his skin as it did every time he had touched Trent in the past.

Max admitted, at least to himself, that he was fiercely attracted to Trent. He knew Trent was straight, even though he'd seen Trent's reaction at the sight of

Asher and Sean kissing earlier, but it didn't stop him from having a crush on him.

He realised they were still holding hands and moved to pull away, hesitating when Trent tightened his grip for a second.

"Do you want to come up?" The words were again whispered as if Trent wasn't sure about asking.

Max was not going to look a gift horse in the mouth, even if it did mean he just made his own life more miserable later when he reminded himself Trent was off limits. "Yeah, sure. I'd love to see the place."

Trent hesitated, and Max had noticed he bit his bottom lip when he was thinking or unsure. Max took the decision out of his hands—even though he should probably have given Trent a way to back out—and headed for the front entrance. He felt Trent following him, and then they were inside.

"Good evening, Mr Walker," the security guard called as they passed.

Trent nodded at him but didn't say anything as they headed for the lift. Pressing level three, Trent stood watching the numbers, while Max watched Trent. He didn't know what to think about Trent's invitation but was going to take it as platonic unless something else happened. Trent didn't seem the type to not know his own mind or body, but you never knew.

Trent fumbled with the lock on his front door when they arrived, then hesitated again before opening it fully. "It's not much."

Max entered to see an open space area housing the

living room, dining area and kitchen and a hallway leading further into the apartment, which he assumed went to the bedrooms and bathroom. Looking closer, his designer eye noticed a minimalist look, although looking again, Max realised this was probably not the look Trent had purposefully aimed for. The furniture looked worn and there didn't seem to be any personal effects except for three photos of his kids.

"Like I said, it's not much." Trent's voice sounded defensive, and Max realised he'd taken his silence for disgust.

"It's a nice open space with lots of natural light. It must be cosy when that fireplace is lit." Max tried to make his voice soothing and enthusiastic without going overboard; Trent would close down on him if he thought he was being insincere. He didn't know him well, but he knew him enough to know that.

"Hmm." Trent walked towards the kitchen area. "Do you want a drink? Beer?"

Max had had enough alcohol tonight. "Coffee? Is that too much trouble?" He saw Trent's shoulders relax slightly and knew then he was probably as glad as Max was that they weren't mixing more alcohol with whatever this was they were doing.

"Sure, coffee is fine."

He wandered around the space to the background noise of Trent bustling in the kitchen. Max noticed nothing was out of place—Trent must be a neat freak. He looked at the view out of the window and saw the building on the opposite side of the road, not exactly a scenic look.

"The view's not great, but the rent is affordable." Max jumped at Trent's voice being so close behind him. He turned slightly, seeing Trent within a few feet of him, holding out a steaming mug.

"Thanks." He took a drink, even though it scolded his mouth. "So, do you like it here?"

Trent walked over to the couch, sitting down and resting an ankle on his opposite leg. "Yeah, it's okay. Like I said, the rent's affordable and the security makes it safe for the kids, so as far as I'm concerned, everything else is irrelevant."

"Where are all your personal belongings?" Max asked, then cringed when he realised that came out sounding like an inquisition. "Sorry, that came out wrong."

TRENT

Trent hesitated. He didn't know how much to tell Max, who was essentially still a stranger. They had met through Sean and Asher and had been out in a group several times over the past year, but they had never been alone long enough for a proper one on one conversation like this.

"I didn't take much from my ex-wife's when I first left. Since then, she has refused to let me take anything else that belonged to me or the kids." He shrugged as if it was no big deal, but it *was* a big deal to him. There were several photographs and artwork he would have loved to take with him, but Trish had been an evil bitch about it from the beginning, so he had given up the fight.

Unfortunately, he couldn't afford to replace anything he'd once had, so he'd had to go without.

"Wow, what a cow. Sounds like you're well rid of her." Max came over to the sofa, sitting down and turning towards Trent so his knee rested on the cushion.

Trent still had no idea why he'd asked Max up to his apartment. He was confused about his motives because, even though he thought he wasn't gay, seeing Asher and Sean earlier had gotten him so aroused his cock had become a very uncomfortable bulge in his jeans. He had tried to find some relief by adjusting himself but didn't want to bring attention to it.

Staring into his mug, he asked, "Do you enjoy designing?" He would be the first to admit he knew nothing about interior design, and he was going to be a total asshole here, but he never realised men did it as a job, he had always assumed it was a woman. Not that he cared, he just hadn't realised.

"Yeah, I love it. Being given a blank canvas and bringing a client's dream to reality is an amazing feel-ing. I can't explain what it feels like. I've known some clients to cry when I've finished because they are so grateful." Max chuckled. "Then on the other hand, you have the ones who swear and bitch all day about everything, and you never get the time of day once you're done. But at least you get paid."

Trent chuckled. "Yes, you can put up with a lot so long as you get paid."

"What about you? Do you enjoy teaching?" Max took a sip of his coffee, eyes closing a little as if it were nectar.

Trent cleared his throat. "I love it. Don't get me wrong, some of the kids I teach are a nightmare, and I would call any teacher a liar if they denied that. But the high that you get when a child who has been struggling with something, say maths, finally understands what you're teaching? Nothing can compare to that. It makes everything else worthwhile." He hesitated. "Well, maybe not the paperwork."

They both laughed. "That's where you met Asher, isn't it?" Max continued.

He nodded. "Yeah, I teach the eight-year-olds. Asher taught the nine-year-olds—class next door."

"Wow, difficult age." Max's eyebrows rose with his wide eyes. "You're braver than me."

"They're not too bad, to be honest. It's difficult for them because age eight is when kids get a hormone surge, so they don't know how to react to things, and everything gets confusing for them. I try to be understanding when conflicts happen, but obviously still be the 'teacher' when I have to be."

"A friendly teacher," Max supplied.

Trent nodded. "Yeah, I suppose so. The kids will probably say different though."

"Do you see yourself continuing to teach? Or is there something else you'd like to do." Max canted his head to the side, making him look adorable.

He looked down at his mug, fiddling with the handle. Adorable? What the heck? "Yes, I love teaching. I may go for a different age range one day, but I don't see myself leaving it completely any time soon." He glanced back up at Max, seeing his gaze on Trent. He sat there caught in Max's eyes, not understanding what was happening or how he was feeling. He frowned and blinked his gaze away, looking down at his coffee again.

Suddenly very sober, he began to talk, but Max beat him to it.

"I think I should redecorate for you. Free of charge, of course. I can just see a few more knickknacks and homely things that could make you more comfortable." Max surveyed the area. "You could have a desk over in the corner by that window…" Max pointed to the very front window of the apartment, "…and use the natural light to do your paperwork. It would be easier on your eyes than using lights. And near those bookcases, you could fit a comfy chair for reading. Putting up some pictures on the walls will make it a little less…sterile." Max winced at his word choice no doubt.

Trent knew what Max saw, but he shook his head. "Thanks for the offer, but I can't right now."

"Why not? It might help cheer you up a bit."

Trent gritted his teeth and rubbed his forehead.

Everyone kept telling him he needed to cheer up, but if only they knew what he was actually going through. They knew nothing about it; but he couldn't get upset with anyone about their throwaway comments because he refused to share those reasons with them. "Thank you, but no." He stood up heading towards the kitchen to rinse his mug.

"Shit." He heard Max mutter the expletive but didn't acknowledge it. He heard footsteps coming closer just as he stumbled and fell against the counter. "Are you all right?" Max asked, reaching out to him.

Trent rubbed his forehead again. "Yeah. I've just got a nasty headache again. Keep getting them, and they're hard to shift." He laughed without humour. "The alcohol probably hasn't helped." He placed his mug in the sink and turned on the tap.

"Maybe you need a trip to a BDSM club! That'll loosen you up." Max laughed. Trent jerked and looked at Max in shock.

"What! No, I'm fine, thanks." Trent shook his head. Where the hell had that come from?

Max laughed again, the sound a little forced. "I'm only joking, Trent. Bad humour, sorry." Max paused. "I'm sorry, Trent. About before. I need to learn tact. It's one of my downfalls." Trent turned to see Max give a shrug and a half-hearted smile.

"One of them?" He raised one eyebrow to show his forgiveness—and disbelief. Max laughed "It's fine. Don't worry about it. I know it all needs doing, I just don't have the funds for it right now."

"I said it would be free—" Max began.

"I know. But I would still need to buy the items you want me to add to the apartment. And I just can't right now. When I can though, you'll be the person I call."

Max looked crestfallen for some reason. "Sorry, Trent. I am forever sticking my foot in my mouth." Max placed his mug on the side. "I'm going to head out. Thanks for the coffee." He turned to go, and Trent let him.

He watched as Max walked to the front door and closed it behind him with a soft click. The silence left behind was deafening. He had no idea why he hadn't stopped Max from leaving. He was conflicted and very unsettled—not by Max's presence—but by how he felt. He didn't quite understand what it was, and it was making him uncomfortable.

He washed up Max's cup and placed it on the draining board alongside his own, staring at the two cups side by side, a startling realisation of contentment flowing through him. He liked the idea of having two cups there as if he shared his life with someone. Trent shook his head at his idiotic thought and headed back to lock up. Once he was sure the front door and windows were locked up tight, he stalked to his bedroom. No lingering feeling of being drunk made it easier for him to navigate his way towards the bathroom. A nice hot shower would help him to sleep—he certainly needed it.

Trent woke four hours later, drenched in sweat, panting with fear. He sat up and swung his legs over the side of the bed, resting his head in his hands, distantly noticing he was shaking. He'd not had a nightmare like this for a while. Ever since the kids had been born, he had suffered with the occasional nightmare—which he assumed all parents did—about losing their children in some tragic event. His had always been a car accident, and every single time, he remembered it vividly afterwards.

He was sitting in the passenger seat next to Trish. Jocelyn and Harper were in the back seat, arguing as always. They were on their way to the beach for the weekend, the car packed with all their belongings. Trent was laughing at something Trish had said, and she'd looked over at him smiling. He stared at her briefly because it wasn't very often she smiled anymore. She gazed back, and then he turned back to the windscreen. Eyes widening when he saw the truck, he shouted out.

Every single time, he woke up just before impact, except this time. It hadn't been Trish driving, it had been Max, and they'd been hit by the truck. He'd woken after holding Max in his arms, broken and bleeding, tears streaming down his face.

He rubbed his hands over his face and stood up. He needed another shower to warm the chill from his bones.

CHAPTER TWO

MAX

Max looked through the paperwork for Mrs Cedar's house redesign. Again. He must have looked through it fifty times already this morning, but his mind was elsewhere. With Trent, to be precise. He couldn't believe he'd spoken to Trent the way he had. They were friends, but not as close as he was with Sean. He should have held back a little with his opinions; Sean always told him to be careful what he said.

He shook his head. He should have just let it go, but he shoved his foot right in the back of his throat. Leaning back in his chair, he rested his head against it and stared at the ceiling. There was no way he could concentrate on the quote, so he decided to go for a stroll. There was nothing more calming for him than walking around the shops and finding bargains. Maybe he'd be able to find something for Trent.

"Stop it, he doesn't want your help, remember," he muttered to himself.

Max stood and walked into the hallway, glancing around him in pride as he always did. His house could have been used as his business card. It was showroom perfect with wooden bannisters going up the stairs, solid wood floors throughout the downstairs and, going up the stairs, wood softened down the centre by a soft luxurious carpet in dark blue.

His furniture was mainly solid wood—thanks to Zak—and what *was* soft upholstery was in blues and browns and greens: his favourites. The white, faintly textured wallpaper was a background to artwork, family photos and shelving. In his lounge, he had four floor-to-ceiling bookcases, full of books on a huge variety of subjects. He had always loved learning and had never stopped, even when he had chosen interior design, he still learned new things on the side. Recently, for instance, he had been interested in the history of artists and had been speaking with Josh about it—Josh had overheard him talking to Sean and explained his career and his love of the same. They had spent many an evening since, conversing about the subject when Josh had been working at Crush on his university breaks.

Max grabbed his wallet, phone and keys as he headed for the door, locked up and drove towards the town centre. His favourite shops were charity shops because they were not only a bargain but sometimes you found some amazing things in there; those were the diamonds in the rough he lived for discovering.

Parking up behind the main road, he walked the short distance, beginning his bargain hunting therapy at the far end of the street. He knew exactly which shops the best ones were to look in, but he still went in every single charity shop, second-hand shop or pawn shop he could find.

Browsing the third place, he stopped when he saw an identical set of bookends. They were ceramic, mainly white, heavy and in the shape of a stack of multi-coloured books. He knew right then, he had to have them. Even though he had told himself not to buy anything for Trent, he just couldn't resist these. He knew Trent would appreciate them—eventually. He wasn't sure how he planned to get them into Trent's house, but he'd find a way. He bought them for the grand total of five pounds and made sure to get a receipt. If he knew Trent at all, when he realised Max was buying things for him, he would insist on paying him back. At least this way, Max could prove how much he spent on each item.

Smiling at the shop assistant, he grabbed the carefully wrapped bookends and walked out of the shop with a grin.

"What's that smile for?"

A familiar voice roused Max from his thoughts, and he looked behind him to see Zak walking towards him with his son in the pushchair.

"Hey! How're you?" Max leaned down to say hello to Dane. "Hey, buddy. What'cha doing?"

Dane smiled a toothy grin and waved a chubby

hand. He was still losing his baby fat at two years old, but he looked so cute with it all.

"Yeah, we're all right. Just getting some fresh air." Max noted the tone of Zak's voice didn't match the lightness of his words.

He canted his head. "What's up?" he asked.

Zak blew out a breath. "Having a few issues at home, that's all." He tried—and failed—for a smile.

"Come on, Zak. You know me better than that. Tell me."

Zak hitched his head to indicate they start walking, and then he began, "Ashley is…" Zak shook his head. "I don't know. Her usual self. In all honesty, Max, I'm thinking of leaving." He blew out another breath. "And taking Dane with me," he continued quietly.

"Christ, Zak. I didn't realise things were so bad. I must admit, I thought it was a bit strange you had to account for your whereabouts wherever you went, but I didn't realise anything else was wrong. How long has this been going on?" Max was dumbfounded. He'd never expected Zak and Ashley to split up; they always seemed so tight. And he was pissed he'd not realised something was wrong.

"Since Ashley found out she was pregnant. I believe she has suffered—quietly—with postnatal depression, but the doctors said she wasn't. She's just angry all the time. Nothing I do appeases her. She gets angry when I work, angry when I'm there, angry when I go out." He shrugged. "I've got no idea what to think."

"Jesus." Max shook his head. "What's tipped you over the edge for you to make the decision?"

"I haven't made any decision yet, Max. I'm trying to figure out what's best for Dane. The books all say that a child develops best being around both parents, but I'm beginning to get concerned for his safety when I'm not there. She takes no interest in him when I'm at home. At all. I'm doing everything for him. I worry that she's not looking after him properly when I'm at work, because his nappies always need changing and his clothes are dirty. I know kids get dirty, but this is a different kind of dirty. God, Max, I sound like an awful husband." Zak's voice hitched, and he looked away from Max.

Max gave him the reprieve and kept quiet, allowing him to collect himself. He'd never imagined things were this bad. When Max had gone out with them both, or in the group, they'd seemed fine. Although Max had noticed Ashley was very reliant on Zak and often cut him off or talked down to him, he'd brushed it off as a married thing. He'd had no idea there was anything else behind it.

"I don't know what the best thing to do is." Zak sounded beaten down.

Max was lost. "I don't know what..." Max suddenly had a thought. "Hold on. What if you could get some off the record advice without anyone finding out?"

Zak frowned at him. "If it would help me figure out what I needed to do for the best, sure."

Max pulled out his phone and searched for the

number he needed. "Hey. I wondered if I could ask a favour?"

"Okay." Max could hear the hesitation in Trent's voice.

"Would you be able to arrange a meeting with your brother for…a friend of mine. Just a chat if you will. He'd like to know his options."

"Regarding?"

"A potential custody case." Max didn't want to say too much. He wasn't sure how much Zak wanted to say so he'd let Zak decide that himself at the meeting.

"Okay. I'll ring Samuel and ask him. Shouldn't be a problem, but I'm not sure when. Can I call you back?" Trent took on a more formal tone as if he was making an appointment.

"Sure. And thanks."

"No problem. Speak to you in a few." Trent rang off.

"He's going to speak to his brother and get back to me. I'll let you know what he says," Max tells Zak.

"Whose brother?"

"Oh, sorry. Trent's brother is a lawyer…Well actually, two of his brothers are lawyers in different areas. It will be Samuel that you'll be speaking to. He'll be discreet."

Zak sighed. "Thanks, Max. That'll help a lot."

"No worries. Always here to help." Max chuckled.

"What were you up to anyway?" Zak asked as they began to walk slowly again. Max had noticed that Dane had fallen asleep during their conversation.

"I'm searching for diamonds," he said distractedly.

He'd just seen a gorgeous green throw in the window across the street. "Hold on." He crossed the road, entered the shop and immediately fell in love with the soft, velvety feel of the large throw, which would look amazing on Trent's cream sofa. Max went to the counter and enquired about it. He bought it and exited the shop, seeing Zak in the same place he left him.

"Find what you're looking for?" Zak chuckled, shaking his head.

"Yeah, sorry. I got distracted."

"Really? I never would've guessed." Zak laughed. "Who's that for anyway? Haven't you got enough throws?"

Max could feel himself getting red. He never blushed, what the hell? "Um, it's for Trent, actually."

Zak eyebrows almost hit his hairline. "I didn't realise he'd hired you to redecorate his place."

Max bit his lip. "He hasn't, exactly." He winced.

"Then why...?" Zak frowned.

Max blew out a breath. "Shit. Okay, I kind of put my foot in it last night, and I'm trying to make amends... even though he told me not to."

Zak shook his head. "That makes no sense, Max. Spill."

"Damn it! All right. I ended up at Trent's house last night—not for that reason—but we began talking while we walked, and we just ended up there. We talked some more while we had a coffee, and I made a stupid comment about his house looking sparse. I offered to redecorate free of charge, and he shot me down. I was only trying to help."

Zak stared at him. "You have the hots for him."

Max stared back. "Maybe," he said like a sullen teenager.

Zak laughed. "Trent is straight, Max. Straight. As in, he likes women. And has an ex-wife!"

"I know, I know. I'm not planning on doing anything about it. I'm not going to force him to be my love slave or anything. He's just a nice guy." Max felt himself getting defensive. "I can't help it if I find him attractive…and kind."

"Okay, sorry." Zak tried to curb his laughter. "So, why are you buying him a throw if he doesn't want your help?"

Max winced again. "Maybe because I'm still going to redecorate, just a little at a time?" he said quietly and ending with a question, expecting Zak to shoot him down.

Zak shook his head. "You are so in over your head; you don't know which way is up."

Max rubbed his forehead. "I know. I'm fucked."

"Just slightly."

He walked a little longer until Zak said they had to get back. Max reminded him about the party that night, then meandered back towards his car. He hadn't seen anything else that had taken his fancy, but then again, he hadn't really been looking after his conversation with Zak. He was an idiot. He should just leave Trent well alone. He'd have to see him at the party tonight, but he could make sure he didn't do anything stupid. He got out his phone and clicked on his app. He would arrange a hook-up to meet him at the party. That should take his mind off Trent.

After the booking was confirmed, he drove home with a spring in his step. Maybe he'd get some work done now.

TRENT

Trent had been searching for his watch when Max had rung. He ended the call and immediately called Samuel's number. He was always more than happy to help when someone needed it, and Trent knew this was Samuel's area of expertise.

"Samuel Walker."

Trent laughed. "Do you even look at the phone before you answer? You'd know it was me if you did."

"Hey, Trent. No, I don't look at it although I probably should. It would save me time and again from talking to people I don't want to." Samuel huffed.

Samuel was two years older than he was and the eldest of the five of them. Carter came two years after Trent did, Luke three years after that, and then baby Ava four years after Luke. Carter went into law as well, just in a different area to Samuel. Luke was a personal trainer and Ava was a police officer, and in a coincidence turned out to be Logan's partner. Small world.

"Yes, it would definitely help you out. Are you busy?" Trent asked.

"Not for you. What's up?" Samuel's voice took on a "take-on-the-world" tone he'd come to expect of his big brother.

"I have a friend who has a friend in need of advice."

"Okay. Do you know what it's about?"

Trent heard rustling and assumed Samuel was taking notes. "A potential custody case. I don't have any more information to be honest."

"Yeah, not a problem. It's my speciality after all. Let's see…" Trent could hear more noise on the other end of the line. "How about tomorrow, say four?"

"Can you pencil them in, and I'll just double check the time is all right and let you know?"

"I'll put it under your name. Teresa will know not to cancel it then."

"Thanks, Sammy." Trent used his childhood nickname for his brother only occasionally, a reminder of their younger years.

Samuel chuckled. "You're welcome, T-man."

Trent smiled. "I'll speak to you in a bit."

They hung up, and Trent called Max. Five minutes later, after Max had rung off to confirm with his friend, he'd rung back to agree the time, allowing Trent to accept the four o'clock timeslot. Max had also given Trent a name to pass to Samuel: Zak. He'd been a little shocked when Max had confirmed who it was, but Trent had not asked any questions. He'd passed the information to Samuel and told him he'd speak to him in a few days.

He resumed the search for his watch. Trent searched the lounge area and when that brought up nothing, he searched through the rest of the apartment. He knew he'd put his watch down before he went out the previous night—it had been itching him, so he'd taken it off for the evening. It was nowhere to be found. He hoped he'd not left it somewhere else as his dad had given it to him—it was a family heirloom.

He sat on the sofa and rubbed his hand over his mouth and chin. This wasn't the first item that had gone missing; a few weeks ago, it was his cufflinks; he still hadn't found them. Trent was beginning to get worried. With the missing items on top of the recurring headaches he'd been having, his mind immediately went down the dementia route. It sounded drastic, but he didn't know what else it could be. He'd already been to see the doctor about the headaches. They'd said he was stressed and tired with work and had prescribed B12—supposedly to help with his memory and to give him an energy boost. Things were still happening though. Not long after starting on the tablets, Trent remembered he'd thought he'd taken too many tablets one day, and then the next day, there was the correct number again. Adding in hallucinations, he didn't know what to think anymore.

He dialled Jocelyn. He wanted to catch up with her; he hadn't been able to get hold of her for that last few days. It went straight to voicemail, and looking at his clock, he realised she was probably in class. Trent left a message asking her to call him when she had a minute. Ending the call, he hovered over Harper's name, then dialled. He didn't expect her to answer but he could always leave another message. As expected, she didn't answer either so he left a brief monologue about how he missed her and would love to see her. Harper hated all the emotion mumbo-jumbo but if there was something wrong with him—he wanted to make sure she knew how he felt.

He looked at the clock again and debated whether to stay at home tonight. His headache made him nauseous, but he decided to grab a banana and some paracetamol and to go get himself spruced up. After all, this was going to be a huge party. Everyone involved had worked so hard, they needed this chance to relax a little.

An hour later, he was ready to go. He couldn't remember whether anyone had said there would be food there, but he hoped there would be. He had nothing in his fridge that would do for a meal. He'd decided to drive to Crush—he'd had enough alcohol last night—and he didn't want to make his headache any worse by having some tonight too.

He expected it to be packed. That night was a three-fold event for Crush: the grand opening of the Garden Bar, a usual Friday night and it was also Valentine's night. If Crush wasn't busy tonight, it never would be in his opinion.

And it was. He struggled to find a parking space anywhere near and had to walk about half a mile. The fresh air had seemed to clear his head, so he didn't complain despite how cold it was. When he got into the bar itself, it was crazy; loud and hot even though it was freezing outside. He pushed his way through the crowd towards the bar, smiled at Charlie and ordered his one and only beer. After his first swallow, he turned and surveyed the customers; somewhere in there were Asher and Logan, he just had to find them.

He decided to look outside first and foremost, especially as he still had his jacket on. Trudging towards the open doors, he nudged past people, known and unknown, until he reached the relief of open air. Flapping his shirt to cool down, he glanced around to find any of his friends and spotted Max. He made a beeline for him, thinking the others would probably be nearby.

He saw when Max noticed him, but Trent didn't see the guy next to him until he stood in front of them. If he had seen him—or at least their positioning—he would have steered clear. Max had one arm wrapped around a six-foot guy with blond, shoulder length hair and the bluest eyes he'd ever seen, and the guy returned Max's embrace. The guy rested his hand on Max's waist and tucked him close. Max was almost resting his cheek against the guy's shoulder; they were that close.

"Hey, Trent," Max said.

"Hi. Sorry I didn't realise you had company. I'll go find Asher. I thought he might be with you." Trent turned to look around from his vantage point but couldn't see anyone.

"They're inside, in a booth. Sean was cold so Asher took him in. You know how he gets everything he wants." Max chuckled at the worst kept secret their group had.

Trent tried to smile. "I guess you won't be getting cold," he mumbled, too softly for anyone to hear. Or so he thought.

"Sorry?" Max's voice held confusion, understandably.

Trent looked over at him, shrugged and said, "I'll go in and find them. Can you tell me roughly where they are?"

Max's frown stayed as he told Trent where they were. He said goodbye, then stalked off into the stifling bar area again.

"I can't believe he's here with that guy. I didn't even know he was seeing anyone. But then why would you, Trent, you don't really talk to him, do you?" he mumbled.

"You talking to yourself or can anyone join in?" Logan's voice in his ear made him jump.

"Shit, Logan. Don't do that!" Trent's heart had been beating hard enough before Logan scared him, now it was frantic.

Logan laughed, then leaned close again. "How else

are you going to hear me in this joint?"

Trent conceded his point. "Where are you all sitting?" he called.

Logan pointed towards the back, possibly their usual booth, and led the way. Trent's heart had returned to normal by the time they reached the others. And yes, their usual booth; they would have it named after them soon.

He threw himself onto the seat opposite Logan and realised he'd lost his beer along the journey somewhere. He didn't even remember putting it down. Another thing to add on to the list of weird happenings.

"What's that frown for?" Asher shouted across the table.

Trent looked up and shrugged. "I'm hot, that's all." He shrugged off his jacket, making sure to put his phone in his jeans pocket instead; that way, he'd be able to feel the vibration if it rang. Not that he expected it to; his kids hadn't replied since he'd left their messages, and in all honesty, he didn't expect them to.

Gemma walked over to their little corner of the world and took a drink order. Trent ordered another beer as he'd hardly started the one he'd misplaced. He'd be all right driving home still. He asked about food.

"The kitchen is open with a full menu." Gemma nodded to the new laminated menus standing in a holder. "I'll take your order when I bring your drinks."

"Thanks, Gem." Trent grabbed a menu and saw a few new things had been added to it. He settled on the lasagne and chips, then looked around at the other guys. Asher was sat in the corner, sideways with his back to the wall and Sean settled backwards against his chest—they were rarely seen apart now, except when their jobs took them in different directions. Logan was sat next to them, arms on the table as he looked around the bar, probably scanning for trouble. As a Detective Sergeant, he worked long hours but was able to swap shifts to make sure he had time with his friends. As far as Trent was concerned, Logan worked too hard and needed those days off more regularly than he got them.

He was tumbled from his thoughts when a body slid across the seat next to him and nudged him further over. He turned his head to see Max, and then the guy from outside slide in next to him. Trent moved as far as the booth would let him, wishing he'd sat where Logan now resided.

"Hi, Max. How have you been?" Logan asked. "Not seen you for a while."

"Good, thanks. Work's keeping me busy, so it's all good."

"I know how you feel." Logan laughed.

"Max, who's your sidekick?" Sean asked with a smile, lessening the potential sting—although they'd been friends for years, so could probably get away with a lot more with each other.

"Oh, sorry. Guys, this is Frederick. Frederick, this is —" Max pointed to each person as he said their name, "Asher, Sean, Logan and Trent."

"Don't forget us!" a voice called.

Two bodies stood side by side next to their table.

Trent realised it was Ethan and Zak, Max and Sean's friends.

"You made it! Grab some seats if you can find them." Sean had sat upright when they'd appeared, joy visible on his face; a far cry from when he was first involved with Asher. Serious emotional issues happened there, but they'd sorted it all out and things couldn't be better.

Zak managed to find a couple of stools, and they parked at the end.

"What have we missed?" asked Ethan. He had been working alongside Sean in the same architectural company last year for his work experience but had been back at uni for this year. He still managed to get out and meet up with them quite a bit, which was good. Trent would hate for Sean to lose another friend.

"Not a lot. Max was just introducing us to Frederick, his date." Asher managed to say that without a smirk in place, but Trent thought he heard it in his voice.

"Oh, nice to meet you, Frederick," Zak said, all polite.

Frederick just nodded as him as if he had no voice. Trent huffed out a breath and rolled his eyes. Gemma chose that moment to come over with their drinks.

"I saw your group had grown so I brought extra beers, hope that's okay?" Gemma knew them well.

"Thanks, Gemma," Logan answered.

"No problem. Are you guys ready to order?" she asked.

"Yes, please. God, I'm starved," Ethan interjected.

Gemma took the order from each of them, except Frederick. Seemed like he wasn't an eating person either.

"Brilliant, I'll get these to the kitchen. You might have a little wait though. Things are crazy as you can see."

"That's fine, Gemma. No rush. Well, not for me anyway," Logan replied.

Gemma walked away as they all countered what Logan had said. "What do you mean 'no rush for you'? There is always a rush for you when it comes to food."

Logan smirked. "I ate before I came out."

Everyone laughed, except for Frederick, Trent noticed. He seemed a bit stuck up to him. He had no idea what Max saw in him.

"So, Frederick, what do you do?" Sean asked.

"Um, I'm an accountant," he said.

Trent raised his eyebrows at that—and the Yorkshire accent that came out with it.

"Wow, that must be exciting." Trent could tell that Sean was trying to get Frederick involved in the conversation, but it seemed like Frederick wasn't interested as he didn't answer except to smile. Max needed to find someone better suited to him.

CHAPTER THREE

MAX

Max could tell this meeting was not going well. He didn't quite understand why Frederick didn't want to engage with his friends—Max had specifically told him he was going to meet them but that they were more bark than bite, and Frederick had said it was fine, but now it seemed like he didn't want to.

He *was* a little shocked at Trent's reaction though. All that huffing and eye rolling he'd been doing had not gone unnoticed. He didn't know why Trent seemed bothered about who Max brought with him. Unless he was just worried about how Frederick was going to treat Max, like Sean was.

Sean knew about Max's predilection for BDSM. He also knew about the app that Max regularly used for hook-ups; that was why Sean was grilling the guy. Sean never outwardly told Max he disapproved, but Max could see that Sean worried every time he told him he went out. He thought Sean believed that one day Max wouldn't come home. Naturally, there was a small chance but the company who owned AN were very stringent with their checking of each applicant. Max had asked the questions when he'd first been accepted and had been happy with the responses. He just wished he could alleviate some of Sean's worries. Unfortunately, he was bound by a non-disclosure agreement.

Their food arrived after half an hour of catching up on each other's lives. Max saw Sean and Zak regularly but Ethan not so much. He'd become closer to Asher, obviously, because he was with Sean a lot of the time. Trent and Logan, however, were still on the outskirts, although he was trying to get to know them better. Logan was a bit harder to pin down because he was always working, but he had managed to speak with Trent many times over the past year, even if they were short conversations instead of meaningful discussions.

That was how his infatuation had started. Trent was gorgeous with his chiselled jaw, barely-there scruff, blue eyes and just got out of bed hair style. If Trent had been gay, Max would have tried it on with him many times. Max realised he was staring at Trent and looked away, catching Logan's eye as he did. Logan raised one eyebrow and cocked his head to the side.

Max blushed and turned to focus on Frederick, who was busy shredding a napkin. He tried to keep their conversation going while he finished his food. He'd known Frederick for a while now, which was why he'd asked for him on the app. They were a good match when Max felt as he was: down and unwanted. Frederick was a perfectly, domineering top and would put Max back together tonight, just like he needed. He realised Frederick had gone silent and glanced over at him when he felt a hand smooth across his back.

"Relax, Max. I'm not playing boyfriend here remember, but if my conclusion is correct, there is someone here you want to make jealous. Even if it's subconsciously." Frederick's quiet voice in his ear, made him close his eyes in mortification. His hand rested on the back of Max's neck, massaging the muscles there.

Max's head fell forward as the massage continued, pleasure and pain coursing through him as Frederick pressed the tense areas. He'd be asleep if this continued for too long.

"Get a room!" Sean shouted. Max's eyes shot open to see the whole table looking their way and Sean grinning like a fool. Sean mouthed, "Payback."

Max laughed. "That might not be a bad idea." He pushed his plate away—luckily, it hadn't been too close to him when he'd dropped his head; otherwise, that would have been embarrassing. "Would you tell Tom congratulations for me please? I've not seen him around yet."

Sean nodded. "Sure. I saw him when we first came in but nothing since. I'll seek him out."

"Thanks." He turned to Frederick. "You ready to go?"

Frederick nodded and stood from the booth, allowing Max to follow suit.

"Nice to meet you, Frederick. Hope to see you again soon." There was the Asher, Max knew and loved, always unfailingly polite. Max chuckled to himself, remembering the exception. Sean had pissed Asher off, and Max had been witness to the epic confrontation that had taken place in Pop's one day last year. Looking at Asher, you wouldn't believe he could hurt a fly, but he certainly took no prisoners when he had decided on something, that was for sure.

Frederick rested a hand on Max's back as he led the way through the throng to the front exit; that was his way of showing he cared but not overtly showing his Dom side. Max knew he would be able to greet friends should he see them, but he also knew that Frederick wouldn't allow him any such thing as soon as they were at their destination. And that was what Max needed tonight. He needed to be free.

The volume of the music muted as the door closed behind them, leaving them in the chilly end of a winter's night. Max shivered, even through the thick coat he'd picked up from the hangers by the front door.

"Come." Frederick's voice brooked no denial, and Max automatically obeyed as he'd been wanting to do all night. He followed Frederick to his car, and Frederick opened the passenger door, indicating Max should get in. He did without delay, knowing their destination was minutes away. His thoughts already began the journey towards his end goal—subspace. He knew Frederick could get him there in next to no time, and he wanted there as soon as possible.

Frederick sat in the driver side and started the engine. "What do you want from tonight? Speak freely."

Max shivered at the cadence in his voice, looked at him and obeyed. "I want subspace. I want to be free. I want to forget. And to remember. And everything in between."

Frederick's eyes narrowed. "You don't know what you want, do you? Never mind. I do. Leave it with me." He clipped Max's seatbelt and his own, then started towards their destination. "I know what you need. You know the rules from now on, don't you?"

"Yes, Master," Max said, eyes lowered to his lap.

The rest of the drive was in silence, and although Max kept his submission complete, his mind whirled with memories of tonight's party. He remembered when Trent had found him and Frederick in the garden; Trent's face had been happy and the smile he'd given Max was...indescribable. The minute Trent saw Frederick, his face had turned to thunder, his body language closed off. He couldn't get out of there fast enough. Max kept trying to figure out what was going on, but he had no idea. He'd had the thought before that maybe Trent was bisexual, but Trent had never confirmed that, so Max had nothing to go on.

"Max." The hardened voice brought him back to the present. He must have missed an instruction. Inwardly, he winced. Not a great start. He kept his head lowered but canted it ever so slightly so show he had heard. "Exit the car, walk two steps behind me as we walk to the entrance. You know the rules once we enter this place." Statement, not a question, so no answer required.

Max opened the passenger door and got out, shutting it again behind him. He waited until Frederick had walked around the car to him, then did as was asked until they reached the entrance. His Master pressed his thumb to the reader, and it turned green.

"I'll be waiting just inside."

Frederick entered and closed the door behind him. The club insisted on every member being identified by thumbprints, so Max followed suit, soon standing next to Frederick once more. Frederick led the way, Max meekly followed behind, head slightly higher than usual to allow him to see in the darkened area without needing assistance.

This was the usual protocol for the AN clubs. Thumbprints identified all members and cameras installed over the entrance doors allowed them to be recorded.

It was a safety precaution the company used to ensure that 'extra' people were not brought into the clubs without having been properly security checked beforehand. Max had heard rumours that it had happened several times, and the members who had managed to get these 'extras' into the club were removed from the premises, deregistered immediately and would not be allowed back in ever again.

This was the type of security that AN had in place to protect its members, and Max was more than satisfied with the safety measures.

Frederick stopped at the counter, talking quietly with the hostess. He received a key, nodded his head and turned towards Max. Max saw all of this while his head was lowered, eyes not quite as low as they should be, which he rectified as soon as he saw Frederick begin to turn.

"Follow me."

Max followed Frederick through the main room and down a corridor to a room. Max had been in this room before—several times in fact—it was Frederick's playground, and Max felt some of the tension seep out of his body at the knowledge of what would happen in this place.

Frederick opened the door and allowed Max to pass. "Strip." His voice had taken on the complete Dom tone now; he didn't have to hide here either.

Max immediately did as he was told, laying his clothes along the top of the dresser placed there for that purpose—and the purpose of holding toys. From this point on, anything Frederick did was up to Frederick. He knew Max's limitations, and Max trusted him. This whole situation wouldn't work if he didn't trust Frederick with everything.

"What is your safeword?"

Standard protocol—checking safewords. "Monochromatic." Max almost smiled when he told Frederick his agreed upon safeword. It was a pun for his own humour. He hated everything to do with monochromatic things; hated the idea of lots of things all being the same colour. Hence the reason for the safeword.

He'd hate to use it—never had so far—but he would if he had to. Same went for his business.

"Good."

Facing away as he was, Max heard rustling, then a blindfold was put in place, eliminating his vision, but enhancing his other senses. More tension seeped out of his body. He heard noises being made, some he could figure out, some he couldn't but he knew Frederick was getting ready. Without his vision, he was limited with what he could do without instruction or assistance. He knew roughly the layout of the room but not enough to keep from tripping over.

Frederick took hold of his arm and walked him to where he wanted him, giving verbal instructions as needed. He pushed Max slightly further forward until he felt a cool, hard surface at his front. Grabbing his wrist, Frederick lifted it and secured it in a strap, tightening it well—the soft inner surface comfortable on his skin. His other wrist was secured the same way. Frederick kicked Max's feet further apart but didn't secure them. Max leaned his head forward against the cool surface, ready to begin his journey.

Max felt a hand glide from his shoulder blades down his spine to his ass. Sharp slaps sounded as Frederick spanked him three times on each cheek in quick succession. Max knew this was just the warm-up and tried not to tense. The stinging sensation slowly died away when nothing else happened, leaving a simmering warmth behind. Max heard a brushing sound as if the wind rustled in the trees, and his mind automatically associated the sound with a flogger.

"Count to ten for me."

Max was given no time to brace himself as the flogger rustled through the air and hit his sensitive cheek. He flinched slightly. "One," he said.

Once more he had no warning, except for the whistling sound. "Two." A beat. "Three." The pain flared in a different area on his ass.

"Four." And another area.

"Five." Same place as before, making it heat up further.

"Six." He wanted to let his head fall back as tension released with each meeting.

"Seven." He knew his ass would be looking very red at this point.

"Eight. Nine. Ten." By the time he got to ten, his body felt loose and warm, and he was ready for more. He knew there was more to come as he was still too coherent. He realised though he wasn't as hard as he usually got, which made him frown and tense again.

"What's wrong?" Frederick asked, his Dom voice still prevalent. "Speak freely."

"It's not working."

"What's not working?"

"I'm not getting as turned on as usual. I'm relaxed and have a nice glow but I'm not as hard as I normally get." Max could feel the tension streaming back into his body with each word he spoke. He rested his forehead against the cool surface in front of him and closed his eyes against the blackness. He just didn't know what was wrong.

"Let's try something different," Frederick said. Max felt hands unbuckling his wrists, and then removing his blindfold. He turned to Frederick and saw understanding in his eyes. He didn't know what Frederick understood, because he sure had no idea, but it was calming to see that Frederick wasn't pissed. "Go sit on the leather table. I'll be back." Frederick left the room, and Max did as he was told. He wasn't completely in submissive mode now, but he still had a little left in him.

Max sat. He wished he could understand what was going on with him. He never usually had trouble, especially when Frederick was at the helm. Maybe he was stressed.

The door opened, and Frederick stalked back in with a tiny, blond sub. "Max, stand. Sub, hands and knees on the table." He paused while the sub did as he was told. "Now make him hard." Frederick came to stand behind Max, both standing in front of the sub. The sub took Max's cock in hand and stroked it a few times before placing it in his mouth. Max closed his eyes against the sensation, feeling pleasure begin to course through him. He lifted a hand and gripped the sub's hair, making him stay against his groin and swallow.

Max felt a whisper against his ear. "This sub likes the crop. Let's see how you both react to it." That exact moment, the crop brushed against his legs, lifting higher until it smoothed across his still sore ass. A short, sharp thwack against his sensitive cheeks made him flinch and moan. The dual sensations heightening his arousal, more so when the image of Trent on his knees in front of him, sucking his cock appeared. He kept his eyes closed, lost in the fantasy of the guy he wanted.

The crop hit him again and again—his ass, his balls, his thighs—then it smoothed across the sensitive skin. Max hissed a breath and bucked into the hot wet mouth. The crop disappeared, but Max was following his fantasy through to its inevitable conclusion. Trent's mouth was amazing, as was the chance for Max to grip his hair and fuck it.

Distantly, he heard the thwack of the crop again and the vibration of the moan against his cock, which was at present in Trent's throat, had him harder than ever. Another hit and the moan sounded different, too high. Max frowned, trying to keep the image in front of him, but another moan had him losing the scene. He opened his eyes, seeing the sub in front of him—not Trent. He lost some of his hardness, much to the panic of the sub, who began to redouble his efforts, not wanting to disobey his master.

"Fuck." Max pulled himself free and walked over to the chair in the corner of the room. Maybe he could watch and get himself off instead.

"Max?" Frederick's questioning tone had him looking at him.

"I'm all right. Keep going." He waved his hand in

dismissal. He should be punished for his disobedience, but at that moment, he didn't care.

Frederick hesitated for a second, then went back to cropping the sub. Max could see the sub was struggling to keep himself upright, his arms were shaking, his cock ramrod straight and leaking between his legs. Max watched as Frederick moved position. As he swung the crop, he saw it hit the sub's cock full on. The sub cried out in pleasure and more precome leaked out. Max began to stroke his cock, fascinated by the view in front of him. Frederick kept hitting the sub in the same area, three times, four times, five before the sub was gritting his teeth and had so much precome leaking, even from where Max sat, he could see the leather padded table was drenched.

He stroked his cock harder, playing with the bundle of nerves underneath—a sure-fire way to get him off.

"Come!" commanded Frederick as he simultaneously pulled out a plug and rammed his cock in the sub's hole. The sub almost screamed his pleasure as his cock emptied. Frederick kept pumping into him, seemingly not far from his own release. Max gripped his cock harder still, stroking faster in time with Frederick's thrusts.

"Ah, fuck!" Frederick faltered, then slowed his hips as he released into the sub.

Max let out a breath and let go of his cock. He was nowhere close and knew it wasn't going to happen, even though his balls were complaining bitterly. He rose and grabbed his clothes from the top of the dresser. He dressed in silence, wincing as he pulled on his trousers and dropped back into the chair with a sigh.

He watched as Frederick took care of the sub, lost in his own thoughts. He had no idea what the matter with him was. All he knew was that it seemed like he needed to picture Trent to be able to get off. Which was wonderful—not.

"Shit." Max shook his head and jumped when a hand came down on his knee. He'd not even realised Frederick had crouched in front of him. He must've been sat there for a while because Frederick would have completed the aftercare with the sub before he'd come back to Max.

"You need a release. You're getting yourself worked up, and it will just make it more difficult if you don't." Frederick looked at him with sympathy. "It's not very often I offer this but let me help."

"It's okay, don't worry—"

"That's an order. If you need it to be." Frederick's voice had hardened.

Max closed his eyes against the possibility of tears and nodded. He opened them again at the feel of Frederick's hands re-opening his trousers. Kneeling on the floor in front of him, Frederick pulled out Max's cock. "Close your eyes and think of Trent. I won't make a sound." Frederick smirked, then took Max's cock in his mouth.

Max began to deny the Trent thing but decided to go with it. He imagined Trent again on his knees, sucking his cock into his mouth; the warmth enclosing around his cock and being swallowed at the back of his throat. A hand grabbed his and reached it to his hair so Max gripped tight, using his hands to control his head. Trent swallowed every time Max's cock hit the back of this throat, the cool air in sharp contrast as he withdrew.

A low vibration started along his cock as he moved in and out, increasing his speed. Soon he lifted his hips and pulling his head towards him as he reached for his climax. He saw Trent looking up at him as his mouth was full of cock and trying to smile, and Max was done.

"I'm coming!" he shouted just before his come began to release into Trent's throat. "Fuck!" He kept pumping until there was nothing left, then he collapsed back in the chair, breathing heavily.

He opened his eyes as his cock was released from the warmth and saw Frederick wiping the corner of his mouth. Frederick looked at him and smirked. "You could have shouted Trent's name. I wouldn't have minded."

"*I* would've. It's disrespectful." Max smiled. "Thank you. I appreciate your help."

"My pleasure." Frederick laughed at Max's obvious disbelief. "I said, I didn't do it often, not that I didn't enjoy doing it."

Max chuckled, then sobered. "I mean it, thank you. I've no idea what's going on at the minute, but I definitely needed that release."

"I know what's wrong, Max. You want Trent, and you can't have him. Your mind is telling you that only he can be the one to give you pleasure. You need to teach it otherwise."

Max studied Frederick. "How did you know?"

"About Trent?" At Max's nod, he continued. "You couldn't keep your eyes off him while we were at the party. When you first saw him, your face lit up. I've never seen you like that. And when he left, you almost deflated. It's not obvious to everyone, don't worry. But the more observant people will pick up on it. Like your friend, Logan. He knows."

"I had a feeling he did." Max blew out a breath. "Oh well. Nothing I can do about that now. I best get going."

"Come see me if you need to, Max. I mean that. You don't need to book, just ring me."

"Thanks." Max left the room, both happy for Frederick's offer and sad because he knew he was in trouble.

As he walked through the common area where members mingle, he had to squeeze past several people. He hadn't realised how busy it had gotten. Seeing a bit of a gap near the entrance, he slowly made his way between the crowd, brushing against people as he went. With an "Excuse me," he brushed past a guy, who had his hand underneath a girl's skirt. The guy turned and pushed Max away from him, hard.

"Woah!" Max raised his arms in a defence gesture as the music immediately stopped, and the crowd turned to watch what happened.

The guy looked around and smirked. "What? You want a piece of my ass? The only way you're getting that is if you kick it—not kiss it." He walked right up to

Max, as close to his face as he could get without touching. Max made sure not to move. "Touch me again—"

His words were cut off as a bouncer yanked on the back of the guy's shirt and bodily dragged him to the exit.

"Hey, you okay?" Frederick stood next to him.

Max sighed. "Yeah, I think so. No idea what that was about. How did you know…"

Frederick indicated the lights above. "The safety strobes were triggered."

Max hadn't even noticed the pink lights were still flashing. Pink lights meant there was an altercation in the common area; different colours meant different areas of the club. At that moment, the strobes turned off, and everyone went back to what they'd been doing before.

"You won't have to worry about that guy anymore. He was clearly new, and reckless, and obviously hadn't read the guidelines."

"What do you mean?"

"Being an initiator in a non-scened altercation on any AN premises means immediate membership termination."

Once Frederick explained, Max remembered reading it in the guidelines. "Well, thanks for the save. I'm going to head home."

Frederick clapped him on the shoulder and squeezed. "Take it easy. You know where I am if you need anything." Then he was gone into the crowd. With another sigh, Max left and headed home.

TRENT

Trent was going to have to get a taxi home. His thought of only having one beer went up in smoke when he saw Max with that Frederick guy. He honestly couldn't remember how many beers he'd consumed by this point, but in his favour was the fact that he could still think coherently. He looked around Crush, noticing there was still loads of customers. He had no idea what the time was, but it felt late. Sean and Asher had gone home already, but Logan kept him company. Although he probably wasn't much use either.

Behind him, he heard raised voices but ignored it until a small voice said, "I said get lost." The voice didn't hold much conviction, and Trent almost ignored it again, but his instincts were pricking at him. He turned to look and saw a guy crowding a young girl, about Jocelyn's age, against the wall. His brain was slower than usual, but not *that* slow. He continued to watch for a few seconds, but he knew he had to intervene when he saw the girl try to push the guy away and the guy just gripped the wrist and slammed it back against the wall.

He slid out of the booth and stood quickly, turning to them without hesitation. "Trent, no." Logan's voice carried to him, but he wasn't going to listen when a girl was being harassed.

"What t'hell d'ya think you're doin'?" His voice didn't come out as sober as he'd hoped.

The guy turned his head towards him without letting go of the girl. "None of your business, old man. Take a hike." He turned back to the girl, getting in her face again.

Trent saw the terror on the girl's face and stepped forward, pulling on the guy's shoulder. "Leave her 'lone."

The guy shook him off. "I said, back off. She's my girl. I'll deal with her." The guy began to pull the girl away from the wall as if he would drag her out of there —which he was probably going to try.

"Stop!" Trent grabbed the guy's bicep and pulled him around to face him, not letting go this time. "Let her go." He was getting more sober by the minute.

The guy pushed at Trent's chest, causing him to stumble backwards, only being stopped by whoever was behind him. He was about to start forward again when an arm sliding across his chest stopped him.

"Martin. Why don't you let the girl go now, eh? And we'll forget this all happened." Logan's voice passed by Trent's ear, and he relaxed marginally.

"She's my girl, Detective. All I wanna do is see her home safe and sound. That's all." The guy—Martin— spread his hands out in front of him, a gesture of innocence.

"Let me be the judge of that, Martin." Logan stepped forward, side by side with Trent now. "Miss, do you want to go with Martin, or would you prefer a different escort this evening?”

The girl looked at Logan, then at Trent, then at Martin as they all looked back at her awaiting her answer. Trent knew the minute she’d made up her mind —and his heart sank.

“I’ll go with Martin. Everything’s fine, Officer.”

Trent saw the look of triumph on Martin’s face, which was quickly replaced with a sheen of patience. “See, Detective. Nothin’ to worry ‘bout.”

“Uh-huh. Miss, I will check on you tomorrow. Please make sure you answer.” Logan’s voice was hard and unflinching, and he saw the panic cross the girl’s face. “What’s your name?”

“Monica,” she answered quietly. “Monica DeLuna.”

“Thank you, Monica. I’ll be in touch tomorrow.”

Martin and Monica left, and Trent whirled on Logan. “Why did you let him go? He was going to hurt her.”

“I know he was. And now he isn’t going to be able to because too many people saw him with her, and I will be checking up on her tomorrow. If she has one bruise to show or doesn’t turn up at all, the finger will be pointed at him by many witnesses. Tomorrow, I will be able to have a talk with her and try to get her to tell me what he’s been doing to her.”

“But—” Trent began.

“No, Trent. There was nothing to be done tonight. All you would have done is ended up in a fight that you wouldn’t have won in your state.”

Trent hated that he was right, so went back to the

booth and sat down. He gestured to Gemma as she passed that he wanted a refill.

"Are you sure that's a good idea?" Logan asked as he sat back down.

"Nope, but I'm going to anyway."

"What's going on with Max?"

Trent coughed up some of the beer he'd just started to swallow. "What do you mean? There is nothing going on between me and Max!" He may have said that a little loud if the number of people who turned to look at them was anything to go by.

Logan raised his eyebrows. "I never said there was anything going on between you. I wondered if you knew anything about the guy that was with him."

Trent shook his head. "Nope, never seen or heard of him before."

"Hmm. He seemed nice enough." Logan stared at Trent, and it made him a little uncomfortable. "He's probably having fun with him right now." Logan laughed.

Trent huffed out a breath. "He should be at home," he mumbled to himself.

"Why should he be at home? Why don't you want him to have fun?" Logan's questions were beginning to annoy Trent, especially when he hadn't meant for his words to be heard.

"Because he's got a lot of work on." The excuse sounded dumb even to him.

His beer came, and he drank some down fast. He needed to forget. Forget Max. Forget Frederick.

Forget Trish. Forget everything. He'd had enough tonight.

One hour later, Trent walked with Logan to his car—all right, against Logan. He couldn't quite keep himself upright.

"I don' even like guys. So wha' the prob'em? I had wife for god' sa'e."

"It's all right, Trent. Everything will work out. You'll sort it out with Max, all right," Logan responded.

"'k."

The next morning, when Trent woke, he had a bass drum in his head, desert mouth and a rolling stomach. He blinked open his eyes, wincing in the light but managing to see a bottle of water and some paracetamol on his bedside table next to his clock. He remembered the walk from the car to his house and up the stairs. But the rest was a blur. He would have to thank Logan for looking after him.

He sat up slowly, not wanting to chance sudden movement in these early stages; he knew only too well what quick motions did to his chances of keeping anything down. He swallowed the tablets and the full bottle of water. Gingerly, he stood hesitantly, needing to use the bathroom. It was slow going but he managed to get there, do his business and get back to sitting on the bed without issue. He glanced at the clock, finally being able to discern what the numbers meant. Eleven o'clock. He hadn't a clue what time Logan had loaded him into bed so couldn't tell how long he'd slept. He'd try to remember to ask him later when he also asked about that girl—he'd forgotten her name.

Trent took a few deep breaths, then stood again and made his way, gently and slowly, down the hallway to the kitchen area. He sat on a stool there and took a few more breaths. The nausea was not abating, but he knew it would take a while. He had no idea how much he'd had to drink last night. A small comfort was that he'd stuck with beer all night, so no mixing drinks to make him worse.

He wasn't sure how long he sat there, staring at nothing until a knock on his door had him wincing again. He wasn't going to answer. Nobody needed to see him in this state.

The pounding continued until a voice joined in. "I know you're in there, Trent. Open the door. I need to make sure you're still alive."

Trent's heart rate increased when he identified the voice as Max. He was the last person he'd expected to hear from. He debated ignoring it but knowing Max, he'd call in reinforcements, and then he'd have everyone turn up.

He got up and walked over to the door. He'd just got there when the pounding started again, making him press a hand against his forehead and his mouth to stop the nausea. Once the noise had stopped, he flicked the latch and opened the door slowly. Max bustled his way in without preamble and turned to look at him.

"Bloody hell. You look like death warmed up." He cocked his head. "Nah, even death looked better." Max chuckled. "Have a good evening, Trent?" He smirked.

Trent glared at him. "What do you want, Max?" he asked as he headed towards the kitchen once again. Coffee was calling his name.

"I come bearing gifts." Max held up a carrier bag.

"What?" Trent was lost. He filled the kettle with water and switched it on, resting against the counter, breathing deeply before opening the cupboard for a couple of mugs. As he put them down, Max brushed his hands away and steered him carefully to a chair at the table.

"Sit. I'll finish the coffee and make you some breakfast." Max turned to busy himself with his self-appointed tasks.

"I don't think I can stomach anything right now, but thanks."

"You will. Once you start eating something, you'll begin to feel better. Trust me."

And the funny thing was, Trent did. He sat there, frowning, trying to figure out what was happening. He must have completely spaced out because the next thing he knew, Max placed a steaming plate of cooked breakfast foods in front of him, and he had his hand around a half-empty mug of coffee.

The smell turned his stomach, but he breathed through his mouth so he could at least attempt to eat as a way of thanking Max. But as he started eating, as Max had predicted, he began to feel better. He'd managed to eat the whole plate and drink several cups of coffee before he realised what he'd done.

"Feel better now?" asked Max.

He looked at him, seeing the smugness on his face, but not caring. "Yes. Thanks for that. I really do appreciate it." He frowned, having a thought. "How did you know I needed breakfast?"

Max laughed. "I bumped into Logan this morning, and he said you might be feeling a little delicate. I offered to come around and make sure you were all right. Logan had police stuff to do but said to tell you he'd see you soon." Max finished off the last of his plate and stood to clear them.

"No, leave them. I'll do it." Trent began to stand but Max's words stopped him.

"Nah, sit, rest up. It won't take me long to wash these up. Tell me what happened last night. Logan told me to ask you about a guy and girl?"

"Trust him." Trent huffed. "A guy was harassing a girl and I tried to stop it. Not my finest moment, I have to admit." He stared at the table, frowning. "She looked to be around Jocelyn's age. It made me mad, thinking that it could've been her in that situation and who would've tried to stop it?" The thought of it happening to Jocelyn made his stomach turn. "I only did what I'd want someone to do if they saw it happening to her."

Max was silent for a moment. "It was brave. A little reckless. But brave. I hope I could say that I would've done the same." He placed a plate on the draining board.

"I'm sure you would've." Trent watched Max as he washed and stacked the dishes before wiping down the counter and setting everything to rights. When he picked up the tea towel, Trent intervened, "Leave them to drain. I'll do it later."

Max glanced over his shoulder at him, then nodded, replacing the towel on the hook.

"How is Frederick?" Trent winced as the name came out in a tone associated with a curse word. But Max just laughed.

"He's fine. Glad to have the weekend free if what he told me of his week was anything to go by."

Trent decided to steer clear of the Frederick subject, he didn't know why he brought it up anyway. "What are your plans for the weekend?"

"I have work to catch up on, quotes to prepare, trinkets to buy, materials to source, blah, blah, blah. My usual weekend." Max laughed without humour. "I don't usually do much else on a weekend. Except meet you lot for nights out when they're arranged. Other than that and my usual nights out, I don't do much except work."

"Yeah, I know what you mean. I have plenty of work to keep me occupied, which I should really be doing now, but there is no way I'll be able to concentrate at the moment."

Max cocked his head. "Hey, how about we go for a walk. Some fresh air might do you good."

Trent knew he should say no. He didn't understand his sudden fascination with Max, or Frederick, or guys kissing, but he knew he shouldn't encourage it. On the other hand, it would be nice to get to know Max better, add another friend to his list. Even though he knew better, he nodded. "Let's do it."

Forty minutes later, Trent had showered—slowly—and gotten dressed for the supposedly chilly morning, and they headed out the door. He kept the pace slow, not wanting to push himself too much to begin with. Max led the way, and Trent followed like an obedient dog. He chuckled.

"What are you laughing about?" Max asked.

"I'd just had a thought that I was following you like a dog would." He laughed again. "Like an obedient puppy." He glanced up at Max just in time to see his gaze darken and him lick his lips. Trent's heart began to race, and he looked away. He had no idea what that was about.

Max cleared his throat. "Am I going too fast?"

"Nah, it's okay. You were right, my head is clearing a little. It's just so damn cold." Trent pulled the collar of his coat upright to deflect the chill from his neck some.

"Yeah, sorry. I should have warned you."

Trent spoke the truth when he said his head was clearing of the hangover. The cold had helped, but the closeness of Max brought a different type of confusion to his thoughts. He didn't remember having any kind of leanings towards men in his past, he didn't know why he was suddenly having these ideas. He shook his head, trying to banish the scenes running there.

"What's wrong?" Max asked.

Trent looked at him and blinked, coming back into the present. "Oh, nothing." He changed the subject. "Where are we heading?"

"I thought we'd walk a couple of streets to the café. Get some real coffee. Not that crappy stuff you have." Max laughed. "Sorry, but it's disgusting."

Trent glared at him playfully but agreed with a shrug. "Yeah, well, it's hot. What more do you want?" He huffed. He noticed Max slide a look at him, but he ignored it. "How did you know about the café here? You don't live around here, do you?" He glanced across at Max, seeing him wince.

Max didn't say anything for a moment. "I...kinda... researched it before I came over this morning." He bit his lip.

Trent laughed. "Was the coffee I gave you *that* bad?"

Max joined him in laughter. "Sorry, but yeah. I have a more refined palette, don't you know."

We might disagree on that, he thought as his mind returned to Frederick. Max can't be that refined. Trent shook his head. *That was bitchy, Trent.*

They crossed the road and entered the little corner café. Max asked Trent what he wanted, refusing his offer to pay, and ordered for them both. They made small talk while they waited and doctored their drinks when they were ready. Exiting the café, Trent realised he felt much better.

"Thanks for this." Trent didn't look at Max as he said it but hoped he conveyed his meaning.

Max bumped his shoulder, making Trent glad he had a lid on his coffee. "You're welcome."

They walked back faster, the cold beginning to seep into his bones.

"Do you have any other siblings? Other than the two lawyers?" Max's question came out of the blue. "We've not really talked about families."

"Yeah, I'm the second of five."

"Wow, big family."

"Not quite as big as Logan's, but yeah."

"Who is older than you?" Max sipped at his coffee.

"Samuel, the lawyer. Then me. After that, there's Carter, who's the other lawyer; Luke, who's a personal trainer; and Ava, who's a police officer and Logan's partner."

"Are you close to them all?"

"Yeah, we all get together as much as possible but obviously differing working hours doesn't always work for us. I think I see Logan more than I see my sister, even though they're partners." Trent laughed. "I don't mind. We'd probably be at each other's throats if we saw too much of each other. What about you? I've not heard you mention family much."

Max was quiet for a moment, sipping his coffee as they neared Trent's apartment. "I have two sisters. Charlotte is three years older than me, and Olivia is four years younger. I speak to them on the phone occasionally but don't see them very often. My parents are…struggling with my life choices. We don't talk much. My sisters chose to stay closer to home than I did."

"You're not from Cambridge?" Trent's eyes widened. He'd honestly thought Max was from around there.

Max shook his head. "Nah. I was born in Ashford. Lived there until I was twenty-two. Decided to go to Cambridge for my degree."

Trent waited for more information, but none came. "What made you choose Cambridge?"

Max blew out a breath. "Honestly? I needed away from my parents. They were not as…open-minded as they appeared to the outside world." He shook his head slowly, watching the pavement as they walked. "To everyone outside of the family, they appeared to be the best parents in the world, loving their son regardless of his sexuality, regardless of his interests, regardless of… everything." He looked at Trent. "But to me, they despised me. They probably would've eventually come around to the idea of me being gay, but the interior design I wanted to study? Nope, no way in hell were they going to allow me to do that where everyone could see." He gave a humourless laugh. "I packed my belongings and picked a place with a good course, and here I am. Best decision I ever made."

"Jesus, Max. What did it matter if you wanted to do interior design?"

"To them, it's a 'girly' course, and one I shouldn't have taken. I'd have been an embarrassment to them, to their social standing."

"What about your sisters? You said they're still there?"

"Yeah, still in the same area. Charlotte keeps the peace for the most part. She's the go-between for me and my parents. She is happy for me to be whoever I want to be, but she doesn't agree that I left."

"What about your other sister…Olivia?"

"Now, Livvy, she took a leaf out of my book. She still lives in the same area, but she's doing her own thing. She's twenty-three now and living in a small house in a village near home, painting to her hearts content. She doesn't care what our parents say. They did a similar thing to her when she told them she was pursuing art, but she stood up for herself and stayed in the same area. She's got balls, I'll tell you that." Max laughed.

Trent smiled, glad to have been able to bring Max around to a happier topic. "She sounds a lot like you."

"Yeah, maybe too much."

They arrived at Trent's apartment and entered the warmth, both sighing with relief. Trent removed his coat and scarf and hung it up on the coat hooks, then meandered over to the sofa. Flopping down, he rested his head back and blew out another breath. He couldn't feel many lingering effects of the drink last night apart from a very dull headache, hopefully the tail end of it. He hoped anyway.

He looked over at Max when he realised he'd not moved from his spot when he'd entered. "You not staying?" Trent's stomach turned at the thought, though he ignored it.

"I better get going. I don't want to overstay my welcome." Max turned to the kitchen and threw his cup into the bin. He moved back towards the door.

Trent tried to think of something to keep him here a bit longer, ignoring his reasons for doing so. Then he had a thought. He sat upright, looking at Max. "Hang on a minute." He stared at Max with narrowed eyes. "Do I recall correctly that it's your birthday today?"

CHAPTER FOUR

MAX

Max rested his hands on his hips and looked over at the bookcase. Blowing out a breath, he answered, "Yeah."

Max was pleased he'd managed to get the bookends onto Trent's shelves while he'd been getting dressed. He didn't know how often Trent went over to the shelves, especially as they only had books and pictures on them, so wasn't sure when he would realise they were there. But at least they *were* there, and they fit nicely too.

He couldn't quite believe how much he'd told Trent about his family. He'd never planned to blurt out all the issues he had with his parents, but it just came tumbling out when he'd asked. Trent probably thought he was a loser now. Little did he know exactly how much Max *had* lost. His parents were not poor, put it that way. Max had had a rude awakening when it had all been taken from him when he'd left. He'd assumed, wrongly it turned out, that his parents would still allow him to complete the course, just so long as it wasn't thrown in their faces. Unfortunately, they'd decided that wasn't enough and had cut Max off completely, throwing him quickly into a student's life of poverty.

Sean had offered to pay for his degree, but Max had been too proud to take it. It would've helped immensely, but he was determined to make a way for himself. And he had. Nothing had felt better than when he'd started making money and was able to start repaying his student loan and rent a place to live. Sean had been a lifesaver in that department too; offering him jobs and recommending him as much as he had. It'd made his life a little easier, a lot quicker. He was proving he didn't need his parents' wealth to be able to live the life he wanted.

Trent's voice brought him back. "Why didn't you remind me? Happy birthday!" Trent came over to him. "What are you planning on doing today?"

He shrugged. "In all honesty, I was going to look around a few art galleries, maybe take a walk through some museums. Nothing exciting." Max loved the art galleries—not that he could afford to buy anything for himself—seeing what people could create from different resources was unbelievable sometimes. The museums fascinated him, all the different objects from way back when. Max loved trinkets and things like that, so the museums were his secret favourite place.

"Max?"

"Sorry?" Max had obviously missed what Trent had said.

"I said, would you care for some company? Or would you prefer to be alone?" Trent fidgeted, not looking at him as he asked. "It's okay if you'd prefer to be alone. I just wondered—"

"That would be great." Max didn't know what had prompted Trent to ask to join him, but he was not looking a gift horse in the mouth, as his mother used to say. It was probably not the best idea to spend the whole day with Trent, especially with how Max felt about him, but he wanted to. Maybe he should think of it as a birthday present to himself.

"Brilliant. Let me get ready." Trent ambled off through to his bedroom, and Max chuffed and shook his head. What Max had left out was that he was booked on to a museum tour that afternoon; Trent was going to have an eye-opening experience, and Max might be able to get a better idea of what was going on inside Trent's head.

They decided to get a taxi to save on trying to find parking on a Saturday afternoon. Trent insisted on paying for it, and Max didn't want to offend him by saying he couldn't.

They got out on the main stretch of road and began the short walk to one of the art galleries Max often went to. Trent had admitted he knew very little about art but was willing to learn. He'd told Max about the few paintings they'd had back when he was with Trish; he didn't know the names of them but from what he'd described, Max bet they were worth a pretty penny.

They entered the gallery, and Max waved to the curator, Karen—he'd been here many, many times now, sometimes to look around, sometimes to source art for his job; he'd become good friends with her over time.

"Wow! These are amazing." The awe in Trent's voice was exactly what Max felt when he came to these places. Give him a room and he could design something extravagant from nothing. Stick him in front of a canvas and nothing would happen. He's just not that way inclined, not like Livvy anyway. It had never crossed his mind to ask Livvy to paint something for his place, maybe he should ask her.

"They really are something, aren't they?" Max's gaze roamed the offerings, seeing vibrant colours set alongside greyscale; his visual palette was overwhelmed. He loved the way the coloured ones weren't segregated to a different area to the greyscale ones. They wandered slowly through the gallery, discussing the pictures and debating the reasons for their preferences. Max found he really enjoyed Trent's company.

"Max! How are you?" Karen came up and hugged him tight. "I've not seen you for a few weeks."

"Yeah, I've been swamped at work."

"And I can see your personal life has taken a good turn too. Who is your gorgeous partner?" Karen was married to the museum, but she also had a wife and two kids at home. She was a gossip like no other and would jump to all kinds of conclusions before you had chance to set her right.

"Oh, this is Trent. He's just a friend." Max just saw out the corner of his eye when Trent looked over at him. He didn't understand what the glance meant; how else was he supposed to introduce him?

"Hi, Trent, nice to meet you. Max's friends are always welcome here." They shook hands. "Would you like a cup of tea or coffee?" She indicated behind her and began walking in that direction, not waiting for their answer.

"She's an acquired taste." He chuckled. "She will start interrogating you soon, so be prepared."

"Thanks for the warning," Trent murmured as they followed in her wake, through a double glass door and into a long hallway that had several doors leading off it. Max saw Karen enter one on the right and knew it was the kitchen area. He glanced over at Trent and chuckled quietly.

"You look like you're heading to your execution."

"Am I not?" Trent replied, half-seriously.

Max shrugged. He didn't know if Karen was about to give Trent the third-degree, but he had a feeling she was. They entered the room and found Karen standing at the counter with the fixings for the different choices.

"Coffee please, Karen," he said as he chose a chair at a table close to Karen's position.

Karen nodded and looked over with a raised eyebrow at Trent for confirmation.

"Coffee, please. Milk, no sugar," Trent said, taking a seat next to Max.

They were silent while Karen made the drinks, and as soon as she sat down with her mug, she started.

"So, Trent, what do you do?" She took a sip of her drink, eyeing Trent over the top of it.

"I'm a teacher," Trent said, looking decidedly nervous. Max smothered a smile within his mug.

Karen nodded slowly. "And how long have you known Max here?"

Trent swallowed audibly and quietly replied. "A little under a year."

"Okay, do you have a partner?"

Max snorted into his mug, trying to hide his laughter. Karen was determined to get everything out of Trent. He wondered whether he should stop her but decided to let her ask a few more questions before he "rescued" him.

"Um, not now."

"Oh, so you had one before. When did you break up?" Karen leaned forward and rested her elbows on the table.

"Five years ago," Trent's voice hardened, and Max knew he annoyed, so he decided to step in.

"What are your intentions with Max?" Karen asked before Max could stop her.

"Jesus Christ, woman. You're as bad as a lawyer, and I should know." Trent shook his head and drank more of his coffee.

"What? I just want to make sure Max is looked after," she insisted.

"All right, Karen, back off. Thank you for caring, but I can take care of myself. I have done for many years. Trent is a friend, nothing more, so get off your high horse and be nice." Max drained his mug and stood. "We better go if we want to see more places."

Trent almost jumped out of his seat in his eagerness to leave and Max had to bite back another smile. He walked around the table to Karen and pulled her in for a hug. "Thank you, hun. I appreciate it but he's a lost cause, I think," he whispered to her.

"Why?" she whispered back.

"He's straight."

Karen pulled back and looked at Max, shock showing in her face. "Really? I never would have guessed with the way he looked at you as you walked through the gallery."

Max felt his heartrate increase with the thought that Trent might want him, but he knew it was hopeless. He had to get over this stupid fixation, and he hoped that today's expedition would help with that.

Karen hugged him again, squeezing him tight. "Keep hope. I'm not convinced." She patted his cheek when they parted, and they all walked out to the main gallery area. They said their goodbyes and stepped out into the chilly street.

"Sorry about that. She's a bit like a mama bear sometimes." Max shoved his hands as deep into his pockets as they could go.

Trent was silent for a moment, then he said, "It's okay. I can understand why she'd want to protect you. It's just difficult sometimes having people I don't know asking questions." He paused. "It feels…"

"Intrusive?" Max finished.

Trent nodded slowly. "Yeah, a little."

"Sorry. I'll tell her to back off sooner next time."

Trent laughed. "I'll believe that when I see it. You're just as inquisitive, you know."

Max laughed too. He looked at his watch. "Come on or we'll be late." Max grabbed Trent's wrist and began dragging him down the pavement towards the Museum of Classical Archaeology.

TRENT

"Late for what?" Trent asked as he scrambled to keep up.

"For the tour," Max said as if that would enlighten him.

"*What* tour?"

Max glanced back at him with a smirk. "You'll see."

Trent didn't like that smirk. He didn't trust Max at that moment. He carried on walking because he was curious to what Max was referring.

They entered the museum, and Max led the way to the desk. He spoke to the lady behind it and got a nod in reply. She pointed to her right, seemingly giving Max directions. He turned and waved for Trent to follow him.

"Where are we going?" he asked when he caught up.

"There is a tour I'm booked on. I've just booked you on too. It's down here, she said."

They turned the corner and came to stand with some other people who were milling around and chatting as if waiting for something. They didn't have to wait long.

"Good afternoon, everyone. I hope you're all doing well today. Welcome to the 'Bridging Binaries' tour. This is the first stop on our tour of the four museums this afternoon. I will be taking you on an exploration of the spectrum of LGBTQ identities that exist across the different ages and cultures. I will be telling stories of non-normative gender and sexual identities using a variety of objects relating to the LGBTQ genre..." the tour guide carried on, but Trent had stopped listening. He turned to look at Max and found him already looking at him, biting his lip and with mischief in his eyes.

"Seriously, Max?" Trent whisper, glaring at him.

"But it's my birthday, Trent," Max said with puppy dog eyes and a pout fit for a drama queen.

Trent rolled his eyes and blew out a breath. "Fine."

Max clapped his hands together quietly. "Yay! This will be fun."

Trent wasn't so sure, but he'd deal with it. Max wanted to do this, so they'd do it.

Three hours later, sitting on the sofa at home, Trent's feet were killing him, but he would begrudgingly admit he'd had fun. The tour guides had been a little by-the-book, but Max had expanded on it with comments, information and funny anecdotes to the different artefacts. Trent found out after they'd finished that Max had been on the tour several times before, but he enjoyed the story-telling aspect of it and said he never got bored. Trent's eyes had been opened about some things—which would forevermore be unremarked upon—but Max was a wealth of information.

He had never had any issues with others being gay or bisexual or lesbian or any other word people wanted to use to describe themselves. He looked at the person's personality, and if they appeared to be kind and polite and, basically, a nice person, then he'd give them the benefit of the doubt. Didn't matter what they identified as.

Now, Trish on the other hand. Well, she hated anything to do with "that world" as she always called it. She hated Asher, and just because Logan hung around with him, she hated Logan too. She would never meet up with them, and whenever she did accidentally meet them on the street or whatever, she would stay as far away from them as she could and not talk—almost as if she was afraid to catch something. Another reason why they'd divorced.

But that didn't matter anymore. The only thing he worried about was her opinions rubbing off on *their* kids. Trent had to believe that the kids knew better. He hoped so anyway.

Thinking about his children made him realise he'd still not heard back from Jocelyn. He picked up his phone and settled back onto the sofa, propping his feet on the coffee table. Max had invited Trent to join him at Zak's house, but Trent had declined, wanting Max to be able to spend his time with his friends. In all honesty, he was partially relieved he wasn't going—he needed a breather from Max's presence. His head was still all over the place and several times during the tour, he found himself thinking about them together, which kept throwing his head in a spin.

He decided to see if he could catch Jocelyn first, and then he'd call Samuel. He needed an ear.

"Hi, Dad," Jocelyn said quietly when she answered.

Trent closed his eyes in relief when he heard her actual voice and not the answer message. "Hey, sweetheart. How are you?"

"I'm all right."

Trent was not expecting miracles with this phone call, but maybe he could get her to talk a little. "How's uni?"

"It's good. Have a lot of work to do but I'm managing."

"That's great. Well, not about the amount of work, but that you're managing." *Trent stop babbling.* "Are you still enjoying it?"

"Yeah, it's great. I'm really enjoying the psychology side of things. I don't mind the work really, it's fascinating." Jocelyn's voice was full of joy and excitement, and Trent was over the moon for her.

"I'm so glad you're enjoying it. You'll make a great social worker. I know you will." Trent loved this girl so much; she was so giving and patient and kind—perfect for the job she wanted to do.

"Thanks, Dad."

Trent cleared his throat of the potential tears he could shed at the almost normal conversation they were having. "So, it's your birthday next month. Any ideas what you'd like?"

"Um, not really. There are a couple of textbooks I'd like to get…"

"I'm not buying you textbooks for your birthday." Trent interrupted. "If you need textbooks, let me know and I will give you the money for them. But I'm not buying them for your birthday." Trent shook his head.

"But I know you don't have a lot of money…"

"Jocelyn. Birthdays are for giving things you'd like to have—not for things you *need* to have. What stupidly, crazy item has caught your eye lately that you decided you'd like to have one day?"

Jocelyn laughed quietly on the other end of the phone, and the sound lifted Trent's heart. This. *This* was what he needed each day to lift his spirit's and make each day worthwhile. The sound of his children's laughter.

"Well, I saw a bracelet the other day, which was gorgeous."

Trent winced a little at the potential price of jewellery, but he'd make sure she had it if that was what she wanted. "Okay, anything else?"

"Um, there's the new film out that I wanted to see at the cinema."

"Sounds good. Okay, I'll have a think. Make sure you send me the description of the bracelet and where you found it—no guarantees I'll get it, but it will give me something to look at." Trent was buying the bracelet regardless, even if it was expensive because Jocelyn deserved it. He'd do no less for his kids, even if they didn't speak to him anymore.

"Thanks, Dad." They were silent for a moment, and then Jocelyn said, "Have you heard from Harper?"

"No, why is everything okay?" Trent sat upright, worry coursing through his veins.

"No, no. Everything's fine. I just didn't know if you ever get hold of her."

Trent blew out a relieved breath, settling back again. "No, she doesn't seem to want to talk to me very much. I'm not sure what I've done to upset her, but I haven't heard from her in weeks."

"I'm sorry, Dad. From what I've heard from her, she seems fine and is working hard at college still. She's loving her languages."

"I'm glad. I wish I could talk to her though."

"I'll tell her to ring when I next speak to her."

"It's okay, Jocelyn, don't worry. She'll speak to me

eventually. I hope." Trent could hear the disappointment in his own voice, so knew Jocelyn could hear it too. He heard noises in the background and instinct told him their call was coming to an end.

"Dad, I'm going to have to go. Class is starting in a few minutes."

"Okay, sweetheart. Oh, when is a good time to ring you?"

"There's no wrong time, Dad."

"Okay, love you, sweetheart."

"Love you, too, Dad. Bye."

Trent waited until Jocelyn clicked the phone off before removing it from his ear. He stared at the dark TV, wishing things were different. He was beginning to bridge the gap between him and Jocelyn now—their conversation this time easier than it had been in a while —but Harper, he had no idea what to do.

To avoid his thoughts derailing, he lifted his hand again and dialled his brother.

"Samuel Walker."

"Even on a weekend, Samuel? You can't check who's calling on a weekend?" Trent laughed. He loved teasing him about working so hard.

"I don't get weekends, Trent. That's for people who aren't lawyers." He laughed with it.

Trent joined him. "Did you get chance to meet with Max's friend?"

"Yeah, I saw him yesterday. I can't—"

"I know, I know. I'm not asking for information. I

just wondered if you were able to help him." Trent knew all about client confidentiality.

"Yes, I can help him."

"That's great." Trent was relieved that Max's friend would be able to get help.

"What's wrong?" Samuel was far too intuitive for his own good, but that was what made him a good lawyer.

Trent debated for a moment what to tell him but decided he needed to be open about it. "I'm going to the doctor next week. For a check-up."

"Why, what's wrong?" Trent could tell he had all of Samuel's attention now.

"I'm not sure exactly. I keep misplacing things or outright losing them. One minute, they're there, the next they're not. When I saw the doctor last time, he gave me B12 to help my memory. It doesn't seem to be working. I'm worried…I'm worried it's dementia or something. I don't know, Samuel. Everything feels different. There's something not quite right."

"Jesus, Trent, why didn't you say something earlier?"

"Because I thought I wasn't remembering where I put them. I didn't think anything of it until the things started actually going missing."

"Does anyone have a key to your place?" Samuel asked, ever the lawyer.

"Only Jocelyn and Harper." Trent got up off that sofa and began to pace around.

"Is there any particular time you've noticed this happening?"

"No, but I've not really been paying attention."

"What's gone missing?"

"My watch, you know the one Mum and Dad gave me, the one that belonged to Grandpa, and some gold cufflinks. There's been other stuff as well, but I can't remember what." Trent rubbed his forehead with his fingers, feeling a headache coming on again. He stopped and stared at the bookcase, not really seeing anything as he tried to work through the issues.

"Well, both of those seem like they are worth money. I'm sorry to ask, and I don't in all honesty believe they would, but are you sure one of your kids hasn't taken them because they need the money or something?" Samuel sounded like he knew the answer already, which he did.

"They wouldn't do that. Both would ask for money with no hesitation." Trent frowned when he thought back to his conversation with Jocelyn. "They'd prefer to go without instead of asking for money." His vision centred in on the shelf, and he looked in confusion. Scanning the remaining shelves, he found everything else in place, but that one shelf seemed wrong. "Holy fuck," he whispered.

"Trent? TRENT!" Samuel's voice came through the phone loudly enough to get Trent's attention.

"I'm here," he said quietly, gaze still stuck to that shelf.

"What the fuck is going on?"

"There is a pair of bookends on my shelf that I don't remember putting there. I've never even seen them before. Shit, Samuel, what the hell is wrong with me?" Trent dropped onto the sofa and rested his head in his hands. He could hardly breathe, his breath was harsh, he was dizzy.

"TRENT!" Samuel's voice seemed like a million miles away. "Fuck, I'll be there in a few minutes."

Trent kept hearing Samuel's voice in his ear, even when he could no longer hold the phone up. Banging sounded on his door and it roused him a little. It took him a few minutes, but he was able to get up and open the door. He looked at Samuel in confusion.

"What are you doing here?"

"Shit, Trent, you scared ten years off my life." Samuel came in a shut the door behind him. He took charge, ushering Trent back to the sofa and sat down next to him. "Right, tell me what happened."

"What happened, when?" Trent was confused. He'd just been talking to Samuel, hadn't he?

"Half an hour ago? What made you go quiet on the phone? You told me about the bookends, and then went silent." Samuel spoke softly as if talking to a scared child.

"Half an hour? I don't remember. I remember seeing the bookends—" he pointed to the bookcase, "and then sitting down when my headache got bad. Then nothing until you just turned up." Trent looked up at Samuel and whispered, "What's wrong with me, Sammy?"

Samuel shook his head. "I don't know, Trent. But

we're going to find out. Today." He stood, withdrawing his phone and made a call while walking into the kitchen area. Trent could've overheard if he tried, but he was too tired. He laid his head against the back of the sofa and rested his eyes.

"Trent?" A slight nudging brought him out of his sleep.

"What?" he asked, eyes still closed.

"You have to get up now. We have an appointment at the hospital in half an hour." Samuel looked down at him, worry creasing his face.

CHAPTER FIVE

MAX

Max pulled up at the kerb at Zak's house. He turned off the engine and looked at their house. Most of the lights were blazing, and it looked so inviting—such a difference from his own house. It must be the having a family thing that makes it so. He headed to the front door and rang the bell.

Immediately, he heard raised voices from inside. They were so loud he could hear the words.

"It's probably the babysitter, Ashley," Zak said.

"I don't want her here. There's no need for her to be here. I am quite capable of looking after Dane by myself," she screamed.

"I know you are, but I thought you wanted a break. I arranged the babysitter because it meant you could have some time to yourself. I was trying to do something nice," he replied, voice sounding soothing.

"Fine! I'm going out then."

Max heard some footsteps beating up the stairs

and others walking towards the door. Zak opened the door, looking weary and winced when he saw it was Max.

"Hey," Max said, quietly.

"Come on in." Zak indicated with his head.

Max followed and closed the door behind him. It was eight in the evening, so Dane would already be in bed.

"Sorry about…" Zak waved his hand. "You probably heard every word."

"No problem."

Zak nodded slowly. "We just need to wait for the babysitter to arrive, which will be any time now."

They both looked towards the stairs when Ashley appeared, sneering at Zak. "I'll be home when I'm home," she said and stalked out the house, slamming the door behind her.

Max winced, hoping Dane would stay asleep. *Bloody hell. This is worse than I thought.*

Another knock at the door made Zak get up again. He answered, and Ethan's sister came in.

"Hey, Max. I hear happy birthday is in order!" She came in for a hug.

"Hey! I didn't realise you were babysitting now! Although, I bet you've had a lot of practise with Ethan and Eric," he said, laughing.

"Definitely. If I can sort them out, I can sort anyone out." She laughed. "I don't do it often, but I love little Dane and it gets me out of the house for a while. If I stare at too many spreadsheets, my eyes will go square." She shrugged. "Gives me a chance to raid someone else's DVD cabinet too."

Zak laughed. "Which you are more than welcome to do, as you know."

Emily smiled. "Yes, I do, and it's much appreciated." She looked around. "I saw Ashley leave."

Zak grimaced. "When I told her you were coming, she decided to go out for the night. Not sure if she'll be home before me or not." He bit his lip. "Could I ask that you stay here until I get back, even if she is here?"

"I can try. She may not let me, though."

"If she kicks up a stink about it, then just leave. I'll pay you now; at least you'll have it."

"No, no. I can wait. Go, have fun, and you can pay me later if I don't see you tonight." Emily smiled at him and motioned for them to leave. "Go!"

Zak gave her another hug, and they left, closing the door quietly.

Once they were situated in the car and Max had started the short journey to Romano's, he asked Zak about the lawyer.

"Did you manage to speak to that lawyer?"

"Yeah. He was really good." He sighed. "I know what needs to be done. It's just doing it that might be a pain in the ass."

Max didn't want to pry when it wasn't welcome, so he just said, "You know where I am if you need anything."

Zak nodded, and they slipped into silence for the rest of the trip.

They entered Romano's and were immediately served by the hostess. She asked them to follow her to their table. Max's eyebrows rose when he saw who is waiting for him. He had assumed it would be the normal crew: Sean, Zak and Ethan, but there was also Eric, Asher and Logan.

"Hey, I didn't realise you were all going to be here," Max said. It was a nice surprise.

"Yeah, we thought you could use some extra friends as you're such a loser," Ethan said.

Everyone laughed.

"Thanks for that, Ethan. Much appreciated," he replied sarcastically, sitting on one of the chairs they'd squashed around two tables. They probably could have done with three tables, but they'd manage.

"I hear we need a happy birthday, Max. Is that right?" Rosalia asked.

"'Fraid so, Rosalia. Another year older but never wiser."

"You'd be surprised how wise you can get in a year," Rosalia said with a small smile. "What can I get you gentlemen to drink?"

After a bit of discussion, during which Rosalia was very patient, they decided upon a couple of bottles of wine to share between them. Rosalia told them she'd get their drinks and be back for their food order.

"Let's decide on our food first, then we can talk. I

don't want to make Rosalia have to wait again," Max said.

They all agreed and spent the few minutes deciding. Then they moved onto different topics.

"What does it feel like to be another year older, Max?" Eric asked.

"Unfortunately, the same as last year," Max answered with a smile. Eric was the youngest of their group and was a big-time actor. He was often off doing a film. He'd been in many blockbusters, and he was only twenty-two.

"Life doesn't get any easier the older you get," Asher said. Sean nodded alongside him. "If anything, it gets harder."

"God, let's not get depressed before we've even started, eh?" Ethan joked.

They laughed as Rosalia came back to the table with another waitress to help carry all the glasses. After they were deposited around the tables and had begun to be filled, Rosalia took everyone's orders.

"Thanks, Rosalia."

"You're very welcome, Max. The food should be here in about thirty minutes or so. Have a good evening."

"So, what news does anyone have for me?" Max asked. "I've not seen some of you for a while."

"Oh, it's been absolutely ages since you've seen us, Max. A whole twenty-four hours. That's an age!" Sean laughed.

It was so good to hear the genuine happiness coming from Sean nowadays. Since he'd met Asher, he'd become more open, more giving with his emotions than in all the time Max had known him. They'd had a rocky start and had almost not worked out, but words provided by a now friend, Owen, had made Sean see the light. It was lucky, too, because Asher had almost given up hope. Now, they spent as much time together as possible and Asher's niece, Janie, who Asher had gained custody of when his sister died almost three years ago, had hit it off with Sean right from the beginning, and their relationship grew every day.

"How else am I going to get to know Logan? It's a good job he's here. I'd been thinking I'd have to go through the police academy to get to know him better. Well, either that or get arrested, and I didn't fancy that option."

They all laughed and so the jokes about what Max would have to do to get arrested set the tone for the rest of the night. Max was really enjoying himself, and he'd finally been able to speak to Logan in more depth. He was a great guy, just a little down on his luck with men. He looked around the table and found that all but Ethan and Zak were gay. He found it funny how gay people seemed to find themselves around other gay people. They seemed to gravitate towards each other. He could understand the reasons behind it. After all, the stigma attached to being gay was still alive and kicking.

Rosalia brought the food out, and they ate with gusto, all catching up with each other. Max hadn't had this level of camaraderie for years, since university, but that was all for show and homework support, not real-life support. He looked around at everyone, suddenly extremely grateful to have these great people in his life.

Max heard a phone ring but didn't pay any attention until Asher answered it with, "Hey, Trent...Oh, hi, Samuel, everything okay?" Asher had one finger in his ear as he pressed the phone to the other ear, and Max shamelessly eavesdropped on the conversation. "Is he all right...what happened...he's never mentioned it to me before...yeah, sure...no, no, it's fine We'll come over to his place now...yeah, okay...see you shortly." Asher hung up and turned to Sean. "Hey, sweetheart, we have to go." He turned to Max. "Sorry, to leave you Max, but we have to head out."

"Is everything okay?" Max asked, worried.

"Yeah, I think so. Trent's been having some issues, and Samuel has asked us to keep an eye on him tonight because he has work to do." Asher and Sean were busy putting their coats on and grabbing their things.

"Can I help?" Max was decidedly more worried now he knew something was wrong, especially as he didn't know what *exactly* was wrong. Trent had seemed fine when he'd left earlier.

"No, don't spoil your birthday. Stay here and have fun. I'll send you an update in a bit." With that, Asher gave him a hug and walked to the exit. Sean followed, after a hug too. Max watched them leave, annoyed that they hadn't let him go with them. He stared at nothing as his mind whirled with the reasons for their sudden departure. Why would Trent need someone to look after him? Was he hurt? Was he ill? Was he drunk? Max had no idea, and it burned his gut that he had no reason to go and find out.

"If it's any consolation, he's in good hands." Logan's voice was quiet in his ear but still made him jump. "Sorry."

Max waved him away. "It's okay. I was miles away." He chose to ignore the comment about Trent for the moment and took a drink of his wine, letting the flavours travel along his taste buds. He was not normally a wine drinker, but Romano's had limited alcoholic drinks so when needs must and all that.

"Max." Logan waited until he looked at him. "He'll be fine."

Max stared at Logan while biting his lip, frowning but nodded. There wasn't much he could do anyway, so he concentrated on eating his food. Maybe he could nip over to see him tomorrow.

An hour later, he received a text from Asher.

Trent is fine. He's suffering from headaches, but he's sleeping now. Don't worry. Happy birthday, Max.

He was still worried, but at least there was someone looking after Trent.

TRENT

Trent sat on the sofa with the TV on, but he wasn't

watching it. He listened to Asher and Sean in the kitchen. They'd been with him, on and off, for the past three days. Since the visit to the hospital with Samuel on Saturday, he'd not been alone for more than an hour. And he was getting tired of it. He understood that they were just taking precautions until he got the test results back, but it was smothering him. He needed his own space back.

He made a decision. He stood and walked to where they were quietly talking—probably discussing him—and spoke firmly. "You two can go home now. It's not that I'm not grateful, I am, but enough is enough. I am more than capable of looking after myself just like I was before this happened."

Asher glanced over at Sean before looking back at him. "I know you are, Trent. That's what we were just talking about. Samuel wanted to make sure you're okay, but we think you are. We're not doctors, but I can't see any reason why you need to be watched, for want of a better word." He smiled and came across to Trent. "But if you feel...I don't know, unsure, confused, whatever, ring us straight away. Got it?"

Trent smirked. "Yes, Doctor."

"Smart ass," Sean replied just as someone knocked at the door.

Trent walked over to answer, raising his eyebrows when he saw Trish standing there. He gritted his teeth and tried to appear calm in front of Asher and Sean. "Hey, what's up?"

She obviously had no qualms about airing their dirty

laundry in front of others as she stalked past, ignoring Asher and Sean, already throwing barbs at him. "You've not answered any of my messages for three days, Trent. I know you have a 'life,'" she used finger quotes, "but I need the money for Harper's uniform. Like yesterday. She also needs some more books." She stopped and turned to him, crossing her arms, her long fingernails tapping her bicep.

He took a breath. "You're going to have to wait, Trish. You know I don't get paid until the end of the month. You can have the extra money then." He waited for the explosion to come as was the usual response when he refused to give her money. He felt bad that Harper couldn't have the uniform straight away, but he honestly didn't have any spare money, everything in his bank was accounted for with bills. And even though he'd said she could have extra money, he couldn't really afford it. Most of his wage was taken up with bills and paying for two kids to go to university. Okay, Harper wasn't there yet, but he'd been paying into a bank account each month ready for when she went. For him to afford the extra things was taking money away from where he needed it. But he'd deal.

"That's not good enough, Trent. She needs them now."

"Then you'll have to pay for them for now, and I'll give you the money when I have it." His gaze flicked to where Asher and Sean were trying not to show they could hear everything.

"I don't have the money! So how the hell can I buy

the stuff for her?" she screeched, then stalked past him again, nudging his shoulder as she slammed the door behind her.

Trent shook his head, looking at the floor with his hands on his hips, wishing with everything that was in him that she hadn't been the one to give him Jocelyn and Harper. He would *never* wish things were different because otherwise they wouldn't be here, but he *could* wish that Trish hadn't been involved. Not much he can do about that now.

"You okay?" Asher asked.

"Yeah, same shit, different day, that's all," he replied with a humourless laugh.

"I'm so glad you got out of there."

"Me too, although doesn't seem much different to when I was with her in all honesty."

"Just remember you now have your independence, which you didn't have before." Asher held up his hand. "And don't try to tell me that she didn't curb your nights out because I know she did."

Trent clenched his jaw and looked away.

"Anyway, we're going to leave you to it."

"Thanks, guys, I appreciate it."

They grabbed their belongings and headed out, waving as they went. No doubt, they'd update Samuel, and he'd receive a phone call shortly. Just as he sat down with a coffee, there was another knock at the door.

"Trish, I told you—" he stopped his words when he

realised Trish had not come back for more arguments. Max was stood on his doorstep. "Oh, hey."

"Hey. Bad time?" he asked with raised eyebrows.

"Nah, come on in." Trent opened the door wider, indicating inside with a cock of his head.

"I can come back."

"No, honestly, it's okay. My ex-wife had just been here, and she wasn't happy when she left so I assumed she was back for more." Trent shut the door. "Coffee?"

"God, yes, please. I had to forgo my cup this morning, and I so need one." Max rested a large bag near the doorway.

"What, even my awful instant stuff?"

Max laughed. "Yes, even your horrible instant stuff will be better than nothing."

"Wow, thanks. High praise indeed." Trent chuckled but went about making what he knew was awful coffee. He just couldn't afford anything better. "So, what's up?"

"Nothing, really. I heard you were under house arrest so decided to spring you. But it looks like someone already did." Max smirked, then sobered. "I know Asher and Sean left on Saturday, but no one knew what had happened. I wanted to check on you."

Trent brought a mug over to Max and indicated the sofa. "I'm all right." He took a breath, trying to decide how much to explain. They'd become closer over the past week, especially with the day they spent together on Saturday, so he decided to tell him the truth. He started slowly. "I've been losing random things over the past few weeks, and I'd been worried that there was something wrong. Mentally, I mean. Dementia, maybe. Or Alzheimer's. Then on Saturday afternoon, I found something that I don't ever remember buying, and it flipped a switch. I was on the phone to Samuel at the time, and when I went silent, he came rushing over. He managed to get me to the hospital for a scan. I'm just waiting for the results." Trent finally looked at Max to see him wide-eyed, mouth open. "You okay?"

"Shit." Max put his coffee down and rubbed his hands over his face several times. He mumbled something into his hands.

"What?" he again, feeling lost.

He came up for air, looking pale. "I said, what did you find?" he asked quietly.

Trent frowned at the question, wondering why it mattered. "Some bookends. On the bookcase. I don't remember buying them—"

"You didn't," Max interrupted softly.

"What?"

Max took a deep breath and let it out in one big gush of air. "You didn't buy them. I did. God, I'm so stupid. I never thought of the repercussions. I'm so sorry, Trent. I was just trying to help, even though you'd told me not to. I wanted to do something for you and didn't think it through properly. I never thought about it. If I'd realised you were having problems, I would never have done it. I'm really sorry. God, I'm such an idiot. I need to stop butting in on people's lives when they tell me not to. Fuck!"

Trent couldn't stop Max's verbal diarrhoea because

he was too shocked to say anything. He just stared at him.

Max stood suddenly. "I'm going to go. I'm really sorry, Trent. I didn't think it through. I won't bother you—"

"Sit down." Trent shook his head. He couldn't let Max believe it was his fault, although he was slightly to blame. "It's not your fault. Well, not *all* your fault." Trent huffed.

"What do you mean?" Max was still standing.

"Sit down. I'll explain." He waited until Max had sat and began. "The bookends threw me, for definite. But there have been other items, which have gone missing in the last few weeks. You weren't to blame for them, were you?" Trent cocked his head.

"No," Max said slowly, obviously not wanting to absolve himself yet.

"Then don't worry." Trent smirked. "But next time, tell me, even if you do think I'll be mad. All right?"

Max nodded, hesitantly, and Trent saw his gaze shoot to the door and linger, biting his lip. "Actually..." Max started.

"You brought something else, didn't you?" Trent laughed, shaking his head and rolling his eyes. "And you were going to do the same thing, weren't you?"

Max blushed and nodded. "Yes, though how I thought I'd get away with it, I don't know." Max looked up at him from under his eyelashes and the look shot straight to his cock.

"Go get it," he said, voice slightly lower from the sudden arousal flowing through his body.

Max stood with a small smile and retrieved the bag, giving Trent time to adjust his cock to sit better behind his zip.

"You don't have to have it if you don't want it," Max said shyly.

"Gimme," Trent replied, hands making grabbing motions.

Max laughed and handed over the bag. Trent opened it to reveal something in a soft green fabric. He pulled it out and laughed when he realised how big it was. When it was fully out of the bag, Trent took his time to look at it. It was a throw, he assumed for his sofa; and it was perfect. Trent frowned.

"If you don't like it, I can take it back."

Trent looked at Max, seeing the distress on his face. "No, it's...I love it. Thanks." He fingered the softness, more than a little overwhelmed with the gift.

"Let's put it on," Max said softly as if he realised this was a big thing for Trent.

He cleared his throat and stood. Max helped him spread it over the sofa, making it instantly look better and more homely. He cleared his throat again. "Thanks, Max."

Max squeezed his shoulder. "You're welcome." They sat down again. "Now tell me about your ex-wife."

"Do I have to?" Trent whined, starting to feel more at ease again.

"Nope, but I thought you might want to."

He sighed. "She came around earlier wanting money, as usual. Granted it was for stuff for Harper, but she drives me crazy."

"That's why you divorced her, wasn't it? Because you couldn't live with her anymore?"

Trent hesitated. No one knew the real reason he left. He had thought it better that his friends just believed that he left because he'd had enough of her. If they knew she'd cheated on him, they would've hated her even more, though why that would've bothered him, he didn't know.

"You don't have to tell me," Max said.

What was it about this guy that made him want to spill his guts? "She cheated on me."

"Oh, Trent." Max reached forward and rested his hand on his knee.

He looked at Max's hand for a moment, feelings swirling through him that he couldn't understand. "It probably wasn't the first time. I came home from school early one day. I was ill, and the head had sent me back. Found them in the shower together, so as they were… finishing off, I packed a bag." He laughed. "She couldn't do anything to deny it, though she tried to tell me I was overreacting." He huffed. "She hasn't changed."

"Bloody hell, Trent. I was right when I said she was a bitch."

"Yeah, she was and still is." He laughed. Trent was still aware of Max's hand on his knee, which he hadn't removed, and suddenly, it became like an elephant in the room. Trent's breath increased as he locked eyes with Max, he wasn't sure if in fear or anticipation of what might happen. What was he thinking! He was straight! He saw Max lean closer, and Trent didn't move. He knew what was going to happen but couldn't either stop it or encourage it.

When Max's mouth touched his, Trent's eyes closed, and he felt the softness of the caress all through his body. When he felt his cock harden, he panicked, standing up so quickly, he knocked over the mugs.

"What the hell, Max!" he shouted as he stormed to get a cloth to clean up the mess. "I'm not gay! We've just been talking about my ex-wife, for god's sake!"

"Fuck!" He heard Max say. He turned back to the sofa and saw Max walking to the front door. "Sorry, Trent." With that, Max opened the door and left, closing it quietly behind him.

Trent stood staring at the door, confused by the feelings that were streaming through his body: anger, denial, want, arousal. The feeling that he wanted Max to come back. What was going on?

CHAPTER SIX

MAX

"Fuck, shit, damn, bugger, blast! What the fuck were you thinking, Max?" Max stormed to his car, shaking his head and took the anger at his stupidity out on the car door, slamming it shut. He leaned his head back against the headrest and rubbed his face, squeezing his eyes shut. He couldn't help but see Trent's face behind his closed lids and feel the softness of his lips. "Stop it." He sat upright and started the car. He had cleared the rest of the day so he could see how Trent was and now he had the luxury of several empty hours ahead of him. Wonderful.

As he drove home, he thought about what he'd just lost. Trent wouldn't come near him now, not unless he had no choice. What the hell had he been thinking? Trent was straight and just because he'd let him hold his knee, he went in for a kiss! *Jesus fucking Christ, Max Hughes!*

Arriving home, he slammed the door of his car again, then slammed the door to his house. If he could find other things to slam too, he would. Max threw himself on his sofa and shouted, "Argh!" He was so pissed at himself. He frowned. No, he wasn't just pissed at himself. He was annoyed at Trent because he'd rejected him.

Max blew out a frustrated breath and checked the time. It was early, but he still had time to get ready to go out for the evening. If he headed for an AN club, he could chill out and watch the others go at it and maybe find a partner for a few hours. Plan made, he stalked to the bathroom to get sorted.

Several hours later, he found himself at Chalice, an AN club about half an hour outside of Cambridge. He was dressed slightly different to his usual fare, as he was not quite sure what he wanted tonight. He wore a black sweater with black tailored trousers visible to others but underneath…a leather chest harness and attached jockstrap. The chest harness felt snug but didn't chafe. The straps fed from a metal ring place in between his shoulder blades, a strap going over each shoulder and going under each arm then were secured across his upper chest by a metal belt hook. Two more straps smoothed down each side into his trousers and attached to the jockstrap. Basically, he was trussed up like a turkey, but he felt decadent.

Striding into the club after using the fingerprint access, he set himself down at the bar, smiling with the feel and sound of the leather straps moving.

"What can I get you?" the bartender asked.

"Whisky, please," he replied.

"You drink that, no one will touch you tonight." A woman was sat two seats down from him, looking at him in question.

He hesitated as did the bartender. He thought he'd come here for some fun, but maybe he hadn't. He knew the rules about alcohol after all. AN had a strict rule that anyone who had drank strong alcohol was unable to take part in scenes or play because it reduces inhibitions and the feel of pain; therefore, someone might agree to more than they could take. He looked at the woman, then at the bartender and said, "Whisky, please." The bartender nodded and walked away.

The woman nodded. "Probably a good call if you're feeling out of sorts. You might take on more than you wanted to."

"May I?" Max indicated the seat next to her. She nodded, so he sat and contemplated his hands, not sure what to say.

"You know, within these walls, I had a sub who'd been with me for a few years. Not in real-life, but here, we would always be together. He's just got married to a beautiful young woman. I'm not hesitant to say that I know it won't last. Why would I say that, I hear you think? Because he's suppressing everything for her. All his urges, his needs, his wants. Everything is being tucked away in a tidy little box inside his head and heart. Don't get me wrong, I'm happy he's found her, but I hate that he'll be unhappy. So, here I sit, waiting for my backup sub so we can give each other what we need without having to hide. I'm a Domme, no being able to hide that, here or in real-life."

Max took a breath and knew he'd been right to come here. "I have confusing feelings for a straight friend. He was having issues, so I went over today to spend the afternoon and keep him company. We got talking about his ex-wife and what a bitch she was. I tried to comfort him. Then I kissed him. I don't know what made me think it was a good idea. We were sat there, eyes locked, and the next minute, he jumps up yelling he's not gay." Max shook his head.

"Not everyone can change the way they've always been. Some people have to work hard to change, some people find it easy, and some people don't want to change. If you've seen something inside him, he may not even realise it's there. Or he does realise and is scared. If he's been straight for however many years and has had no inclination at all towards men in that time, this may come as a surprise, and with it a struggle, for him."

"I thought I saw interest, and not just on this occasion, but maybe I was wrong."

"And that's what's worrying you." Max stared at her open mouthed. She laughed. "You're worried on two counts. One that you're wrong and this guy is straight, therefore, you've blown your friendship into the wind. The second count is that you're worried you're right. And if you are, what does that mean for him? And for you. Because if he is bisexual and is only just realising it, he may not choose you."

Max closed his eyes and dropped his head. A slim hand rested against the top of his head, stroking through his hair. He felt her lean closer.

"Trust your instincts. Follow them where they lead you. Regardless of the final destination, you will arrive where you need to be."

Max felt someone come to stand close by. He lifted his head, dislodging her hand, to find a face he recognised but didn't know by name waiting beside the woman. He was dressed in a suit and looked a little harried.

"Sub." The woman nodded to her submissive, then turned to Max. "My name's Staci, by the way." She held out her hand.

Max was glad to know her name, but he replied, "Thank you for your time, Mistress," as he shook her hand and bowed his head to her.

"Such manners." She smiled. "I will leave you to your evening. Think about what I said, and come find me if you need anything, Max."

He watched as she left with her sub trailing behind her. It was only after she left his sight, that he wondered how she knew his name. He turned to his drink but decided he wasn't in the mood tonight. He pushed the drink away and stood. He caught the bartender's eye and indicated he was finished.

"Mistress Staci has already settled your bill, Mr Hughes."

Max's eyes widened. "Oh. Please tell her thank you."

"I will. Have a good evening."

Max huffed and shook his head, then turned to leave. He had a lot to think about. As he exited the club, he headed towards his car, which was parked a couple of streets over. As he got to the end of the building, he was yanked into the alley by his shirt and thrown to the floor.

"You made me lose my membership!" The guy shouted and threw a fist towards Max. Although Max was fit, he didn't stand a chance when he was already off kilter.

Max recognised the voice but couldn't put a face to it. He put his hands up in front of his face as the guy's fists rained down on him. He felt the punches hit his head, stomach, arms. After a few moments, the guy's weight was gone, and Max laid back breathing heavily, cradling his nose, which he thought was broken.

"You're all talk, you are. Getting me thrown out of the club! Who do you think you are!"

All the breath in his lungs was expelled when he was kicked in his stomach. Max groaned as the kicks kept coming: his stomach, his side, his legs, his face. He tried to roll to protect his front but ended up getting stomped in the kidneys instead. He didn't know which was worse.

One consolation, Max thought, he knew who he was.

After a few more minutes of the kicking and stomping, Max realised he couldn't feel much at all, which he distantly worried about. Then the blows stopped.

"Now, who's got issues, eh?" The guy spat in his face, then Max heard footsteps retreating quickly.

Max groaned as he tried to find a position that didn't hurt. He knew he was in trouble but couldn't move enough to go and get help. He didn't know how long he'd been there before he remembered his phone was in his pocket. With every movement sending knives up and down his body, he removed his phone and placed it in front of his face. He couldn't see well enough to open the app and press the button he needed to, but he did know that he'd programmed number one to redial the last number. Using his limited vision to figure out the correct button, he dialled and pressed the phone near his ear.

"Hello?" A hesitant voice answered, and Max closed his eyes the rest of the way when he realised Trent was the last person he'd called. "Max?"

"T-Trent?" Max's throat felt like glass.

"Max? Are you okay?" Trent's voice was a balm to his soul.

"Trent…need…help," he managed to get out, every breath sending shards through his torso.

"Max? Where are you? What happened?" Max could hear panic in Trent's voice but could do nothing to alleviate it.

"Chalice…alley," he croaked.

"What's Chalice? What alley?"

Max coughed wetly, feeling himself losing consciousness. "Club…Chalice…alley…" Then he saw nothing but black.

TRENT

"Max? Max! Answer me! Shit!" Trent looked at his phone and saw it was still connected. "Max!" He had no idea what or where Chalice was. He didn't disconnect but hoped to god he could find him. He had no idea what was wrong, but he could tell Max was in pain. He opened the search tab on the internet and searched 'Chalice club'. A dozen results came up but the closest one was half an hour away and was a BDSM club. After the throwaway comments Max made the other day, Trent had a feeling that was the right one.

He ran out of his house after grabbing his keys and began the drive. He could hear nothing on the open line, which kept Trent worried sick for the whole journey. He debated whether to ring anyone else to help him. He wasn't sure why Max had called *him* in the first place, especially with how they'd left things. But regardless, he would be there to help him in…eight minutes. God, this was taking forever.

Finally, he pulled up on double yellow lines near the

club. As he got out, he saw a bouncer throw someone out the door and shout for them to stay away. Not the kind of club he planned on frequenting. He scanned the building, trying to figure out where Max might be, then decided to end the current call and redial Max's mobile, hoping he'd hear it ringing.

A few seconds later, a very quiet ringtone began. Trent followed the sound around to the right of the building and down an alley. As he saw a human-shaped lump on the floor, he began to run.

"Max!" He knelt next to him, breath catching as he saw the state he was in. He wasn't sure what to do. He gently stroked Max's hair, talking to him but he wasn't getting any response. He had to decide: try and move him to the car or call an ambulance. He gently turned Max to his back, eliciting a groan from him and very slow movement.

"Max?" He saw Max trying to open his eyes, but they were both mostly swollen shut.

"Trent?" Max's voice was hoarse, but Trent heard him.

"Yes, Max. I'm here. What happened?" Max didn't reply but tried to get up, hissing and slumping back down when it was obviously too painful.

"Help…me…home," Max croaked.

"Max, you have to go to hospital! You're black and blue!"

"No!" It would have come out as a shout had he been at full fitness.

"Fuck, Max! Please, let me take you to hospital," Trent pleaded with him.

"No…home."

"Fuck! You're such a stubborn asshole. Fine, then you're coming to my house."

"Phone?"

Trent looked around and found Max's phone on the ground next to them. He tucked it in his pocket, then lifted Max into his arms and got unsteadily to his feet. He walked to his car, careful not to move him too much, and then laid him on the back seat, giving him some bundled up tissues to hold beneath his nose. Trent ran around to the driver's side just as someone came walking out of the club towards them. The guy waved as if to get his attention, but Trent was not interested. He just wanted to get Max home. He pulled away and headed in the right direction. It would be a trek back, but he had to hope that Max would be better closer to home rather than here.

The trip home seemed to take even longer because he drove carefully, but eventually they arrived. He carried Max to the lift and down the corridor to his apartment. Luckily, the night porter didn't spend his time in the front entrance to the building; otherwise, Trent would've had a lot of explaining to do. He still might if anyone looked through the CCTV videos at any point. Unlocking his door was fun, but he managed it, closing it with his foot.

Trent laid Max out on his bed, hearing no protest of any kind from Max. He was out cold again. Trent decided to remove some of Max's clothes, so he didn't overheat now he was out of the cold weather. Once he removed his coat, he left Max while he got some paracetamol and water for him. By the time he returned, Max was awake again.

"Hey, how are you doing?" Trent sat on the edge of the bed carefully, trying not to bounce too much.

"Okay…phone?"

"Oh, yeah, hang on." Trent left the tablets and water on the bedside table and went for his own coat which he'd taken off when he'd gone for the water. He retrieved the phone and handed it to Max.

Max held it up to his face, close, groaned and dropped his arms back to the bed.

"Do you want me to do something on your phone?" Trent asked.

"Yeah…AN…open."

Trent opened Max's phone, then pressed the AN button. "Passcode?" Max lifted his thumb so Trent turned the phone so Max could reach. "Okay, what now?"

"Red…button."

Trent saw it. "What, I just press it?"

Max nodded, then winced in pain. "Not a…call…a message."

Trent raised his eyebrows but did as asked. He saw the red icon turn green and blinking so told Max that.

"Thanks." Max wheezed, so Trent passed the water to him, helping him sit up a little to take a sip. As he laid him back down, he felt something underneath

Max's sweater and wondered what it was. He decided to have a look at his chest to see if there were any visible marks—and see what was underneath. He lifted Max's sweater, gasping when he saw the bruising, then all the air left him when he saw the leather harness. Trent's immediate reaction was not appropriate for the situation, but try as he might, his cock would not calm down.

"Fuck!" he mouthed.

Max tried to pull the sweater back down, but Trent had a question.

"Do you want the hospital or doctors to see this?"

Max hesitated, then shook his head.

"Then shall I help you take it off?"

Max nodded slowly. Trent helped Max take off the sweater, trying to ignore the hisses and groans of pain coming from Max. Once it was done, he let Max rest for a few minutes before trying to figure out the harness.

"Undo front...clasp," Max croaked. Trent was sure Max had some broken ribs.

Trent did as Max said, rolling him to each side to take it off his shoulder. He eyed the remaining leather heading down into his trousers, not sure how to do that bit. He looked to Max. "How do I...?" He indicated Max's trousers.

"Don't...worry...leave it," Max said.

"No, I don't mind. I just don't know how it works."

"Need to...get naked..." Max smirked, then hissed as the cut on his lip began bleeding again.

Trent blushed and closed his eyes in embarrassment.

"Joking…undo trousers…unclip strap…each side," Max said.

Trent cleared his throat, then moved his hands to Max's zipper. He bit his lip as he lowered the zipper, then spread the trousers wide. He noticed the clips and unfastened them quickly, then redid the trousers.

"There…not so…difficult…was it?" Max huffed, then groaned.

"Serves you right," Trent replied haughtily. He folded the harness up and moved to his wardrobe. "I'll put it in here for now, in case we get visitors."

As he closed the doors, there was a knock at the front door.

"No idea who that will be at this time of night," Trent murmured.

"Might be…for me," Max said.

"Okay, if you say so." Trent headed towards the front door and found a guy carrying a medic bag.

"Mr Walker?" he asked.

"Yes, can I help you?"

"I'm here to see Mr Hughes."

Trent stared at the stranger, feeling that life was becoming a little surreal. "Sure. This way." He led him to the bedroom. "Max, you have a visitor."

The medic went right to work, checking Max over, asking questions, generally being a doctor. At the end of the examination, the medic insisted Max was to go to the hospital.

"Please remember the guidelines, Mr Hughes. Keep

the location of the incident vague when you talk to the police, which you will undoubtedly have to do. The information I've gathered here and whatever you send through when you are feeling up to it, will be sent to the owners. They will find who did this, and you'll be notified. I would suggest someone stays with you for a short period of time during the investigation." The medic talked quietly; Trent thought maybe he wasn't supposed to hear.

The medic stood. "Mr Hughes, it's been a pleasure. Remember the guidelines for talking to friends as well. Small non-descript ideas work best." He looked at Trent. "Although, that might be impossible with this one."

With that, he nodded and left. Trent heard the front door shut, and he stared at Max. "What the hell was that about?"

"My personal…medic," Max joked.

"Fine, whatever. Sounds like you're not allowed to tell me anyway. Let's get you ready for hospital. I'll carry you to the car." Max didn't argue, so Trent knew he was in pain. That's when he realised the paracetamol were still on the bedside table. "Shit, Max, I didn't give you the pain relief."

"It's okay…get some…at hospital."

After struggling to get Max back into his sweater, Trent manoeuvred Max into the back of the car again and drove to the hospital. He abandoned his car in the middle of the road and got Max out, carrying him through the doors of A&E. A nurse saw him straight away and called for a gurney where Trent laid him out to more groans.

"What happened?" a doctor asked him.

"I…I don't know exactly. He was at a club, and I got a phone call from him asking me to go get him. He sounded in pain. When I got there, he was in an alley. Like this." Trent indicated Max's body.

"What's his name?"

"Max Hughes."

"Are you family?"

"I'm…" Trent knew what would happen if he said no, "his boyfriend," he finished quickly, trying not to blush or wince at the lie.

"Okay, head over to the reception desk so the nurse can fill in some details, and we'll get you some information as soon as we can." The doctor and nurses wheeled Max away from him, and Trent watched, his heart aching, though he didn't know why.

As Trent sat waiting, after giving the nurse as much information as he could, he thought about who to call. Eventually, they'd figure out he wasn't Max's boyfriend, and they'd need someone else. With everything Max had said about his parents, he knew they were not worth a call but maybe his sisters? When he realised who he needed to call, Trent rolled his eyes and retrieved his phone.

"Hello?"

"Logan, I need your help."

"Sure, Trent. What's wrong?"

"I'm at the hospital with Max. He's been beaten up outside some club."

"Fuck. Is he okay?"

"I don't know, Logan. We've not long been here. But he looked…a mess."

"Shit, Trent. I'm on my way."

"Thanks. Could you ring Sean for me as well, please?"

"Sure thing. See you shortly."

After Trent hung up, he rested his head against the window behind him. He tried not to think about what Max looked like under that sweater. *That harness was… nope not going there.*

CHAPTER SEVEN

MAX

Max remembered Trent placing him on the gurney and being wheeled off, but he couldn't remember being placed in this room. He'd awoken a short time ago to the sound of beeps and the smell of disinfectant; not his favourite. There was natural light filtering through the windows, so he knew it was morning, or almost. As he scanned the room, he saw a figure slumped in a chair next to him in what had to be the most uncomfortable position. Trent was sat with one leg over the arm of the chair and his head must have been resting on his hand at one point, but that hand was now squashed between his chin and chest. He was going to have a crick in his neck when he woke up.

He couldn't believe Trent was still there. Max had expected him to leave the minute he'd been taken away from him. Although he probably should have known better. Trent wasn't the type of guy to leave someone in pain.

"He hasn't left since you got here." The quiet voice made Max jump. He hadn't thought to look around the rest of the room once he'd seen Trent. Logan continued, "He kept pestering the doctors and nurses for more information until they finally let him stay in here with you."

"I'd expected him to go home," he croaked.

"I assumed you would. Instead, he kept watch until I told him to sleep and that I'd watch over you while he did. Even then, he wasn't happy about it."

They kept their voices quiet as they talked.

"How are you feeling?" Logan asked.

Max catalogued his injuries. "It's hard to tell to be honest. I ache everywhere, I can't see brilliantly through one of my eyes and my nose hurts like hell. But I can breathe a little easier."

"The doctor has given you some painkillers to help, which could be why you're breathing easier. I didn't hear everything he had to say—you'll have to ask Trent —but you have deeply bruised ribs and a lot of other bruising. Your nose wasn't broken, though they originally thought it was. I would've been surprised if you hadn't been in pain."

"What are you doing here anyway?" Max winced with the way that came out. "Sorry, that was rude. I just meant—"

Logan laughed softly. "I know what you meant." He calmed, then looked at Max with a serious expression.

"He was worried about you. He didn't have any information about what had happened to you, and he didn't know…if anyone was after you." Logan smirked. "I'm the brawn…with a gun and badge."

Max turned his gaze to the ceiling, realising how much he'd put on Trent and sighed, wincing when his ribs protested.

"What happened last night?" Logan's question hung heavy in the silence.

Max debated what to say. He knew he had to adhere to the guidelines and limit AN's involvement. He wasn't sure how to explain it away when there was a police detective questioning him. "What has Trent told you?"

Logan laughed. "That's not how this works, Max."

Fuck. He wished he knew what Trent had told him. He'd have to stick close to the truth. "I was beaten up outside Chalice in St Neots."

Logan's eyebrows rose. "The BDSM club?"

Max nodded slowly. "Yeah."

"Nice place."

"Usually."

"What made you visit there?"

"It's one of my go-to places when I need to get away."

"And you needed to get away last night?"

Max could tell Logan was in full investigation mode now. "Yeah." Max rolled his head to look at Trent and was silent for a moment. "I crossed a line I shouldn't have crossed…" Max turned back to Logan, "and I needed to find my feet again."

Logan looked between Trent and Max several times before he nodded slowly, obviously reading between the lines of his words. "Do you know who beat you up?"

Max looked him squarely in the eye and lied. "No, I have no idea."

Logan stared at him for a moment, then bit his lip and nodded. "Most people, when they've been beaten within an inch of their lives, are spewing information left, right and centre, hoping that any piece they give will help the investigation. You, on the other hand, I have to pry information out of. Usually, that means you're hiding something." Logan paused to let that sink in. "All I'm going to say is that you need to think carefully about what you're not saying. I can only help you so much, then my hands are tied."

Max locked gazes with him and nodded. Something passed between them, but Max was unsure exactly what. It was as if they both had similar secrets.

A ringing phone broke the silence and made Trent jump to sitting, then groan as he grabbed at his neck. The noise stopped after a moment.

"Have a nice nap?" Max teased. Trent's gaze flew to his, and he saw his eyes light up. He wished he would look at him like that every time. Max's heart pounded, and he was glad he was not linked up to a heart rate monitor. Trent stood from the chair quickly, wincing again.

"Serves you right for sleeping in such a comfortable position," Logan quipped sarcastically.

Trent glared at him, then the ringing began again. Max realised it was Trent's phone when he pulled it out of his pocket. The grimace on Trent's face identified the caller without any words. He pressed a button and pocketed it again.

"How are you feeling?" Trent asked. He sat on the edge of the bed, hesitantly. Max really, *really* wanted to put his hand on Trent's thigh, which was so close to him, but he refrained. Just.

"I'm all right. A bit achy, but I'll live. Thanks for—"

Trent's phone rang again, and he cursed. "Sorry. She'll just keep calling if I don't answer. Let me take it outside, I'll be back in a minute." He reached forward and squeezed Max's hand, then left the room.

Max was shocked that Trent had touched him like that after their conversation last night, even something so basic.

"I don't know what's happening between you both, but I know how you feel about him." Logan's voice came closer as he headed to the bed. Max refused to look at him. "He's a little lost, Max. I have no idea what's going on in his head at the minute, but you need to give him time. I'm not saying he's gay or bi or straight. I have no idea what he is right now. My best advice would be to just be there when he needs it, when he doesn't, when you need it. Just be around him and let him figure it out himself. Pushing won't do anything. And it may, in fact, make it worse."

Max did look at him then. He could see the sincerity in Logan's eyes and the camaraderie. "Thanks," he whispered.

Logan nodded and walked to the door. "Oh, one more question. Are you worried about your safety?" Logan pinned him with his gaze as he asked the question.

Max bit his lip. The medic had told him he needed to be with someone, but he didn't think that meant he needed protection. He shook his head. Logan stared at him for a moment, then nodded again. "See you soon." Then he left.

A nurse came in not long after, Max could still hear Trent outside his door on the phone. The nurse took his obs, chatting generally about things. Trent came back in looking sour faced.

"Everything okay?" Max asked, worriedly.

"Yeah, just Trish being Trish." He winced. "I am going to have to leave for a couple of hours though. Will you be okay?"

Max was disappointed but understood that Trent had his own life to live. "I'll be fine. I have the nurses to keep me company." He smiled at the nurse, and she blushed.

Trent rolled his eyes. "I'm sure you do. I'll be back in a couple of hours then. Your phone is in the drawer next to you if you need it." He hesitated.

"Trent, I'll be fine. Go." Max shooed him away, withholding a flinch at the harsh movement.

He nodded and turned for the door.

"Mr Walker?" The nurse called his name, and Trent turned to her. "You can kiss your boyfriend goodbye, I won't mind."

Max choked as he repeated, "Boyfriend?" and looked at Trent. He saw him clench his teeth and finally realised how Trent had managed to get them to let him in here. With Logan's words ringing in his ears, he decided to let him off the hook. "It's okay, he's not big on PDA's. I'll see you later. Sweetheart." He couldn't help the smirk that crossed his lips when he tacked on that last word. He couldn't resist a little dig.

Trent blushed but stood staring at Max. Then he walked slowly over to the bed, looking down at him. Max could see him chewing on his lip and was confused what he was thinking about. Max's eyes widened as Trent's face lowered towards his. He scanned Trent's face for any indication of what he was thinking. Then he felt Trent's soft lips against his own in a brief caress before he pulled away again. Max gasped, eyes closed from the unexpectedness of it. When he opened them, he saw Trent was still close, looking at him. "Wha—" Max tried to talk but was stopped by Trent's lips against his own again, this time a little harder and a little longer. Max wanted nothing more than to grip the back of Trent's head and plunder his mouth, but he restrained his urge. This was more than he could have ever hoped for, even if it went against Logan's opinion.

Max took a chance. He opened his mouth a little and stroked his tongue across Trent's lips. Trent paused, then opened a small amount. Max's heart rate increased exponentially, he couldn't believe he was kissing Trent —or rather Trent was kissing him. Their tongues touched, and Trent deepened the kiss a little more. It was only when a groan fell from Max's mouth that Trent pulled back and stared at him.

He could read shock and panic on his face. Max pushed up, ignoring the pain, and pressed one last kiss to Trent's mouth. "Go," he whispered, feeling his lip begin to bleed again.

Trent turned around and left.

"Wow, now I understand why he doesn't do PDA's, everyone in the vicinity would get hot under the collar." She laughed even as her face flushed red.

Max gave a small smile as he wiped the blood away. "Yeah, they would." Because he certainly had. What the hell was that all about?

TRENT

What the hell what that all about? Trent thought as he walked out of the hospital and towards his car. Logan had moved his car when he'd arrived, which had still been parked on the double yellow lines, but amazingly hadn't been ticketed. He couldn't believe he'd kissed Max.

When the nurse had mentioned about kissing him goodbye, Trent's heart had begun to pound and his brain had whispered, *if Max had been your boyfriend, you'd have kissed him goodbye.* So initially it had been to keep up the pretence, so he'd be able to get back later to see him. But once he'd kissed him, he had no idea what had come over him. It was the first time he'd properly kissed a guy, if he discounted the kiss they'd had last night, and he'd enjoyed it. His cock had too.

He was so confused. He didn't understand how he could've had a reaction to Max when he'd only ever had a similar reaction to women before. At least, he thought he had. Trent blew out a breath as he unlocked his car. He had to shelve this for a later time to think about.

The phone call he'd received had been Trish, yelling at him for not giving the money to her like he said he would. He didn't know how many times he'd told her he didn't have any until the end of the month, but she wouldn't listen. He was going to speak to Samuel. He hated asking for money, but he needed Trish off his back. He went to his big brother to help bail him out of this drama.

Trent pulled up to his old house and cut the engine. He didn't want to go in there. Ever since she'd had it re-decorated last year, it hadn't felt like his home. Although saying that, it hadn't before either. It was only having the two kids there that made it anything close to home.

He knocked on the door—he'd made the mistake once of not making his presence known and never would again.

Trish opened the door. Every time he saw her, she looked so far from how she looked as a young woman. She was still a brown-haired, Spanish beauty with Mediterranean skin tone, a button nose and large brown eyes. He had always thought her mouth showed how strict she was as it was thin and sharp, though now they looked definitively plumper. Her make-up was done with a precision known to supermodels, whereas before it used to be natural looking. Her clothing style had changed too. Gone were the jeans and comfortable tops; they were replaced with tight fitting dresses and pencil skirts. He had no issue with anything she had done, but he hardly recognised the woman he'd married. No wonder she didn't have any money to pay for Harper's things if she kept using it to "preen" herself.

"Have you got the money?" she spat out.

"Some of it," he replied, waiting for the explosion. He didn't have to wait long.

"You're making us look bad, Trent," she snarled.

"What are you talking about?" He had no idea where the outbursts were coming from lately.

"Do you want Harper to walk around town looking like she wore hand-me-downs? What would everyone think? I'd be the laughing-stock of the town."

Now he understood. It was all about her perceived "status" within the town. It was all her parents' fault. Before Trish had been born, they had moved from a coastal town in Spain, where they were highly thought of, to Cambridge, and they still truly believed that their status was at the same level here as it was in Spain. Over the years, he had tried explaining to Trish that things didn't work the same way here, but it had been so ingrained in her beliefs that he could never dissuade her.

"Don't you roll your eyes at me! Ever since you left, you've been dragging us through the mud with you. We would have been better if you've had left and never come back."

Trent had enough. Trish had put him down for years while they were married, but he was beginning to find his backbone. Now he was on his own, he knew what he wanted—kind of—and it wasn't her and her "status." He didn't even think Jocelyn and Harper wanted it. But Harper was stuck until she'd finished college. Once she was at uni, it would be easier for her. At least, he hoped it would.

"Well, if I'd done that, you wouldn't be getting any money right now, would you?" Trent snapped back.

He almost laughed at the shock showing on her face. When they'd been married, he had let her walk all over him, but now, he didn't give a damn.

She straightened her spine, looked down her nose at him and held out her hand.

Trent shook his head and handed over the envelope. "You get one-fifty, that's all. If you need more, you either find it yourself or wait until I get paid." With that, he turned and walked back to his car.

He laughed. If she was so worried about her reputation, she really shouldn't have had a yelling match on her own doorstep. He could already see one of the neighbour's curtains twitching. He heard the front door slam just as he reached his car. Yet again, he realised he was better off without her. Max's face swam to the front of his mind. He wouldn't regret him. The thought flew through his head. He wasn't sure what to do with that.

He drove home to grab a shower and a change of clothes, grabbing some extras for Max in case he didn't have any. He hesitated at the underwear. After seeing Max in that strap harness, he wasn't sure whether that was his usual or just something he wore for the club. He decided to pack some briefs anyway, and if Max didn't want to wear them, he didn't have to.

The thought of the harness though made him think of it stashed in the wardrobe. Trent took it out and laid it on the bed. It was almost like the kind of thing you'd wear on a bungee jump. He remembered the sight of Max with the straps fitted snugly over his chest and down his sides and he wondered what they'd feel like. With a slight hesitation, he took his t-shirt off, then lifted the harness from the bed and slid it over his arms to his shoulders. The feel of the cold leather against his warm skin made him come out in goosebumps. Making sure the straps sat flat against his back, he felt for the clasp. Tightening it, he let out a breath, then felt his way to the straps hanging down by his hips. He had no specially made jockstrap to clip them too, but he did have his jeans, so clipped them to his belt hoops.

Once he was completely fastened in, he took a deep breath and let it out slowly. If didn't feel as strange as he expected it to. The leather had warmed to his skin temperature, so the only time he felt them were when he moved. If he tightened them to fit him as it should, he would probably feel it more, but he wouldn't do that as they were set for Max's measurements. He walked to his bathroom and stood in front of the mirror. He just stood there, looking at the floor, feeling like the minute he saw himself in it, something would change.

He took another shaky breath, then lifted his gaze. All the air went out of his lungs at the sight of his tanned skin in sharp contrast to the black leather. He felt himself getting hard again. He was right; something was changing inside him. Trent had felt as if something had broken inside him over the years, but seeing himself like this felt like coming home, like something was being fixed, like he was beginning to see the real him that had been there all along. Which didn't make a lot of sense when he'd not been inclined towards BDSM before.

He could probably understand why he'd gone "into hiding" when he was younger if that's what he'd done. With Trish getting pregnant when he was twenty, he'd had no time to just be. He'd gone from a university student to working full-time and a father within the space of a year, and then another child two years later. He loved his kids and would do anything for them, but maybe now was his time. Maybe. He just needed to figure out what to do with it.

His gaze followed over his body one more time, then he removed the harness and placed it back in the wardrobe. He was still half hard. Trent was sure there was something bad about getting hard and soft so many times within a short period. His emotions were doing almost the same thing, up and down.

He glanced at the clock and realised he'd been away from the hospital longer than he'd planned to. Trent quickly got dressed again and grabbed the bag with clothes for Max and some magazines and books, then picked up his keys and headed off to the hospital.

Trent heard voices just as he pushed his way into the hospital room. His gaze went straight to Max and saw that he sat a little more upright against several pillows. Max turned to look at him, a smile lighting his face.

"Hey, you," Max said. "I knew you'd be back sooner rather than later."

"Well, what can I say, I can't keep away from you," Trent answered sarcastically, at least that was the tone he tried for. He saw Max's eyes widen slightly and flick to the side. That was when Trent remembered he had other people in his room. He turned to the visitors and saw Sean, Asher, Zak and his son sat watching them with almost identical grins. He felt his face heat but smiled, ignoring them. "Hi, guys. How are you?" He set the bag he'd brought next to the bed; he'd tell Max about it later.

"We're good. We heard you've had an adventure," Asher answered, the concern in his eyes belying the lightness of his words.

Trent glanced over at Max, seeing him give a slight shake of his head, which Trent assumed meant he hadn't told them the specifics of the previous night. He sat himself in the seat he'd occupied this morning and decided to keep the tone light. "You keep telling me I need to get out more."

"Yeah, but hospital visits were not in the plan." Sean raised his eyebrows at him, daring him to quip a remark.

Trent pointed at Max. "Blame him." He turned his gaze to Zak's son. "Hey, buddy. What'cha got there?" Dane looked at him, frowning for a second, then jumped off his dad's knee and ambled over to him, chatting in the way only two-year-olds can, but holding out his toy to show him. It took him back to seeing Jocelyn and Harper being like this, small chubby legs walking as fast as they could across the floors, mumbling and chatting along the way. He frowned, wishing he had more photographs of them at that age, but Trish had them all. A fresh wave of anger spread through him, but he pushed it down to deal with another day. He'd had his fill of thinking about her today.

Dane trotted back across the room to his dad, and Trent concentrated on the conversation around him.

"—did Logan say? Has he found anything out yet?" Sean asked Max.

Max sighed and rubbed his forehead, chuckling gently. "Sean, Logan left like three hours ago, give him a chance. I know he's good, but I don't think he's *that* good."

Sean blushed—Trent wasn't sure whether it was from anger or embarrassment—and sat back in his chair. "I know. I just..." He blew out a breath, and Asher curled his arm around his shoulders. Trent watched as he comforted Sean, whispering in his ear, and Sean leaned into him. Envy burned through him unexpectedly. He hadn't felt that in a long time. After his breakup, he'd been glad to be alone, and it had held him steady for the past five years. Now though, things were changing, and he wasn't sure if it was for the better or not.

CHAPTER EIGHT

MAX

Max watched as a gamut of emotions passed over Trent's face as he stared at Sean and Asher. He wished he knew what Trent was thinking at that moment. It was almost longing, but Max wasn't sure. Trent turned and caught Max looking—he wasn't going to hide it. That kiss earlier had done a number on him, and he was all kinds of turned around. He cleared his throat.

"Everything all right in the outside world?" he asked, wondering if Trent would tell him what he'd run off to sort out.

"Yeah," he said with a sigh. "All sorted for now."

Max raised his eyebrows at his vague answer, and Trent chuckled.

"Trish. Being a pain in my ass, as always," he explained.

Max nodded but frowned. He didn't like the sound

of that woman. Everything he'd been told about her, from Trent and the other guys, was awful. She sounded like a bitch who only cared about herself. He hoped he'd be able to control himself if he ever met her, but he made no promises.

"Has the doctor been in to see you yet?" Trent asked.

Max nodded. "Yeah. They've said it's mainly bruising. My ribs are the worst, deeply bruised. They have said I can go home when I have someone to stay with me for at least three days." Max rolled his eyes and sighed. "No one will put up with my shit for one day, let alone three!" He chuckled.

"You can stay with me," Trent said, then his eyes went wide as if he hadn't meant to offer.

Max would love to take him up on that offer, but he wasn't sure it was in Trent's best interests to have Max there with him. Luckily, Max could dissuade him because he had to work.

"Thanks, but you'll be working. I'll figure it out. Even if I have to stay here for a day or two." He didn't like the idea of it, but it was better than nothing.

"It's half term. I'm not working this week." Trent shrugged. "The offer stands."

"It's a good idea, Max. I'm rammed with appointments this week, and Asher has all the kids for the holidays so we can't do it. And…" Sean glanced at Zak, "I'm sure Zak has enough on his plate with his little one there. Ethan's at uni all week, and you know full well, Logan will be working too."

"Yes, thank you for letting Trent feel like he's my only option. I'm sure that makes him feel a lot more wanted." Max let the sarcasm hover in the air to hide his own opinion. Sean blushed.

Trent laughed. "I guess I'm it then, Max."

"No, I'm not going to put you out when you have a week off to relax. I'll call Livvy and see if she can come up for a few days. If not, maybe Charlotte can."

Trent leaned closer to Max, lowering his voice. "Max. I'm offering, it's not a problem. If it will make you feel better, I can stay at yours. I'm just trying to help." He sat back again and stared down at his hands.

Max immediately felt bad for making Trent feel uncomfortable. He closed his eyes, shook his head and said something he would likely regret. "If you are one hundred percent sure, I'd appreciate it."

Trent glanced up, studying him for a moment, then nodded. "No problem. Shall we get you ready to bust this joint?" He didn't wait for an answer, just smirked as he stood. "I'll go speak to the nurses." With that, Trent whirled out the room, taking some of the oxygen with it.

Max stared at the door for a few minutes, trying to figure out how he'd managed to get himself into this mess. Then a voice interrupted his thoughts.

"Earth to Max," Sean said.

"What?"

Sean and Asher chuckled. "I said, are you really all right going with Trent?"

Max nodded. "Yeah. I know I don't know him as

well as I know you, Asher, but I know him well enough. I just didn't want to intrude on his free time." And he didn't want to risk the chances of getting too close again.

He'd had the opportunity to think about that kiss before everyone had turned up about an hour ago. It had been delicious, but Max had decided it had to be a one-time thing. He knew his personality, and he would push and push for Trent to give him everything he could, even if he wasn't ready for it, and Max didn't want to do that. He could tell that Trent was battling something—excluding his ex-wife—and he didn't want to make it worse by pushing him further than he wanted to go. If Trent was gay—or bisexual, or whatever else—Trent needed to figure it out himself without any input or meddling from Max.

Trent walked back in the door with a doctor following behind.

"Okay, Mr Hughes. I'm happy for you to leave so long as you stay with your boyfriend—" Max saw Sean and Asher glance at each other in confusion at that word, "—for at least three days, four would be better. You need to rest your ribs, so avoid lifting anything heavy or straining, stop playing sports or going to the gym for the moment and avoid lying or sitting still for long periods of time. You'll want to breathe shallowly because it hurts to do otherwise, but I'll need you to breathe deeply to ensure your body heals properly." The doctor paused as he looked at Max's chart. "If you're unsure of anything, please call, and I'll talk you through it."

"Thank you."

"Let's get this paperwork filled out, and we can get you sorted. Do you have a change of clothes to get into?"

Max looked to the ceiling. "No—"

"Yes, he does," Trent interrupted. Max looked at him. "I brought a bag of stuff in case you needed something." He saw a faint red blush on Trent's cheeks.

"Great." The doctor moved closer to Max and began talking him through the discharge paperwork.

What felt like ten hours later, but was, in fact, just over an hour, he shuffled painfully to the bathroom with a nurse to get changed. Sean had offered to help but the nurse had come in and taken control. He probably would've refused Sean anyway, no point involving friends in your state of undress unless you had to. Then the realisation that he would probably have to have Trent help him with things like this screamed through his mind. Oh, shit. What had he agreed to?

The process of undressing and dressing was a painful process, and one he would have to learn to breathe through—he definitely couldn't do it on his own though so *would* need Trent's help. The same with bathing, but that was something he could attempt on his own to begin with to save face.

Once he was ready, he stood as tall as he could, breathing through the pain and walked out of the bathroom, the nurse following, then leaving the room altogether. His swollen eye skewed his depth perception, but he saw Trent straight away talking with Sean and Asher. They seemed to be having a disagreement. When Asher noticed Max walking towards them, he nudged Sean, and they all turned to him.

"You look better clothed," Asher said, then blushed and stammered, "I just mean you hide your injuries better when you're wearing clothes. God, Asher!" He muttered the last bit as if to himself and rubbed his face.

Max laughed, then groaned. "God, don't make me laugh." He cleared his throat. "I knew what you meant, Asher."

"Ready to go?" Trent asked.

He nodded. "Yes, definitely ready. And thanks for the clothes."

Trent's gaze looked him up and down in assessment. "They fit you well."

"Should I be concerned about you having clothes my size?" Max teased.

Trent blushed. "They're my older clothes, from when I was with Trish. I've bulked up a bit since then."

Max looked him over and couldn't believe him ever looking different to what he did then.

Sean cut the tension with his words. "Right, we're

heading off. Make sure you come over to ours in the next few days, and we'll feed you."

He smiled at the thought of seeing his favourite girl. "Will Janie be there?"

Asher laughed. "Yes, Janie will be there. You will no doubt spoil her rotten as always." He looked at Sean. "Remind me to limit her treats the day they come so she doesn't have too many!" He laughed again.

Everyone joined in. Max had become close to the little girl when Sean and Asher's relationship was beginning and struggling. He loved her as if she was his own. She was such a beautiful girl, inside and out, and so sensitive to others' emotions. It was never a chore when they asked him to babysit or when she appealed to him to play with her.

Asher, Sean and Zak said their goodbyes, Dane waving madly as they went out the door, and then it was just Trent and him, standing awkwardly in the middle of the hospital room.

Trent cleared his throat and broke the silence. "Do you have any things you need to collect?"

"Just the bits I came in, although the clothes are covered in blood, so need a good wash...or throwing in the bin. I've not looked at the state of them yet."

"Where are they?"

Max indicated the cupboard by the bed, and Trent opened it, collecting a blue bag.

"Okay, let's go." Trent held open the door and indicated for Max to go first. He walked slowly, trying to remember what the doctor said about allowing his body to move in normal motions instead of restricting it. It hurt, as the doctor had said it would, but he knew it would be better for him in the long term. It was slow going, but they managed to get to the entry waiting room.

"Let me go and fetch the car and bring it so you have less distance to walk. Sit down here for a breather."

Max didn't object. He felt liked he'd walked a marathon already, sweat dotted his forehead, and his breath was raspy. As he sat waiting, he thought about what was going to happen once he got to Trent's house —at least he assumed that was where they were going, they never agreed completely when they'd discussed it earlier.

Trent returned and put an arm around Max's back to help him get up and kept it there as they started walking, which Max was grateful for. That slight help eased the weight on his back, and it helped him to breathe more freely. Getting into the car was another fun chore, twisting his body was painful, and he was sweating again once he was sat down.

Trent crouched down next to his open door. "You okay?" His brow pinched, making Max want to smooth it with his finger.

Max nodded slowly. "Yeah. It's just taking a lot out of me. Guess I have this to look forward to for the next few days or weeks." He rolled his eyes.

"We."

Max rolled his head on the headrest towards Trent. "What?"

"*We* have this to look forward to. Not just you."

Max stared at him and spoke quietly, "Are you sure you know what you're getting into?" He didn't intend for there to be a double meaning to his words, but he realised it could be taken a different way. He waited to see which way Trent would take it.

Trent stared back for a few seconds, and Max saw a faint blush tinge his cheeks. "Nope," he whispered. Then he stood and shut Max's door, walking around to the other side to drive them away from the hospital.

Max had no idea which version of the question Trent had answered—maybe both. He'd deal with it later. He was exhausted.

TRENT

Trent knew they hadn't agreed on a place for Max to rest, but he was taking him to his house. He remembered what the medic had said and thought Max would be safer away from his own house, therefore Trent's house was the better choice. He'd also realised he loved the idea of Max being in *his* space, which was monumentally stupid. He had no idea where all these thoughts were coming from over the last few days. It had only been just under a week since Crush had opened its Garden Bar and he had taken Max to his house for the first time. So much had happened in that small amount of time.

He suddenly recalled they had a birthday party to attend this weekend. Charlie was the bartender at Crush and had been there for a couple of years if Trent remembered rightly. As Sean had been the architect for the Garden Bar's refurbishment, Trent had been spending more time there because Asher had been spending more time there, for obvious reasons. He'd gotten to know Tom and Ginny, Charlie and Josh, and Analise really well during the last few months, and so he, Sean, Asher, Logan, Max, Zak, Ethan and Eric had all been invited to Charlie's party. It wasn't a huge get together as such, he'd been told, just friends getting to know each other in amongst the public customers too; they weren't shutting the place down for the night— although Tom had insisted, but Charlie had threatened to not turn up if he did.

Trent huffed a laugh. "Did you—" he began, then glanced over and saw Max was asleep against the car window. He smiled at how he looked, mouth agape, dark lashes resting on his cheeks. He looked forward again, scared he'd go off the road if he looked for as long as he wanted to.

He couldn't believe Max was going to be in his space for the next few days. He was back at work on Monday. There was plenty of holiday days leftover though. He remembered the doctor's caution of complications. He'd take his holiday days if Max needed him.

He arrived at his house and parked the car in the allocated spot. Looking over at Max again, his heart seized in his chest. He was *gorgeous*. Trent sat there for a few more minutes under no illusion that he was giving Max more time to rest, but in fact, was just watching him like a crazy man. He had even twisted a little in his seat so he could watch him more easily and rest his own head in his hand.

When Max coughed, then groaned in pain, Trent jumped into action and flew around the car to help him however he could.

"Shit, Trent. That fucking hurts," Max moaned, clutching his waist and breathing slowly but deeply as the doctor ordered.

"I bet it does. Come on, let's get you upstairs." Trent grabbed the bag and threw it over his shoulder, then eased Max out of the car and keeping his arm around his waist, but it was slow going. Trent debated his next words but decided to offer anyway. "Would it be easier for you if I carried you?" he asked softly.

Max slowed until he stopped and looked over at the doors of the building, then at Trent. He grimaced, then said, "Would you mind?"

Trent shook his head quickly. "I don't mind, although I don't know if it will be any more comfortable than what you're already feeling."

Max tried for a smile. "It can't hurt much more than it already is."

Trent double checked Max's face before bending down to reach under his knees. As he took Max's weight, Max groaned and clutched his arms around his own waist. Trent proceeded down the hallway to the lift, and then out of the lift to his apartment. He could see and hear Max was in pain, but there was nothing he could do about it—and he hated it. He slowly stood him back up outside his front door, keeping hold of him tightly as Max regained his breath and his equilibrium. He only realised after a minute that he was stood there with both arms around Max and his head resting against the side of Max's head as he rested it on Trent's shoulder. Max had what felt like a death grip on the back of Trent's shirt too.

Trent knew he should pull away, but he couldn't. Max was the one who eventually lifted his head and looked up at Trent. "Thanks," he whispered.

"No problem," Trent whispered back. He felt the need to close the distance between them, and he almost did, but Max's eyes widened, and he pulled away a little faster than he should have given the groan that came out of his throat. Trent unlocked the door and led Max to the sofa, allowing him to get himself in a comfortable position—on his nice new throw—before he returned to close and lock the door behind him.

"Would you like a drink?" he asked as he removed his coat and hung it up above his newly removed boots.

Max cleared his throat. "Yes, please," he answered.

Trent went about getting coffee, a glass of water and a glass of juice for him. He could've asked him what he wanted, but he knew Max would already be feeling a little out of sorts being at someone else's place and probably wouldn't feel comfortable asking for what he actually wanted. So, he took the decision out of his hands. Okay, it wasn't the coffee that Max liked—and Trent may have to remedy that sooner rather than later—but it was hot, and it had caffeine in it. He made a note that he'd have to go food shopping now he had a guest. He mentally winced at the state of his bank balance, but he'd make it work.

Placing everything on a tray—he'd put some biscuits on there too—he took it over to Max and placed it on the coffee table.

Max chuckled. "You expecting company?"

Trent felt his face go warm as he realised Max was laughing at how much he'd brought over. "I wanted to make sure you had something you wanted." Trent shrugged as if it was no big deal. Although he had no idea why it *was* a big deal.

"I think you covered it." Max smiled at him, and Trent's heart rate increased as did the blood flow to his cock.

He looked away, busying himself with the contents of the tray, until his phone rang. It came up as an unknown number and usually he wouldn't answer but something made him take it.

"Hello?"

"Mr Walker?"

"Speaking."

"Good afternoon. My name is Dr Stone from the hospital. It's regarding your test results."

Trent sucked in a breath, not sure what he hoped for. "Yes, what do they say?"

"Everything is good, Mr Walker. There are no signs of any brain damage or anything that would cause what was described. At this point in time, I would suggest that it's stress related. Try and sleep well, exercise more and eat well. See how that helps. If you still have problems in a few weeks, come back to see us. I'll leave an open appointment for you for the next six months. Any issues or questions within that time, just ring up and we'll book a time to see you again."

"Okay, thanks, Dr Stone."

"You're welcome, Mr Walker."

They hung up, and Trent stared at his phone for a moment.

"Everything okay?" Max asked.

"Yeah. That was the hospital with my test results."

"And?"

"Everything's clear."

"That's brilliant news."

"Yeah."

"You don't sound happy about it."

"It's only because if it's not that, then what the hell is going on?" Trent shook his head. "Never mind, I'll deal with that another day. It's not going anywhere." He turned to Max, seeing him gingerly reach for a biscuit before looking over at him.

"Thank you, Trent. I appreciate this more than you know. Even if sometimes it may come out as sarcastic or snarky, I do appreciate your help."

Max's quiet voice made Trent stare at him. He saw in his eyes the struggle Max was having with being in someone else's care. "I know you do. Just do me one favour?"

"What's that?"

"Make yourself at home. Please. I haven't got much, but for the time you're here, it's yours too."

Max bit his lip and looked down at his hands, eyes looking suspiciously wet. His nostrils flared, and he gazed back at Trent as he sniffed. "Thanks," was the wet reply.

He nodded, then decided to change the subject. "So…film night?" he asked.

Max sniffed again and smiled. "Sure. Line 'em up."

Max made a valiant effort to watch the film Trent put on, but he was almost asleep at the halfway mark.

"Hey," he said, prodding Max gently. "Time for bed, sleepyhead." Trent smirked slightly as the phrase he used to use for his daughters slipped out.

Max blinked a few times before he seemed to focus on Trent. "Hey, you." He sounded drunk.

Trent snorted. "Come on, time for bed. Let's get you sorted." Trent had talked with the doctor and nurse about what Max was and wasn't likely to be able to do, and he knew Max was going to try and do it himself anyway. But Trent had decided he was just going to take charge, regardless of Max's refusals; otherwise, he was going to hurt himself further ,and Trent couldn't live with that.

He lifted Max upright and held him while he got his balance, then almost carried him to the bathroom. He hadn't been to Max's house to get any clothes yet, so he'd have to wear Trent's again. Not that he minded. He left Max alone for five minutes so he could do his business but didn't allow him too much time to get himself into trouble. Even that short time, gave Max enough to be trying to remove his shirt by himself.

"Here, let me help," Trent said.

"I'm okay—"

"Max, let me help."

"I'm fine—"

"Max! Let. Me. Help." Trent's voice came out like an order, and immediately, Max dropped his arms and looked to the floor. Shit. His mind flew back to the vision of Max in the harness and being outside a club and his comments about BDSM. *Holy fucking hell. Is Max a sub?* Trent closed his eyes, rolled his lips inwards and breathed through his nose for a moment to regain his composure—and to try and reduce the existence of his hard-on. "Let's get this shirt off. Slowly does it. No fast movements or you'll hurt yourself more." Together they manoeuvred the shirt off and the trousers, leaving Max clad in boxers. "Do you want a shower now or in the morning?"

Max lowered his eyes again and whispered, "In the morning, please."

The soft voice and lowered eyes screamed submission, and Trent had never realised how sexy that was.

"Come on. Time for bed." He wrapped his arm around Max's naked waist and helped him to the guest room. Both bedrooms in the apartment were good sized and the guest room had two small double beds in there —for his kids usually. They were always made up for if the kids decided to turn up, so he knew everything was fresh. Pulling back the covers, he helped Max lay down and covered him over again. He crouched down next to him. "Shout me if you need anything, Max."

"I'll be fine," he said.

"I know you will." He decided to take a chance. "But shout at me if you need anything; that's an order." He almost gulped as Max's eyes lowered, and he seemed to shiver.

"I will," he whispered.

Trent didn't know what made him do it, but he leaned forward and kissed Max's forehead, then stood and walked away. He left the door open a crack and went to the living area to tidy up before he headed off to bed himself. He hoped he'd be able to sleep tonight.

CHAPTER NINE

MAX

The following morning, Max tried to get out of bed again. He'd tried once in the night and ended up shouting for Trent because his body had become stiff from non-movement and every tiny motion hurt. He was mortified that he couldn't do the simple things himself. As he rolled to his side, he winced and rested a moment. When his breath returned, he pushed his arms underneath him and pushed up, trying to keep his back straight to ease the pressure on his bruised ribs. It worked a little, but he was still sweating by the time he'd gotten upright.

He was about to attempt to stand when a knock sounded and Trent walked in, shaking his head. "I told you to shout me."

Max couldn't say anything, breathing hard as he was so just waved a hand at him. Trent laughed. "Would you like a shower?"

Max would've loved a shower, but having a shower meant having Trent in there to help him, and he didn't know if he was ready for that or not. He shook his head.

Trent raised his eyebrows. "You're going to have to let me help you in there sooner or later," he said.

Max closed his eyes, resigned. He may as well get this over and done with. He nodded.

"Better. Let's get you standing. Then you can have a breather before we walk to the bathroom." True to his words, Trent helped him every step of the way; it was slower going this time. If anything, Max needed the help more today. The bruising must have set in completely because he felt like he'd been hit by a truck.

Trent helped Max to sit on the toilet—there was no way he'd be able to stand without support—and left the room to get some towels and clothes so Max could have some privacy for a few moments. While he did, he thought about how they were going to do this. Max knew that this was a bad idea. There was no way he'd be able to keep his reaction to Trent a secret, not if Trent helped him in the shower. But he couldn't see any other way for him to get clean—he still had dried blood on his body—and there was no way he'd be able to stand by himself for the time it would take him to wash.

Trent knocked on the bathroom door, and Max called for him to enter. Max saw Trent had changed into some swimming trunks. Fuck, he looked hot in those.

"How are you doing?" Trent asked.

"So-so," Max replied, being honest for a change. It wasn't like it would change the outcome.

"All right, then. Let's get the water warming up, and then we'll get you in."

Max was reassured by the matter-of-fact tone Trent took. If Trent could be calm about it, then Max could be too. He hoped.

A few minutes later, Trent stood in front of him. "Come on, let's get you in the warm water. Hopefully, it will soothe your muscles a bit." He turned Max to face the shower and stood behind him. Max felt his hands on the waistband of his boxers, and then they were being lowered. Max closed his eyes, fighting the sensation of having someone else's hands on him. Trent supported him as he lifted one foot, then the other and to step under the shower. Max could feel Trent's presence behind him, but they did not touch anywhere except for where Trent's hands held.

Trent grabbed some shampoo and began the leisurely task of cleaning Max's hair. Max closed his eyes in bliss. He got lost in the sensations as Trent rubbed the soap across his skin. Max could hardly feel the touch, as soft as Trent's hands were being, and he felt himself relax as the warmth of the water soothed his aches and pains.

Trent left no skin untouched except for one area. After he had washed every bit he could, Max felt Trent stand behind him, then the soap was held in front of Max.

"Here, I'll help hold you up, and you can wash the

rest," he said in a shaky voice. Max took the soap and began to wash his cock as quickly as possible as Trent held his hips for stability. When he leaned forward slightly to reach his balls and ass, he hissed with the pain again—he'd momentarily forgotten with how much the water had helped.

He heard Trent blow out a breath. "Hold on, let's try it this way." Trent stepped closer, resting his front against Max's back, and he realised Trent was hard. He was careful of where he put his hands, wrapping them around Max's waist. "Lift your leg and rest it on the edge of the shower, you'll be able to reach without bending." His voice seemed matter of fact, but his fast breathing was a giveaway that he was not as calm as he sounded.

Max closed his eyes and gritted his teeth, trying to stop his reaction, which he knew was impossible. The feeling of being held, of Trent's body flush with his back, of his covered cock resting against his lower back, made that a fight he lost. His own cock rose, and there was nowhere to hide. He quickly washed and reached to put the soap back on the shelf. As he leaned forward, his ass pressed harder against Trent, unintentionally. Maybe Trent did feel something for him. But then he remembered the reaction Trent had when Max first kissed him, so he ignored it. He could use it as a fantasy later, if needed.

"Finished?" Trent asked.

Max nodded. There was no way he could do anything about his cock now.

Trent let go of him slowly, holding his waist until Max got his balance. The warmth had relaxed him a lot but being there with Trent had worked him up. Trent reached around him to turn the shower off.

He felt Trent step out of the shower, and Max braced himself to have to face him. After a couple of minutes, he heard Trent say, "Come on, the towel's warm."

Max took a breath and turned, hearing Trent's breath catch and seeing his eyes widen as he took in Max's state. Trent stood with a towel wrapped around his waist, wet swimming trunks on top of another towel on the floor. Max held onto the side of the shower as he walked forward, careful not to move too quickly, which in turn made sure that Trent had a long look at his erect cock.

Trent cleared his throat and began to dry Max off gently. Whenever the towel brushed against his cock, he bit his lip to hold in a moan and tried to silence his intakes of breath. Once Trent had dried most of him, he stood in front of Max again and held out the towel.

"Let's do the same as last time, I'll hold you and you can dry." He walked behind Max and wrapped his arms around him again, allowing Max to rest his back against Trent's front. Trent's towel did not stop Max from feeling Trent's hard cock, and he sucked in a breath as he dried off, both at the feeling of Trent and at the sensitivity of his own cock as he dried it.

When he'd finished, he attempted to wrap the towel around his waist but hissed in pain. Trent took over, wrapping it around him and tucking the edge in—not an easy feat with a hard on. Once he'd done that, he grabbed another smaller towel and rubbed Max's hair, then his own.

"I think we're done," Trent said.

Max didn't say anything. He couldn't. That was the most anyone had ever taken care of him and, regardless of his cock's reaction to it, he tried to hold on to the feeling of being looked after. And to hide the fact that he was close to tears. He was an emotional wreck.

"You okay, Max?" Trent asked, resting his hand on Max's shoulder.

Max nodded and rasped, "Yeah."

"Okay, let's go to my room, and I'll grab you some clothes of mine for now. I'll nip over to your place later and grab some of yours if that's okay?"

"Sure." Max didn't know what else to say. Trent ignored the elephant in the room, and Max struggled with his emotions.

Trent helped him across the hall to his bedroom and deposited Max on his bed. At any other time, Max would've been happy for this to happen, but not now. He was ready to run—for Trent's sake.

Trent dug out a t-shirt, some joggers and boxers and helped Max to dress. Again, it was a case of ignoring his cock, which although wasn't as hard as in the shower, was still not easy to tuck into clothes. Then he turned and got himself dressed, allowing Max some semblance of distance—at least until the towel dropped as Trent pulled on his boxers and Max saw his ass.

"Fuck," he breathed, his mind on how much he

could worship that piece of perfection. Too soon, Trent hid it under his clothes.

"Right, let's go get some breakfast. I'm sure you'll be needing some pain relief, too, won't you?" Trent asked, helping Max to his feet again.

"Yeah, everything hurts a lot more than it did yesterday."

"That's probably because your bruising has set in and you've had no paracetamol since last night. I'll get you some, and hopefully, you'll feel better by the time I have breakfast ready." Trent deposited Max on the sofa with the remote within reach and headed off to the kitchen area.

Max shifted a little until he was comfortable and rested his head against the back of the sofa. He was tired already, and he'd only been up for an hour. Trent came back with pain relief, which he gratefully swallowed with a glass of water. Then Trent headed off again, probably to make breakfast.

He must have dozed a little because he woke when Trent nudged him gently, saying, "Max? Breakfast's ready."

Max took the proffered hand and stood with a wince. "Fuck. I'm going to have to keep moving. I understand what the doctor meant about not staying in one position for too long. Every time I stay still, I seize up." He stretched a little, hoping to alleviate some of the pain. It wasn't as bad as it had been, so the paracetamol must be working.

They sat in the kitchen and ate the omelettes Trent

had made. Making small talk while they were eating, Max asked about Trent's kids and regaled Trent with tales of the characters he'd met whilst working, especially the handsy female last year. She still made Max cringe now when he thought about it.

"Right, if you are okay for me to do it, I'm going to nip to your house and get some of your things. If you can write me a list of what you need and where I'll find them, I will grab them," he said as he took the dishes to the sink.

"You don't have to. I can get Sean to do it. You're doing enough already."

"I don't mind at all, but if you'd prefer Sean to do it, then that's okay. I know it's not easy letting someone you don't know very well into your home."

Max laughed then groaned. "You mean, like you have?"

Trent creased his brow, looking at Max. "What?"

Max pointed to himself, then around the apartment. "You just said it's not easy letting someone you don't know very well into your home. I'm here. In your home. It's not any different from letting you into my home."

Trent smiled slowly. "Yeah, I guess you're right."

"And anyway, we're close buddies after showering together." Max threw that in as a joke. Trent stared at Max for a moment, then turned back to the sink.

"Yeah, I guess we are," he said, then cleared his throat. "Okay, well, there's a notepad near you, so get writing."

Max heard the slight order in his tone and shivered.

He was a switch but, by god, did Trent's voice make him want to submit every time. And Trent knew it. Max hadn't been able to hide his reaction to it last night because he hadn't been expecting it, and therefore, he had also not been able to restrict his response to it. He'd submitted automatically to Trent's orders and knew he would follow them, regardless of the outcome.

TRENT

He drove towards Max's house, trepidation singing through his veins. Even though he'd made the offer, he was worried about what he'd find. Knowing Max's inclinations, he didn't know what to expect. It certainly wasn't what he got.

He closed the front door behind him and stood in the doorway to the lounge, mouth open, gaze surveying his surroundings. Max's lounge was the epitome of what Trent would call earthy. Dark wood floors and furniture, interspersed with a blue rug, green throws over the brown leather sofa and the cream marble fireplace and walls, giving it some lightness. The numerous shelves were littered with books and the walls with art and photographs.

He looked closely at a few of those, seeing a younger Max with who he presumed were his sisters. Trent was being nosy, and he continued through the house giving himself a tour. The kitchen was bigger than his but maybe small compared to some, but Max had made it work with cream coloured base and wall cupboards, giving him plenty of storage, and complimenting it with an amazing red glossy oven.

The dining room had bronze style artwork hung on the cream walls with brown and cream curtains and a dark wood table, chairs and floor. The conservatory was again in browns and creams with additional sofas and a recliner.

Trent walked up the stairs to the first floor, looking at photos along the way; they covered the whole wall, and he was careful not to knock any. He saw Max grow up on the climb of those stairs, and it was a strange thing. He didn't have many pictures of growing up, maybe he could ask his mum for some.

Reaching the landing, he saw five doors. Max hadn't said which was his, so he went to the first one and saw a well decorated green bedroom that didn't look lived in. The second was another bedroom, this time in shades of brown. The third was the bathroom. He hit jackpot at the fourth bedroom. Blues and dark browns continued in here, but there was a more lived-in feel to this room, which was confirmed by the items on the bedside table and the rumpled sheets.

He didn't want to linger too much in Max's bedroom; he felt like he was getting a glimpse he shouldn't be. He grabbed Max's duffle bag from the top of the wardrobe as Max had instructed and laid it on the bed, feeling a certain sense of déjà vu from when he left

Trish. He searched the chest of drawers and wardrobe for the items Max had listed, and then hit the bathroom for his toiletries. Once all those were packed away, he headed to the lounge to get some of the books he'd requested. Trent was amazed by the variety of subjects and with how much they had in common. He made a mental note to mention it to Max, and maybe they could discuss history as that was Trent's favourite subject and seemed to be an interest for Max, looking at the shelves full of historical novels and non-fiction.

Just as he placed some books in the bag, a knock came at the door. He debated answering it or not, as it wasn't his house, but someone had probably seen him walk in anyway.

When he opened the door, he saw an elderly lady stood there.

"Can I help you?" he asked.

"Yes, please. Is Max here?" she said.

"No, he's not at the moment."

She narrowed her eyes. "Who are you then?"

Trent bit his lip to keep from smiling. So, Max has a neighbourly busybody. That should be fun to tease him about later.

"I'm Trent. Max is staying with me for a few days."

She clapped her hands together and put them to her smiling mouth. "Oh, how wonderful. I can't believe he's finally met someone. I never thought it would happen, you know. He was always alone, except for those 'people' he brought back late at night. It wasn't good for him. I told him that several times, but he wouldn't listen. Oh, I'm so happy he's found you. What do you do, Trent? How long have you been together? Would you like to come around for tea one day? I bet Max is over the moon with you. I can't wait to tell everyone that my Max has a boyfriend. Oh, how wonderful!" she finished as she walked off down Max's drive.

Trent was stunned. The woman hadn't even stopped to let Trent answer her questions. He had never heard so much come out of someone's mouth so quickly before. It was only as she got to the path and threw back, "Tell Max to bring you around on Sunday afternoon!" with a wave that he tried to shout a denial back at her.

"I'm not his boyfriend!" he called to no avail. She just waved and carried on, no doubt heading to set the rumour mills alight.

"Well, shit." Trent stood there for a second longer, then shook his head and closed the door. He chuckled to himself. He had so much to tell Max when he got back home.

They sat on the sofa in Trent's house, drinking hot chocolate with a film on in the background while Trent regaled Max with his adventures.

"Oh my god. She didn't?" Max covered his eyes with his unoccupied hand, groaning, this time not in pain.

He chuckled. "That's Mavis. She lives a few doors down and means well, but she's right nosy."

Trent noticed Max said this with love, not in an unkind way. They obviously got on well, and he could just see them bantering back and forth, chatting like old biddies.

"Well, she told me to tell you to bring me around on Sunday afternoon!" Trent laughed when Max groaned again. "I'll let you explain on Sunday."

"Thanks! I thought you were my friend! She will go on and on about how I should've kept you on a leash to make sure you didn't run. She'll never let me hear the end of it. I should make you come with me so I can keep her off my back for a while."

Trent laughed although the idea of having Sunday lunch with Max and his old biddies sounded nice. Real nice. Too nice.

He must've been quiet for too long because Max said, "I'm only joking. I won't throw you to the wolves."

Trent looked over at him and saw he'd finished his drink. "Let me take that." He took the mug and placed it, with his, on the coffee table. He leaned back again, resting his arm along the back of the sofa. It was only as he did it that he realised his fingers were quite close to Max and the effort it took not to touch him was immense. All he had to do was extend his fingers and he'd be touching Max's neck. He frowned down into his lap, not moving his arm yet in case Max figured out he was uncomfortable.

He still couldn't understand where these thoughts were coming from. He couldn't ever remember being attracted to a man before, but then had he ever really had the chance to sow his seed. He looked at Max again, seeing his gaze on the screen. His heart beat so hard, he was worried Max could hear it or even feel it from where he sat.

Biting his lip, Trent knew he had to decide. His breath came fast as he extended one finger towards Max. The first touch made Max jump and glance over at him. Trent saw him swallow hard, and then look back at the TV. He ran his finger along his neck, making goose-bumps appear, and watched as Max closed his eyes and leaned his head a little further forward. Trent didn't know what he was doing, he was just following his instincts. Another finger joined the first, smoothing up and down Max's neck and hairline.

"What are you doing, Trent?" Max whispered.

"No idea," he replied.

"Do you even know what you want?"

"I don't understand what I want," he answered honestly. "All I know is how I feel when you're around."

"And how is that?"

"Confused. Light. Horny." He paused when he had another realisation. "Home," he whispered.

Max looked across at him at that, eyes wide. They stared at each other for a few minutes, neither breaking eye contact.

"Can I kiss you?" Max whispered.

Trent shook his head but seeing the hurt in Max's

eyes made him clarify. "I want to kiss you," he said softly.

Max's eyes widened comically, and Trent would have laughed if he hadn't been so focused on his admission. Max nodded.

Rising from the sofa instead of scooting across so he didn't bounce Max, he moved closer then sat down sideways next to him, leg resting on the sofa between them. He didn't want Max twisting too much and hurting himself further.

He couldn't believe he was about to do this, but if he was honest with himself, it felt right. He lifted a hand to cup Max's cheek and brushed against his skin with his thumb. "I don't know what I'm doing," he whispered.

"It doesn't matter. Just kiss me." Max's breath cascaded across Trent's face.

The first brush of their lips brought back the memory of Max's first attempt at this, when Trent rebuffed him. A fleeting thought that he must remember to apologise for his reaction came to mind before the reality crashed in. He was kissing Max.

Trent started with just little pecking kisses before Max groaned and pressed his lips harder. Then Trent licked at Max's lips for entry, knowing this was the turning point. Permission given, his tongue thrust inside, twining along Max's, and their kiss deepened further. Trent cradled Max's head, not wanting him to move too much and exacerbate his injuries. He sucked Max's tongue into his mouth, then licked inside his mouth again. The kiss went on longer than Trent intended because he couldn't get enough.

He pulled back when he was breathing so hard, he thought he'd pass out. He sat in the same position, holding the back of Max's head, gaze roaming across his face. Fuck, he was gorgeous.

Max's eyes opened slowly, and he stared at Trent. "Wow," was all he said.

"Are you in pain?" Trent asked, when Max winced.

He chuckled. "Nope, can't feel a thing. Except for how hard my cock is right now."

Trent glanced down between them and saw Max tenting his joggers, same as Trent was. He huffed a laugh. "Almost as hard as you were this morning," he said with a smile.

"Fuck you!" Max said without anger. "You were rubbing all over my body, what did you expect to happen?" He laughed. "I was so sure I'd spill just from that."

"I had to stop myself from reaching for you," Trent admitted.

"You should have." Max looked at him, then nodded. "But you weren't ready."

Trent shook his head. "No. I have to admit, Max, I have no idea where these feelings have come from. I've never felt like this for a guy before. I really don't understand what's going on."

Max reached up to cup Trent's cheek. "It's okay. We'll figure it out together. And if you decide it's not right...then I'll deal. I—" Max cut himself off. "Do you want to tell anyone else? Or speak to someone else about us? I'm sure Asher would listen. Or even Logan because he knows I'm hot for you," he said with another chuckle.

"I don't know at the minute. Can it just be me and you for a while?"

"Of course. Though remember the party on Saturday. If things go how I'd like them to, I don't know if I'd be able to keep my hands to myself. Although I would if you insisted."

"Just give me until then to try and figure out what's going on. Is that okay? Sorry, I feel like I'm pulling you in one minute and pushing you away the next." Trent rested his forehead against Max's.

"It's fine, Trent. You need time to sort out your head. I understand."

Trent pressed his lips to Max's again briefly.

They spent the rest of the afternoon, laid on the sofa —Max flat on his back, Trent on his side beside him— watching TV, talking history and books, with intermittent standing and moving so Max didn't seize up again. And kissing. Lots of kissing. Trent couldn't remember the last time he'd enjoyed an afternoon quite as much as this one.

The following day, they made their way across town to Sean and Asher's place for dinner. Sean had called them the night before ordering them to come over for a home cooked meal, which Trent looked forward to. They'd survived on takeaways for the last few days, not because neither could cook, but because they didn't want to cook. Trent had gone shopping for a few essential food items, like bread, ham and cheese to tide them over at lunch times.

They arrived on time, which was a first for Max apparently. And that was confirmed when Sean opened the door, then stood there with wide eyes and mouth. "You're here!"

Trent chuckled. "Well, you did invite us. Of course, we're here."

"No, I mean...on time! Max is never on time. In all the time I've known him, he's never been on time."

Trent looked at Max. "By any chance, are you always late?"

Max looked sheepish but nodded. "Almost always."

"Are you going to let them in, or are you going to let all the heat out of the house instead?" Asher's voice carried down the hallway from the kitchen.

"Sorry, come on in," Sean said.

Trent and Max stripped off their coats and shoes in the foyer before following the scent through to the kitchen.

"That smells amazing. What's for dinner?" Max shuffled in and sat with a small grimace, which was less pain-filled than it had been the previous day.

"Spaghetti carbonara," Asher said with a grin.

"Thought you might need something slightly healthy to tuck into."

"I don't know what you mean," Max said. "We've done well with Chinese and pizza takeaways this week, Trent, haven't we? They're healthy...they have vegetables on or in them."

"Yeah, not sure you can get away with saying they're healthy, Max," Sean said as he walked into the room with a little lady following behind.

"Max!" Janie leapt towards him, but on instinct, Trent caught her around the waist before she could jump on him. "Uncle Trent, put me down!" Janie said, laughing.

"I will, pipsqueak, but you need to be careful of Max. He's got a few bruises on his tummy and face." He carried on when she stopped struggling and looked at Max. "He's okay, sweetheart, you just need to be careful, that's all. Okay?"

Janie nodded. "Yes, Uncle Trent." She walked up to Max. "Hi, Max." Her face was one huge grin.

"Hey, darling. Look at you! You've grown since I saw you a couple of weeks ago. Have you been sticking your feet in compost so you'd grow quicker?" Max looked at her with a twinkle in his eye, making Janie and the rest of the room, chuckle.

"Don't be silly, Max. I'd get muddy feet."

Max sighed. "Yeah, I guess you would. Never mind, then." He closed his arms around her for a hug and kissed her head.

Trent watched the interaction with a smile. Max was

amazing with her. He'd seen him in action before, but each time, it blew Trent away how well Max got on with kids. He hoped, one day, Max had a family of his own with loads of kids running him ragged.

"Food's ready," Asher said.

"Oi, pipsqueak!" Trent waited until Janie looked at him. "Where's my hug?" he pouted.

Janie ran up to him and jumped into his arms. "Love you, Uncle Trent," she said in his ear, squeezing him tight.

"Love you, too, pipsqueak." He let her jump back down, and they all sat around the table.

During the meal, they kept the conversation light. With Janie being there, they couldn't discuss "adult" subjects, like how Max's case was doing, but Trent could tell them some funny things that happened at school the previous week. When they'd all finished eating, Janie asked if she could go and watch the end of her movie, which Asher agreed to.

"Now we have no little ears, have you heard anything from the police, yet?" Sean asked, leaning forward.

Max shook his head. "No, not yet. It's likely to take a while, Sean. They're not going to find whoever did this within a couple of days. If they did, I'd be surprised."

"I'm going to chase it up with Logan when I see or speak to him next. I don't know what shifts he's doing so it probably won't be until tomorrow, but hopefully, he'll have some information by then," Trent said.

"How are your injuries?" Asher asked.

"Not too bad," Max said. Trent snorted. "All right, they could be better, how's that?"

"Still an understatement," Trent argued. "He's black and blue from chest to groin. It hurts for him to sit too long; it hurts for him to stand too long. Stop pussy-footing around, Max."

"I'm okay, Trent. Stop worrying. You're like a dog with a bone." Trent knew Max was exasperated with him, but he wouldn't change his ways, and Trent also knew that Max liked his fussing, even though he'd probably deny it with his last breath.

Trent shook his head and looked at Asher and Sean, who wore identical "what the hell is going on" expressions. He bit his lip. Maybe him and Max had become too comfortable with each other over the last few days. Although, if they were going to make a go of this, then everyone would know soon, anyway. Trent tried to ignore their expressions and asked Asher about the kids he looked after. They spent the next half an hour talking about their individual jobs and funny anecdotes. Trent really had had a good time, although he'd struggled throughout to keep his hands to himself, after being so free to touch Max the previous day.

He just needed a little more time to think about what this meant. He was fairly certain he had no issues at all with being...whatever he was...he just didn't want to let Max down if he came across something he wasn't comfortable with.

He'd speak with Logan tomorrow, but maybe he could speak with Asher now.

"Asher?" He waited until he had his attention. "Can I have a quick word?"

"Sure." Asher turned to Sean. "I'm just chatting with Trent, make sure Janie doesn't sneak in for ice cream." He pinned Sean with a look, which Trent interpreted as "make sure you don't give Janie ice cream."

They picked up their coffees and walked into the back garden, through to the garage conversion that had been completed last year. Asher had wanted to separate his childminding business from his personal home and had employed Sean to draw up the architectural plans for it. It was how they'd met. The conversion had been a godsend to hear Asher talk about it, and his business had benefited from it.

Closing the door behind them, they sat at the table designated for the children's dinner. "What's up?" Asher asked.

"I like Max." Trent just laid it on the table.

"I know you do." Asher looked confused.

"No, I *really* like Max." Trent tried a little inflection in his voice, hoping Asher would get the hint without him actually having to say the words.

Asher continued to look confused for a second while he inspected Trent's face, then Trent saw understanding dawn in Asher's eyes. "Oh!"

"Yeah, oh."

"All right. How do you feel about it?"

"Confused. Unsure. Content." He paused thinking. "Did I mention confused?" he said, chuckling.

"I can imagine. How did it all come about?"

"Well, I've been feeling confused for a while, but ever since…" Trent paused, feeling his cheeks heat at the reason for his initial confusion.

"Since when?"

He took a breath. "Ever since you and Sean got together, I've watched your…interactions, and they've been…hot. God, this is so embarrassing." Trent put his head in his hands, his face hot to the touch.

"Oh. Okay. Thanks for that." Asher laughed a little self-consciously if Trent heard right. "And it has you confused about whether you like guys or not."

Trent could tell that was a guess from Asher's point of view, but he'd hit the nail on the head with it. He nodded. "I don't want to string Max along if I'm going to realise in a few days, weeks, months that I'm not gay and it was just…I don't know…an experiment, or whatever."

"Firstly, you would never do that to Max. Secondly, there isn't really much I can tell you. There's no guide to being gay. Everyone feels differently to the next person. What I would say is that you need to trust your instincts and your feelings. Think about how you'd feel if you could never see Max again. That the moment we left the kitchen, you'd never be able to set eyes on him again. How do you feel about that?"

Trent thought, and his heart rate and breathing increased; he began to shake and shook his head.

Asher smiled. "There's your answer."

Trent blew out a breath, trying to calm his thoughts and remember Max was only a few steps away. He had never had that reaction to anyone before. Except the more he thought about it the more he realised he had. "My kids," he stated.

Asher looked at him in confusion, once again. "Your kids?"

"I was just thinking I'd never had that reaction to anyone before. But I have. I have that reaction whenever I think about not seeing my kids. Fuck, Asher. I'm in way too deep, aren't I?"

"Nah, you're right where you're supposed to be." Asher covered his hand and squeezed. "Don't overthink things. Take everything one day at a time. And make sure you talk to each other. Communication is key."

Trent nodded, biting his lip. "Thanks."

"Not a problem. Are you going large with this, or keeping silent while you work things out?"

"Silent for the moment. I was going to speak to Logan tomorrow, but I don't really think I need to now." He laughed.

"Probably not, but it wouldn't hurt."

"Maybe." Trent stood. "I best get Max back home. He'd happily stay, but I know when he's in pain. He refuses to take painkillers unless I tell him to."

"Stubborn fool."

"Yes, he is."

They grabbed their cups and made their way back to the kitchen. Max locked eyes with him as soon as he entered, and he finally felt his heart rate get back to normal. Max raised his eyebrows in question, and Trent smiled.

"Let's head back, Max."

"All right." Max winced when he tried to stand, and Trent stood behind him, holding his waist to help him. "Thanks."

"No problem," Trent said.

"Thanks for having us over. Dinner was great."

"Janie! Max and Uncle Trent are going now. Come say goodbye," Asher shouted.

Janie came in holding an empty bowl. "Bye, Uncle Trent. Bye, Max," she said as she placed it on the table.

Trent bit his lip, and he looked over at Asher and Sean, seeing Sean look guilty, and Asher shaking his head. "Bye, pipsqueak," Trent said as he blew a raspberry on her cheek.

"Bye, darling." Max kissed her cheek while Trent held her.

They walked to the car, and Trent helped position Max in his seat. He had a lot of thinking to do, but he thought he knew what his decision was going to be.

CHAPTER TEN

MAX

They spent the next day kissing, touching and generally smooching whenever they could. Trent would not go any further though because of Max's injuries. His bruises had changed to a blue-black colour, so he looked worse than he felt. They still hadn't slept in the same bed, Trent said he was worried he'd roll over and hurt Max in the night. Max was beginning to get frustrated, but he had said he would give Trent space, so he tried to keep his word. It was difficult though because he wanted Trent with a passion he'd not felt in a while.

He hadn't sensed that Trent had changed his mind about them, but he'd not opened up again since their initial kiss. Max wanted to push Trent down on the bed and have his way with him, but he knew he had to be careful. His injuries were not even close to healing yet, and he didn't want to be off work longer than necessary.

It was Charlie's party tonight, and Trent was driving. He said he wanted to be able to drive Max home if it was too much for him. Max was going to try and change his mind though, not that he thought it would do any good. Trent was stubborn, that much he had realised in the last few days living with him.

"Right, I'm going for a shower. Take it easy while I'm gone." Trent leaned forward and kissed Max briefly and walked off.

He had noticed that Trent showed affection more readily now. He wasn't hesitating, he just did it—and Max loved it. He bit his lip. He debated whether to join him in the shower. He jumped up from the sofa and walked quietly to Trent's room. Once he'd realised Trent was already in the bathroom, he walked in and undressed. Listening at the bathroom door, he heard the flow of the water change and knew Trent was under the spray. Twisting the handle slowly, hoping to make no noise, he opened the door and slipped in, closing it behind him. Trent faced towards him in the shower but with his eyes closed as he washed his hair. Max took a moment to gape at the beautiful sight of the man.

He walked closer and just as he was about to climb in, Trent opened his eyes and jumped. "Fucking hell, Max! You scared the shit out of me!" He shook his head and smiled. "You just couldn't be patient, could you?"

Max shrugged. "Patience is not one of my strong suits." He smiled.

"Come here." Trent beckoned him with a hand, and Max wasted no time in climbing in with him.

Turning so Max was under the spray, Trent wrapped his arms around him, and Max reciprocated. He rested his head on Trent's chest and let the water beat down on his back. It was nice to just be held for a change.

He lifted his head. "Thank you."

Trent frowned at him. "For what?"

"Being you. Being open to change. Being…just being you."

Trent looked at him, gaze roaming his face. "Let's get you washed," he whispered and reached for the shampoo. He washed Max's hair, making him feel so relaxed he could've probably fallen asleep. Then he grabbed the soap bar and washed his body, careful of his bruises. This time though, he didn't miss a spot. He turned Max around, so he faced the spray and wrapped one arm around his waist, then with his other hand, he gripped Max's cock making him gasp. This was the first contact his cock had with another part of Trent's body, except for pressing against him previously.

Confident strokes had him hard as steel in no time. Trent stroked up, twisting his hand under the head, then down, twisting back again. He repeated this several times until Max was babbling incoherently. Trent let go briefly, and Max tensed for denial, but Trent repositioned his hand, so his fingertips were on the sensitive part of his cock. Max felt Trent's gentle fingers rub against that part until he bucked in his arms.

"Fuck, Trent. I'm so close. Please. Please let me

come. Please. Oh, god. Ah, fuck! Please!" He was trained not to come unless he had permission, and he hoped Trent realised that. Although they weren't in a Dom/sub relationship, Trent had become that to Max ever since he'd used *that* voice on him. It was ingrained in him that he could not come unless his Dom gave his permission. "Please, Trent. Please!"

Trent bit down on Max's earlobe. "Come."

That voice reverberated down his spine and along his cock, enabling his climax to spurt all over the shower tiles. Max couldn't remember the last time he'd come that hard. His ribs were screaming at him with how hard he was breathing, but it was worth it.

"Fuck, Trent." He sagged against him until he felt Trent hard against his ass. He smiled to himself.

He turned around and dropped to his knees before Trent could say a word. Within seconds, he had Trent's cock in his mouth. He knew if he'd given him a chance, he would've said he didn't need it, even if he did. If Trent told him no, then he'd pull away, but he hoped he didn't.

He licked the head, feeling it jump beneath his palm, flicked his tongue against the slit and sucked the head like a lollipop. Then he opened his mouth and sank Trent into him. It was a heady feeling, being someone's first experience, he wanted to make Trent feel good, to hopefully not change his mind about them. He knew a blowjob would not change someone's mind, but if Trent hadn't felt this connection between them, then he may have denied himself completely. At least now he had more information to base his decision on.

Max smiled around his cock. He pulled off with a pop and stroked with his hand while he got his breath back. He rested Trent's cock against his tongue and moved back and forth, teasing the underside until Trent grabbed at his head.

"Ah, fucking hell," he whispered, hips bucking into Max's mouth. Max looked up at him and locked gazes as he took him deeper down his throat and swallowed around him. "Shit, Max. Do that again." Max did. Trent's hips bucked into Max again and again. "Holy hell, that's feels good. Swallow me, Max. Fuck, yeah. I'm nearly there. Fuck."

Max held onto Trent's hips and kept his mouth around his cock, sucking with every withdrawal. He let Trent use his mouth as he wanted, breathing through his nose.

"Fuck, that's it, come on." He thrust a little harder, and Max gagged. "Oh, fuck. I'm coming!" That must have been too much because the next second Trent released into Max's mouth, and Max drank every drop. When Trent stopped bucking and sagged against the wall, Max leisurely licked him clean until Trent became too sensitive. "Fucking hell, Max," Trent gasped.

Max stood and helped Trent to turn into the spray, then he washed Trent's hair and body for him. Once clean, he gave him a kiss and got out of the shower to dry off. He'd leave Trent to think about everything while he got dressed. As he was about to leave the bathroom, Trent called his name.

"I'm going to speak with Logan tonight. Can you bear with me while I do that?" Trent's voice had taken on a worried tone, but Max smiled.

"Of course, I can. Just remember to talk to me before you make a final decision. Please." With that, he blew Trent a kiss and walked out.

Max was able to dress himself now at least. He chose a simple outfit of blue jeans and a black shirt, mainly because they are easy to get on and off and slapped on some aftershave. Ready almost as quick as usual, he headed out to the living area, stopping in his tracks when he saw Trent in black jeans and an emerald-green shirt. He looked divine.

"Wow, look at you, hotshot. That shirt looks amazing on you," said Max, practically drooling.

Trent blushed. "Thanks. You look good too."

"I thought I'd go the same colour as my bruises." Max laughed when he saw Trent's expression. "Stop frowning, it's a joke."

"I know, sorry, I'd just been thinking about how you haven't heard from the police yet. I'll speak to Logan tonight and see if he can tell me anymore. I don't like not knowing where this creep is."

Max walked over to him and cupped his cheek. "I'm

fine, Trent. No one is looking for me, it's just a random act of violence, I'm sure. The police will figure it out."

As Trent looked at him, Max saw the need for answers in his eyes. "Okay."

"Are you ready to party like it's the new millennium again?" Max asked, gaining a chuckle from Trent.

"I'm too old to party like that now."

"Hush, you're not old. You're only twelve years older than me." He wrapped himself around Trent, resting his chin on his chest and looking up at him. There wasn't a large height difference but enough that Max had to look up a bit. "You've still got good stamina," he whispered before he claimed Trent's lips again. He couldn't get enough of his kisses, how one minute they were soft and exploratory and the next they were hard and demanding. It fit Trent's personality.

Trent pulled away after a short time. "We're going to be late."

"And?" Max answered, running his hands down to Trent's ass and squeezing, making him arch into Max.

"Fuck, Max, you're insatiable." Trent took his mouth again, this time leaving no prisoners. Once he was done, he said, "Hell, Max, you look like you've just been thoroughly fucked with your red, swollen lips and sleepy eyes."

"Make it true," he answered unapologetically.

Trent smiled. "No."

"You're always saying no to me," he pouted.

"That's because you always request things at the

wrong time, and I'm older and wiser than you are." Trent smirked. "Time to go."

"Fucking hell." Max adjusted himself and followed as Trent made his way to the door.

Twenty-five minutes later, they were sat in their usual booth in Crush with Sean and Asher, Zak, Ethan and Logan with their food order on the way.

Max could see Trent hadn't been happy when he'd ordered a beer, but he hadn't taken any pain relief for this particular reason and told Trent that. He could tell Trent didn't like it. Trent wasn't drinking because he'd driven, so Max made sure to alternate between beer and water, so he wasn't too wasted for when they had to go home. He'd had a brief conversation with everyone about his injuries, so they were up to date, but then he'd changed the subject. He couldn't tell them much anyway.

"So, how are things between you two," Zak asked.

Max looked over at Trent to see if he was listening, and he was talking to Logan. "Quite good actually," he said quietly.

Zak raised his eyebrows. "How well is quite well?"

Max felt his face warm a little. He didn't know why because he'd always been happy to talk about sex and stuff before. Maybe it was because Trent meant so much to him, he didn't know. "Third base."

Zak smiled. "It's serious then?"

Max felt his smile fall. "Kind of." He tried to explain without giving away too much of Trent's personal business. "Understandably he wants to go slow, and he said he's going to speak with Logan tonight. He's not told me exactly what he's worried about, but I think he's worried that he's not gay, and he's going to hurt me. Which I'm happy to hear—that he doesn't want to hurt me—but I wish he'd relax a little more. Kinda go with the flow."

"I'm sure he will relax once he has some answers. Logan will help him. Give him time."

"I'm know. I'm just—"

"Impatient. Yeah, I know." Zak laughed.

"Anyway, how's things with you?" He'd not heard from Zak since their last get together.

Zak looked strained at the topic. "Not great. Ashley is spending more and more time out, and I'm either home with Dane or Emily is babysitting. It scares me that I don't trust her."

"Have you spoken to the lawyer again?"

"Yeah, we've been in touch a few times." Zak laughed, shaking his head. "He's refusing to let me pay him."

"Wow, that's good of him."

"Yeah, but I feel bad asking him things when I'm not paying him. I don't want to take up too much of his time."

"I can understand that."

Zak blew out a breath. "Anyway, onto brighter subjects, please."

Max laughed. "Like what?"

Zak shrugged. "I don't know. How about your business?"

He rolled his eyes. "I've had to put everything on hold at the moment because of the 'incident,'" using finger quotes, "so I'm having to rearrange a lot of things. Hopefully, I can start back doing stuff on Monday. Trent will be going back to work, so I will be back home—where all my paperwork is, I might add. Trent refused to pick it up when I asked him to the other day." He shook his head. "He is so stubborn."

Zak raised his eyebrows again. "Like someone else I know."

He glared at Zak. "Shut up."

"Hey, now, what's all this?" Trent leaned over and nudged Max's shoulder with his own. "Why does he have to shut up?"

"No reason."

"Max says you're stubborn. I was enlightening him to the fact that so is he." Zak didn't care if he dropped Max in it if his smile was anything to go by.

Trent laughed. "I am definitely stubborn. And also right."

Max sat back in a huff. He wanted more alcohol. He sat forward again. "Let me get past, please."

"Why?" asked Trent.

"I need more alcohol if I'm going to deal with all of you."

"No, you don't."

"Yes. I. Do." With that, Max pecked him on the lips and squeezed past. It was only when he was walking to the bar that he realised what he'd done. *Shit, shit, shit.* He grimaced, not daring to look back at what he knew would be a Spanish inquisition aimed at Trent. *Sorry, Trent.*

TRENT

Well, fuck. As much as he liked the fact that Max was happy to kiss him in public, he had just outed him to the whole table. Trent looked around at the shocked faces—all except Zak, who looked smug and Asher, who already knew—and decided to be honest.

"A couple of days ago, although I've been confused for a while. It just happened. No, I don't know where we're going. We're still working things out. I have no idea what I'm doing." He paused, looking down at his hands. "I like him." He waited a beat, then looked up. "Does that cover all of your questions?"

Everyone was silent for a minute, then burst out laughing. It was Trent's turn to be shocked then.

"It took you long enough," Logan said, clapping him on the back. "I thought Max was going to an early grave with all the pining he was doing." He handed Trent his beer. "I think you're going to need this tonight."

Trent tried to wave it away. "I'm driving."

Logan pushed the beer back. "Get a taxi, pick up your car tomorrow. There, sorted."

He blew out a breath and downed the beer.

"Thanks," he said as he wiped his mouth. "I should've got Max to get a whole round."

"You must be psychic then," said Max as he brought a tray with enough drinks for everyone, including Trent. "I saw you down Logan's beer, so I thought you'd be off driving duty now." Max squeezed across to get to his seat. "I am so sorry I kissed you. I didn't think—" he began, quietly.

Trent kissed him to shut him up and garnered a few catcalls from the table's occupiers. He didn't care. Now it was out in the open, he felt freer in a way. He was still a little confused about what it all meant, but he liked Max, a lot, and he wanted to make sure he gave it his all. He didn't want to mess Max around or hurt him.

As he pulled away, Max leaned into him. "Is this a coming out party now?" he said, chuckling.

Trent laughed. "I suppose in a way it is. But let's not tell anyone, I don't want to steal Charlie's thunder."

They spent the next few hours drinking, laughing and being with their friends and each other. They stole the odd kiss here and there, touched hands or legs occasionally and looked at each other often. Trent had never felt so relaxed.

Charlie came over as the night ended to thank them for his gift. The friends at the table and Tom and Ginny had all banded together to get him a long weekend break in the Lake District, and he was over the moon with it. Charlie was also very drunk, much to his boyfriend's amusement. Josh told them Charlie didn't drink very often as he was always the one behind the bar instead, so he was going to enjoy Charlie's hangover tomorrow. As they were about to leave, Charlie caught sight of someone and called them over.

"Johnson! Hey, come over and meet my friends!"

Trent laughed at his exuberance. The guy came over, smiling and gave Charlie a hug before moving his attention to the table.

"Hey, nice to meet you all," Johnson said.

Josh made the introductions, and Trent noticed Johnson's eyes widen when they got to Max. He looked over at Max and saw Max with a similar look.

"Everything okay?" Trent whispered in his ear.

Max nodded. "I've seen him around before." Which Trent took to mean in the BDSM circuit.

Trent listened as Logan talked to Johnson about work when Johnson's mobile rang. "Sorry, let me just answer this. Won't be a second. Hey, Adam…Yeah… Seriously? What the hell, man. You know you can… Yeah, all right…text me the details…See ya. Sorry about that."

"No problem. Everything okay?" Logan asked.

Johnson blew out a breath. "Yeah, my best mate is coming to town. Not seen him for ages. He always just drops by unannounced. I never know his whereabouts from one day to the next." At Logan's puzzled look, he expanded, "He's a photographer, so travels a lot."

"Sounds nice. You'll have to bring him around here to meet us one night. We'll get him inducted into our ways in no time." Johnson laughed at Logan's remarks.

Max nudged his arm. "Shall we head home?" he

asked. Neither had drunk a large amount, but Trent had a nice buzz going. Trent nodded and reached to get his phone. "'S'okay. I'll ring a taxi."

Max received a text twenty minutes later saying their taxi had arrived, and they said their goodbyes, promising to catch up again soon. Trent was more than happy to repeat tonight's fun; he hadn't felt as included for a long time. He frowned, he didn't mean that they *excluded* him, but he'd struggled to find where he fit, at least that's what it had felt like. Now though, he'd felt part of it. He wasn't sure if it was the relationship with Max that had caused it or if something had changed inside of him to help him feel more alive.

He'd spoken to Logan at the party briefly. He'd explained his worries that he'd hurt Max if he changed his mind later. Logan's advice was simple, if it feels right and good to him, then it's fine; if he feels uneasy, wait. It was advice he was going to try and take.

He'd also asked him about Max's case. There was no news, which Logan was pissed about. There was nothing that pissed Logan off more than no leads on a case. Which then reminded him to ask about that guy and girl from last week. Logan had confirmed the girl had been in one piece still and he planned on checking up on her a few times over the next few weeks, just to make sure she stayed that way. Martin had not been happy about it though, Logan had said with a smirk.

The taxi deposited them outside Trent's building, and they entered the apartment without incident. The fresh air had helped sober them a little. When the door closed behind him, he turned to find Max staring at him, an unreadable look on his face. They stood staring at each other for a few minutes before Trent swallowed and took a step towards Max. He wasn't sure where he wanted the night to go, but he still felt the same pull to be as close to Max as possible, so he didn't fight it. He eventually stood toe to toe with him, still gazing at him.

Max lifted a hand and rested it against Trent's stomach, then slowly moved it upwards over his chest to finish against the side of his neck. His other hand followed a similar route but ended with Max's fingers cupping the back of his head, tangled in his hair. "Kiss me?" Max whispered.

"Forever." The words came out before Trent knew what he was going to say, and although they shocked him, they felt so right. He slipped his arms around Max's waist and lowered his head. Before he made contact, his gaze roamed Max's face. "Mine," he breathed and sank into a kiss that quickly turned from soft and gentle to hard and passion-filled.

Trent's head spun with the taste and scent of Max; it was all around him. He wasn't sure if the alcohol in his system was making him more relaxed or more reckless, but he lifted Max, who linked his legs around Trent's waist, and walked towards his bedroom. He wasn't sure what he was ready for, but he wanted Max in his bed tonight, that much he did know.

Twice along the way, they paused to gasp for breath, but soon started again until Trent's knees had knocked into his bed. He pulled his head away, stepped back and lowered Max to the floor. He stared in his eyes, trying to find something—he didn't know what—but finding an awareness that settled him for some reason. He smoothed his hands up Max's chest and to his shoulders, sliding his leather jacket off and into a heap on the floor. Following the jacket, his hands glided down Max's arms until he linked their fingers together.

"Only what you're happy to do," Max whispered, still gazing into Trent's eyes.

Trent gave a small smile and lowered his head again, kissing him once, then again in thanks. After that, their kisses turned slow and deep as they divested each other of their shirts and shoes, no hurry in their movements, just a deep realisation to Trent that he was really going to do this with Max. He felt nervous but also as if his nerve endings were alight. He'd never felt this type of connection to anyone, especially not Trish.

He banished that thought the minute it entered his head, not wanting her to intrude on this moment. Fingers caressed down his spine, making him arch and release Max's lips with a moan, and he buried his face in his neck as Max's hands continued under the waistband of his jeans to cup his ass. Max used it to pull Trent closer to him, and their kiss turned more passionate as they rubbed their bodies against each other. Trent pulled his mouth away again, breathing heavily and walked Max backwards until the back of his legs hit the bed. He pushed a little more, indicating he wanted Max on his bed, and he complied, lying back on his elbows, looking up at Trent, waiting for his next move.

Trent had no idea what he was doing, but he followed his instincts. He knelt on the floor at the bottom of the bed between Max's legs and leaned forward to kiss the skin of his stomach. Max groaned with the touch, emboldening Trent to continue. His hands ran up Max's legs until he reached the waistband and looking up at Max, he reached for his button. It undid easily, and he dragged the zipper down slowly, enjoying the anticipation of unravelling what he knew was underneath.

"Trent…hurry," Max whined.

Trent licked along the waistband, purposefully drawing it out further, then as Max lifted to allow the motion, he pulled them down with his briefs, freeing his cock, which bounced upright against Max's stomach. He yanked the clothes off the rest of the way and threw them behind him, staring at his cock the whole time.

Leaning forward, he rose on his knees to get closer. He'd never given a blow job before, but he knew what felt good for him, so he'd start there. He reached with his hand, slipping his fingers between Max's cock and his stomach, holding it steady as his tongue traced from base to tip. He swallowed Max's taste and wanted more, so he repeated the motion, this time sucking the head into his mouth, eliciting a groan from Max.

Max flopped on his back on the bed, and Trent saw him grip the covers hard enough his knuckles were white. He took this as a good sign and continued a couple more times. The third time, he sucked the head in, he took more into his mouth, hollowing his cheeks as he pulled back off again, his hand stroking up at the same time.

Trent took his cock in again, this time swiping his tongue over the underside of it.

"Jesus, Trent," Max moaned, breath heaving as he bucked up in response. "Fucking hell."

Taking note of Max's responses, made Trent feel more confident he was doing okay, so he kept sucking, using his tongue and his hand.

"Fuck. You have to stop, Trent. I don't want to come yet." Trent hummed in denial while Max's cock was in his mouth, and Max groaned loudly. "Please, stop," he said.

Trent slid his mouth off and looked at Max; his pupils were blown wide, his cheeks were rosy, and he gasped for breath. He crawled up Max's body, kissing skin as he went, then rested his lower abdomen against his cock, making sure his jeans didn't hurt Max, and kissed him. He still couldn't believe he was doing this and that he was okay with it all. At least so far.

They stayed in that position for a while, kissing leisurely, hands roaming. Max slid his hands to Trent's jeans and undid the button, then used his hands and feet to strip them off him. Trent lifted his head and breathed deeply as their cocks rested together between them. He stared at Max as he thrust gently, seeing an answering flare in his eyes before Max gripped Trent's head and pulled him down for another kiss. Trent continued to thrust, rubbing their cocks together, their kisses getting deeper and harder and faster.

Breaking off again, he rested his face in Max's neck. "God, you feel amazing, Max. I never understood..." he stopped realising what he was about to admit and not sure if he was ready.

Max wrapped his arms around Trent's head. "I know."

And Trent believed he did.

Max pushed at Trent's shoulders, rolling him to his back and straddled him. His bent legs were either side of Trent's hips, their cocks still touching, and he lowered down to his elbows, hands bracketing Trent's head. Max was close enough that they could share breath, and Trent found he loved it. He ran his hands up and down Max's spine and legs, anywhere he could reach.

"Thank you, Trent."

Trent frowned. "What for?" He hoped they weren't finished already.

"For trusting me. For letting me in. For allowing me this. If this is all I can have, thank you."

Trent realised Max thought he wouldn't go any further. He hugged Max to him and decided to lay it on the line regardless of if he was ready. "You trusted me first with your secret about liking me. You let me see you, instead of what you show everyone else. You allowed me to help you when you didn't want it. I haven't given this to you, I have given it to both of us."

He paused. "And I have no intention of stopping." With that, he pulled Max closer and kissed him with everything he had.

He had listened to Logan's advice and everything felt right and good. If that began to change, he would speak up. But if it didn't, well let's say, he was sure he'd enjoy the result.

CHAPTER ELEVEN

MAX

Max couldn't believe Trent's words. He honestly hadn't thought Trent would want to go any further than just playing as they were. He was blown away.

Returning Trent's kiss, he circled his hips against Trent's, rubbing their cocks together, unable to stop the moan that sounded. His mind was fuzzy with the lack of oxygen, and he broke away. "Wait, wait. We have to talk practical for a minute." Max was not going to have sex with Trent until Trent knew exactly what was going to happen. He thought Trent knew about it all, but he couldn't in all conscience carry on without making certain.

Trent slammed his head back against the pillows as he thrust against Max's cock. "Why?" he gritted out.

"Because I need to know you know what's happening."

Trent took a breath and let it out slowly, looking at Max the whole time. "Okay."

"Right, so you know how guys have sex right?"

"Bloody hell, Max, of course I do!"

"And you know about the need for lube and stretching before anything else happens, right?" Max petted Trent's chest to calm him.

"Lube, yes, stretching, um, no," he admitted, eyes leaving Max's before returning with a faint blush added to his cheeks.

"Okay." Max cleared his throat. "Right, well, I'd like you to fuck me," he said quietly, "if you want to, that is?"

Trent bit his lip, his cheeks reddening more when he nodded.

"All right. I'm going to need to be stretched before you fuck me, all right?" Max decided to be matter of fact about it all so he wouldn't sound patronising. At least he hoped he wouldn't. "Either I can do it, or you can do it. What do you want?"

Trent was quiet for a moment before he cleared his throat and said, "Can you do it. But can I watch? For next time."

Max felt his smile grow as he realised Trent wanted this to continue and not just be a one-time thing. "Sure. Do you have any lube?"

Trent nodded and indicated the bedside table. Max reached across, opened the drawer and took out the half-empty tube.

"Okay, I'm going to turn around and show you how

to stretch me." He chuckled. "I feel like we've swapped roles and I'm the teacher." He turned around so he straddled Trent's legs backwards. He had never had someone watching him when he'd done this before, so he was out of his comfort zone. Opening the tube, he squirted some lube on his fingers and reached around to his hole, spreading it around.

"Fucking hell, Max," he heard Trent say.

He pushed the tip of his finger in his ass, bearing down and allowing the intrusion. He'd had this done to him many times and always loved the sensations of something bridging his hole. Closing his eyes at the feeling, he pushed in and out for a few seconds until he could get his whole finger in with no burning. Then, after looking around and seeing Trent's wide-eyed gaze on his ass, his mouth open and his hand absently stroking his own cock, he pushed two in and did the same, little by little he was able to take the intrusion until his fingers were easily slipping in and out.

Max knew he had to stretch himself a bit further because of the size of Trent's cock, but his own was so hard he wasn't sure how much he could take. Suddenly, it was taken out of his control. Trent reached for the lube, and Max heard the tube click open and close before Trent's hand removed Max's and replaced it with his own. He felt the cool slippery gel against his hole, and then Trent's finger pushed inside.

"Ah, god, yes," Max cried as he pushed back gently, meeting with Trent's hand. Trent quickly added a second finger, making Max keen with pleasure. Trent pushed his fingers in and out for so long Max thought he'd die from the foreplay of it. "I need it, Trent. Another one."

"I don't think…" Trent trailed off. Max looked around and saw the concentration and frown on Trent's face.

"I'm fine, Trent. Another finger, otherwise, it'll hurt when you fuck me." He knew what to say to make Trent obey. There was no way Trent would purposefully hurt Max.

Max moaned when Trent's fingers left his ass, but they were soon back with a third. The burn was back but with Max bearing down and Trent going slowly, he was able to get all three in. He slowly withdrew and pressed in again, repeating it until the fingers went in easily, and Max pressed backwards in faster motions.

"Fuck, Trent. I'm ready. Please."

At that, Trent gently flipped Max over on to his back, being careful of his bruises, and turned him so his head was back at the top of the bed. "Hold onto the headboard," Trent ordered in that voice Max knew he would do anything to hear.

He reached his hands up and gripped one bar in each hand tightly and opened his legs, exposing himself to Trent, who had positioned himself between his legs.

Trent reached across to the bedside table for a condom, and then for the lube again. Max watched as Trent ripped open the packet and sheathed his cock, then covered it with lube. He knew Trent had listened to everything he'd said and was grateful.

Trent hesitated after that and rested his hands on each side of Max's body. "Tell me what to do to make this good for you," he whispered, frowning.

Max let go of the headboard for a moment and wrapped his arms around Trent's neck. "Anything you do will be amazing. Please don't worry so." He kissed him leisurely, bringing some of the passion back and leaving some of the practicality at the door. "Put your cock against my ass," he broke away to say, and Trent reached a hand down to do what Max said. "Press in slowly, I'll bear down, and you'll feel resistance, but keep going." It was a struggle to talk as he felt Trent comply. He moaned as Trent began to breach him.

"You okay?" Trent asked.

"Yes, keep going," he panted.

"Fuck, you're so tight, I don't know if I can."

Max felt it the moment Trent breached the tight muscles and sank further into him more easily. The burn was there as Trent was easily bigger than even three of Trent's fingers, but it was a welcome burn. Trent kept pressing in until Max felt his balls touch his ass, then he stopped.

"Holy fucking hell, Max."

Max let go of his head and cupped his face to kiss him again. He loved the feeling of Trent inside him. It felt different from other people, and he'd had plenty, not that he could remember a single one of them at that moment.

"Move, Trent. Fuck me," Max pleaded.

Trent lifted onto his hands and looked at Max. His eyes narrowed. "Hands on the headboard."

Fuck, he thought as he did as he was ordered, *that was so hot.*

As soon as Max had tightened his hands on the bars, Trent began to withdraw. Max felt Trent's cock stroke his insides as he pushed back in. He could tell Trent controlled his movements, and Max wanted him to lose that control. So, the next time Trent pressed in, Max lifted his hips to meet him.

"Fuck. You're so tight. It's never felt like this before. Jesus."

Max saw stars as Trent changed his angle. "God, Trent, right there, oh, hell, fuck!" He was not going to last if Trent kept that up.

Trent's movements increased in speed, balls slapping his ass as his cock pistoned inside. "God." Trent moved one of his hands and wrapped it around the back of Max's neck. It brought their faces closer together, and Max lifted his head for a kiss. Trent laid on top of him and wrapped his arms around his back and to his shoulders, lifting him enough to still hit Max at the right place. They didn't really kiss, just left their lips pressed together as Trent pounded into him. The extra friction on Max's cock from being stuck between them took Max right to the edge.

He broke away, "Fuck, I'm gonna come. Please, Trent!"

"Come," Trent demanded as he continued at the

same pace, not changing anything, which made Max hit his peak seconds later. "Trent!"

"Holy hell. Fuck! Max! Ah!"

From a distance, Max felt Trent's rhythm falter before he wrapped Max tighter in his arms and his cock completely in his ass. Max let go of the headboard and wrapped Trent in his arms, wanting to be as close to him as Trent seemed to need to be to him.

They stayed that way for a few minutes as their breathing returned to normal.

Trent pulled back first, moving a hand down to his cock, probably to hold onto the condom as he withdrew. Max moaned as he did, and Trent kissed his lips.

"I'll be back." With that, Trent went into the bathroom. Max laid there, his heart rate slowing down, ribs aching a little with each deep breath and hoped Trent didn't regret what they'd just done. For Max, it was amazing. He'd not had sex in that position very often, it was too close, too emotional. But he hadn't thought twice about it with Trent. Anyone would have thought Trent had been fucking guys as soon as he hit puberty. He just hoped Trent was able to reconcile his feelings and thoughts.

He supposed he'd have to wait and find out when he came back out.

TRENT

He threw the condom into the bin and washed his hands, then stood looking at his reflection for a moment. He didn't know what he was looking for. Maybe he thought he'd be freaking out about now but checking his feelings, he felt great. The sex he'd just had with Max had been the most mind numbingly amazing sex in his whole life; he hadn't realised what he'd been missing.

Trent shook his head. He really had thought he'd be freaking the fuck out now. He was just eager to get back to Max. So he did.

Opening the door, he looked across seeing Max in almost the same position he'd left him in. He chuckled at the sight. "Worn out?" he asked.

"Fuck you," Max replied without heat.

"You already did, and I can't do it again right now."

"Funny."

"I try." He walked over to the bed with a damp cloth and climbed back on, situating himself on his side, right next to Max, resting his head on his hand. His other hand, the one with the cloth, he placed on Max's stomach, making him twitch. "You okay?"

Max laughed and took over wiping off the mess he'd made of himself. "I should be asking you that question."

"I'm fine. Surprisingly." He decided to be honest. "I went in the bathroom expecting to freak out and didn't want you to see it."

"And did you?" Max turned his head to look Trent in the eye.

"Nope." He popped the 'p', smiling as Max's eyebrows rose.

"Really?"

"Really. I'm fine with it."

Max stared at him for a moment, then a huge smile lit his face, and he jumped onto Trent, knocking him to the bed and throwing the cloth onto the table. Wrapping him in his arms, Trent nestled his head in Max's neck and held him tight.

"I'm so glad." The words were muffled coming from Max's mouth; his face was buried in Trent's neck too. "I was so worried I'd pushed you too far."

"Nah, it'll never happen."

Max pulled back slightly. "You might not think that when you realise what kind of things I like." He bit his lip, which Trent realised he did when he was unsure of something.

"Why don't you explain it to me. I'll try to ask questions rather than freak out...at least until I get the whole story." He smiled to soften the words.

Max chuckled, then sobered. "I'm scared you'll run."

"I'm scared I won't be enough for you." Trent confided this in a whisper. "There, we're even."

He wrapped his arms around Max again and turned them, so they were both on their sides.

Blowing out a breath, Max kept stroking a hand through Trent's hair, while Trent kept his hand on Max's waist, the featherlight touch of his fingers up and down, raising goosebumps.

"I'm a switch." He paused. "Okay, if I'm going to talk about this, I need to explain a lot. Now I'm going to assume you have no knowledge of this stuff unless you tell me otherwise. Please don't think I'm patronising you, I'm not. I just want you to know what makes me tick."

"It's okay, Max. Explain it however you need to. I know a little about BDSM but not a huge amount. So assume I know nothing." He leaned forward and kissed him.

"All right. God, I don't really know where to start." He rubbed a hand over his face.

"Start at the beginning. What got you into it?"

"In all honesty, I kind of fell into it. I knew I was gay from when I was young, and even though I told my parents at that early age. They waved it away and ignored it. When I hit puberty, there was no denying it, even for my parents. They told me in no uncertain terms that if I wanted to 'frolic' with men, I had to do so out of the area. As soon as I had my driving licence, I was out every weekend. Not for hook-ups, not all the time, but for fun. It was a break from the rigidness of home."

"Sounds like they kept trying to put you in a box."

Max nodded. "Yeah. Anyway, this one time I was out, I got fed up with the bar I was in, so I went walking around to see what else was there, and I ended up going into a club. At first, I had no idea what it was, but then a demonstration started. I still remember it vividly now. A guy was laying on his back on a wooden box, arms and legs cuffed to the sides so he couldn't move. Another guy wore nothing but trousers, which were undone with his cock hanging out. I couldn't hear everything but every time the guy in the trousers spoke, I trembled. I could feel myself wanting to obey him. As the scene progressed, I walked closer. When I was there, I could see everything in clear detail and hear every word. Looking at the guy chained to the box, I could see myself ordering him around. To put it mildly, I was confused. I sat down right there and watched to the very end. When they walked off the stage after, I still sat there. Eventually someone came over and asked if I was okay." He laughed. "When we talked about this meeting later, he said I looked at him as if I'd mentally left my body."

Trent smiled. He could understand the imagery.

Max continued. "The guy, Kieren, talked to me and listened to me for the rest of the night. It was only as the club closed around us that I realised we'd been talking for about four hours. I apologised and got up to leave. Kieren told me to come back the next night and he'd help train me. By the time I left that night, I'd figured out I was a switch, and I could both dominate and be submissive, depending on my mood. Kieren taught me how to do both."

Trent felt jealousy swirl through him. What the hell? This guy was from years ago. "So where is Kieren now?"

Max smiled. "He's still back there. Or at least he

was the last time I spoke to him. We keep in touch on the phone, messages mainly. When I moved up here, I didn't get to see him for a while."

"It's good you had someone." He forced his voice to sound even, though he wanted to get rid of this guy who had so much of Max's past.

"Anyway, that's when it started. And I've just carried on. I researched places here and found some nice ones —and some not so nice ones—but it got old quickly. Then I found an app—"

"The one from the other night? That you needed help with?"

Max nodded. "Yeah." He bit his lip. "I can't give you a lot of information because the guidelines are really rigid to protect all the members. But basically, this app shows different places for hook-ups, scenes, events and stuff like that. Once I'd applied and been accepted, I never looked back. It was perfect for what I needed."

"And what did you need?"

"To be who I wanted to be or to forget who I was, depending on my needs."

"So, it taught you to be free."

Max looked at him, eyes wide. "Yeah. You get it?"

"I get why you do it. But what do you do exactly?" Trent was a little concerned that he would not be able to give Max what he needed. He'd watched the occasional porn video about BDSM, but he didn't see the allure. But maybe he was looking at the wrong thing.

"Well, that's a loaded question." Max laughed. "Um, so it's all consensual, so things are agreed beforehand for everyone before they get together. If I'm the dominant, I might spank a submissive, tie them up, edge them, sometimes there's sex involved, sometimes not. There are lots of other things as well, but they are the basics. Aftercare is a very important part of being a dominant."

"What's aftercare?"

"It's when the dominant takes care of the submissive until they have returned to their body, for want of a better word. You see, when a submissive is really into a scene, endorphins will flood their body making them feel high, a bit like being on drugs. This high—called subspace—can last a while, depending how far into it they get. It's the dominant's job to make sure no harm comes to the submissive while they are in that state. It could mean cuddling them, making sure they drink and eat something, getting them washed and dressed. Again, it's something that would be discussed before the scene actually starts."

"That's pretty good. I hadn't thought about what happened afterwards."

"It's a really important part of a scene and one that a submissive might find hard to begin with, having to rely on others. For me as a submissive, I like the feeling that I don't have to think, that my Dom is taking care of me the way he believes I need to be taken care of. Sometimes, I need spanking, sometimes fucking. It varies, like I said, with the mood I'm in. And I have specific people now, that I go to if I need to do that. It's hard to find people to trust so when you do, you keep hold of them."

Trent thought back to the men he'd seen Max with before, nothing standing out as someone he thought Max would have that type of relationship with. At least until he remembered last week. "Frederick." A statement, not a question.

Max scrunched up his nose and mouth, then nodded. "Yeah, he's one of my Dom's."

"Why was he at the party then? I thought he was your boyfriend."

He saw Max blush and bite his lip again. He looked down and wouldn't meet Trent's eye. "I brought him to make you jealous," he whispered so quietly Trent had to strain to hear him.

He laughed out loud, rolling onto his back. "Bloody hell, Max."

"What! I liked you, and I didn't know what else to do. I was also trying to distract myself. I knew you were straight, so I thought you were off limits." Max moved over and rested his chin on Trent's chest.

"Well, it worked. I was out of my mind and had no idea why. I couldn't figure out what was wrong with me and why I was bothered who you were with." He shook his head. "And you obviously had no boundaries because you kissed me still believing I was straight!"

It was Max's turn to flop on his back. "I know! I was stupid!"

Trent rolled over onto him, bracketing his head with his arms. "No, you weren't. Obviously. Since we're here, aren't we?" Trent lowered his lips to meet with Max's and slowly teased him.

After a few minutes, Trent pulled away. "I need some sleep. Get under the covers."

Max jumped into action, and Trent spooned behind him, content for the first time in a long time.

CHAPTER TWELVE

MAX

Max woke slowly, feeling overly warm. Reaching to push the covers off, he dislodged an arm that had been resting on him but over the covers. His eyes widened as he remembered what happened, and he turned his head slowly to look behind him. Sure enough, there Trent was, peaceful in his sleep. His mouth was slightly open without a hint of drool anywhere, the lines in his face had smoothed out, making him look younger. He itched to touch him but didn't want to wake him after their late night.

"You stare at me much more, I'll think you have a crush on me," he said, his voice like gravel and eyes still closed.

Max smiled and turned around to face Trent, he pressed their lips together, making small pecks, nothing too heavy. He was so excited that this had happened; he couldn't believe it. And he bounced as if he'd had too much sugar.

"What are we doing today?" he asked.

Trent made a growling noise. "Nothing. Absolutely fucking nothing. I am not setting foot outside this apartment until tomorrow morning," he grumbled, rolling onto his back and taking Max with him.

"Okay." He was content to stay here as well. He had to remember to call Mavis and tell her they wouldn't be making it to dinner though.

They laid in companionable silence for a few minutes, and Max thought Trent had drifted back off until he spoke again.

"What's got you so jittery this morning?"

"I'm just happy."

"You'll bounce away if you're not careful."

"Sorry."

"'S'okay. Right, I'm awake." Max would beg to differ. Trent's eyes rolled as if he struggled to stay awake, so Max decided to go a fetch some coffee—decent coffee—and bring it back.

"Go back to sleep. I'll fetch coffee and be back soon." He kissed Trent and left the bed.

"Don't be long."

Max smiled as he got dressed, he felt a little stiff from the remaining bruises, but last night, he'd hardly felt them at all.

He grabbed Trent's keys off the side and headed out the door. Walking quickly blew away a lot of the cobwebs, and he was soon on his way back again loaded with coffees and food; it should wake Trent up a little.

Entering the apartment with Trent's keys was a new experience but not an unwelcome one. It was a little overwhelming how different things had become in the past week. Max was happy about the turn of events, but he was also a little concerned that Trent was going to change his mind after he'd experienced this for a short time. He knew Trent wouldn't do it on purpose, but Max was afraid to put everything in.

Oh, who was he kidding, he was all in, he thought with a grin.

He placed the food and drinks on the table, taking off his jacket and draping it over the back of a chair. He walked through to the bedroom, seeing Trent laid with his back to him, covered partially with the cover. The expanse of his back was on show, and Max was mesmerised by the definition there. He knew Trent worked out, maybe not as much this week because he'd been keeping Max entertained, but he usually went every other day if Max remembered correctly.

He stood beside the bed and ran his hand up Trent's back to his shoulder. A hand grabbed his and pulled him over Trent's body; Max bounced onto the bed beside him with a laugh. Trent rolled him over and spooned him from behind, wrapping his arms around him.

"Hello," Max said laughing, appreciating Trent's warmth after being outside in the cold.

"Hmm. Too many clothes," Trent growled out,

pulling at Max's clothes until he was laid in his briefs. Trent tried to take them off too, but Max protested saying he wanted coffee. "Coffee?" Trent asked, peeking through his eyelashes.

Max laughed again. He hadn't laughed like this—in a relationship—in so long. "Yes, coffee is in the kitchen. Come on, get out of bed, lazy ass."

"I'll give you lazy ass!" Trent proceeded to roll on top of Max and tickle and kiss and rub against him, getting them both worked up.

Max pulled his head away. "Coffee!!" he shouted. He tried to distract Trent; he wanted to talk to him before they get caught up in the motions again.

Trent rested his head in the crook of Max's neck and stayed there for a minute before lifting his head and kissing Max gently. Then he pushed himself up and stood, cock standing upright. And looking delicious.

"Seen enough?" Trent said with a smirk.

"Never," Max answered honestly.

Trent leaned down to peck a kiss on his lips and walked to the bathroom. Max let out a breath once Trent had disappeared. He really did need to speak to him and make sure he was okay with everything that had happened last night. He appeared to be fine, but Max didn't want to make the mistake of not checking.

He stood and walked to the kitchen with just his briefs on, rearranging his cock a bit now it wasn't so hard. He got some plates and spread out the food he'd brought—croissants, muffins, pancakes and some fruit bowls. Then he turned the radio on to the local station while he waited.

Trent walked into the room in boxers, eyes widening at the sight of the food. "Did you buy the whole damn shop?" he laughed.

"Nah, I left a few crumbs for the other customers."

Trent chuckled as he pointed between the two cups. Max passed Trent's to him, watching his throat as he swallowed, which in turn made him swallow hard. He was sexy as fuck. Trent sat down and picked up a croissant, stuffing some into his mouth.

"Thank you for this," he said when his mouth was empty again. "You didn't have to buy breakfast."

"I know I didn't, but I wanted to." Max didn't know how to ask what he wanted to ask so decided just to blurt it out. "Are you—"

"What's wrong?" Trent asked at the same time. They laughed.

"Nothing's wrong. I just wanted to ask if you were okay with everything that happened last night? I know from your actions this morning that you seem all right with it, but I wanted to check and make sure." Max couldn't look at Trent, not wanting to see anger or laughter in his face at his insecurity.

Trent's hand covered his own, and he squeezed. "Look at me."

Max dared a look up and visibly relaxed at the serious look on Trent's face. He should have known Trent wouldn't laugh or be angry at him. Insecurity is a hard emotion to ignore sometimes.

"I loved every minute of it. Yeah, okay, it is a bit overwhelming because I hadn't expected *us* to happen. But once I'd come to terms with that fact that I like you...a lot...everything else is easy." He chuckled. "Well, a little easier, I should say, not easy. I just came out to all our friends. For me, that says I'm happy. That I know what I want." He turned serious. "I'm not saying I won't have issues; I'm still learning new things about myself. But from where I stand at the moment, I'm not going anywhere."

Max relaxed a little. He was unsure what issues Trent was talking about, but he was happy with everything else he said. He'd just have to trust that Trent would talk to him if there were any problems.

After that, they took the fruit bowls to the sofa and put on a film to watch. Before they'd even got halfway through, they were laid on the sofa kissing and rubbing against each other again.

Trent pulled away quickly and turned towards the door. Max hadn't even heard it open.

"What the fuck are you doing here?" Trent asked in anger.

"I should ask you the same thing! What the hell do you think you're doing, Trent? What? Suddenly you're into men now? Are you that starved of attention that you have to go this low? I'm fed up with you cheating on me in this little love nest of yours. Especially with that degenerate! I am so glad Jocelyn and Harper didn't see you like this. God, what will people think!"

Max was confused. There, in Trent's apartment, was

the woman for whom he'd redesigned nearly her whole house last year. The one who'd tried it on with him every day, and then got pissed off when he'd refused her.

And apparently, she was Trent's ex-wife. At least that was what Max assumed.

He sat up, pulling the throw over his almost nakedness. Trent wasn't bothered, although is erection had waned now so he wasn't showing as much as he could have.

"What the fuck are you talking about? We divorced five years ago! You have no claims over me now, so shut the hell up!" Trent stalked to her and stood towering above her.

"What are my parents going to say? If they hear about this, Trent, it will devastate them. How can you sink so low as to fool around with people like him?" She sneered over at Max. He didn't see any recognition in her eyes, so maybe she didn't know who he was.

"Fuck you, Trish! Get out!" Trent pointed to the front door.

"Trent, honey, don't be silly. We can get over this, just come home. I've been allowing this little…experiment…of yours, but enough now. It's time for you to come home where you belong. Then we can forget all about this."

She moved forward as if to touch Trent, and Max held his breath waiting to see if he'd let her. He had no idea what was going on. She seemed far too confident that Trent would come home to her and it shook Max's reality. Maybe Trent *was* only experimenting and didn't really care about him. Max wanted to look away from the train wreck in front of him, but he couldn't seem to do it. He had to know.

Trent slapped her hands away and stepped back, making Max's breath leave in a rush. "GET OUT!" Trent grabbed her arm and pulled her to the door, throwing it open and pushing her through it. "Leave me the fuck alone, Trish!" Then he slammed the door and stood braced against it, breathing as if he had run a marathon.

Max kept quiet; he didn't know what to say anyway. He was worried about Trent's reaction to her presence. One thought went through his mind though, he now understood why Trent had spoken about art he'd previously owned that Max would've said was expensive. It made sense with *this* woman being his ex-wife.

Trent turned and walked closer, standing with his hands on his hips and blew out a breath. "I have no idea what her problem is." He looked over at Max. "I'm sorry, Max. I'm so sorry you had to see that. I'd like to say that was a unique experience, but lately that seems to be the sum of our interactions."

Max stood and wrapped his arms around Trent. "It's okay." Max felt him shaking and held him tightly, the worry easing some with Trent's reaction. He hadn't expected this. He hesitated, realising he had to admit he knew her. "Thing is, I know her."

Trent stared at him. "What? How?"

"I did a job for her last year—redecorated the house. I'm assuming your old house," he added quietly.

Understanding dawned in Trent's eyes. "I wondered who she'd managed to get to do it. Small world." Trent gave a laugh lacking humour. "Jesus, this is fucked up. I'm going to get dressed."

Max watched as Trent walked away and disappeared into the bedroom. He sat back on the sofa and rested his head against the back of it, looking at the ceiling. This was not how he envisioned the afternoon panning out. Now, he just had to find out what the hell was going on with Trent and Trish. Was Trent really experimenting? He wasn't sure he wanted to find out the answer.

TRENT

Unfortunately, Trent had to go back to work the following day. After dropping Max off at his own place yesterday, he'd lost himself in catching up with the work he had pushed aside when Max had come to stay. He'd managed to get completely up to date, which was a first.

He walked into the staff room at seven-thirty, ready for the meeting that happened every week; usually it was after school, but on the first day back, they always did it before to catch any issues before school started.

Resting his bag on a chair, he headed for the kettle. The coffee at school wasn't much better than what he had at home, but it was better than nothing, especially as he'd hardly slept last night. His dreams were interspersed with Max, Trish and being chained up. He reckoned he barely had four hours all told.

Taking a sip, he moved his bag and sat down. From his glance around he could see there were still around few people missing, as usual.

"Hey, Trent. How you been?" Claudia Freeman sat down next to him, cradling her mug. Claudia was the year one teacher and a complete gossip. Trent inwardly groaned.

"Hey, good thanks. How was your break?" he asked politely. If she was talking to him, she either had something to tell him or something to ask him.

"It was amazing. Colin and I went to Spain for five days. It was beautiful."

"Sounds good." He took another sip of his drink, hoping she'd get to the point of her chat.

"It was. We went out this weekend as well." He saw that she was staring intently at him. "There was a party happening in a bar we'd never been to before, but we loved it. They had this newly opened Garden Bar; it was absolutely beautiful."

Trent's heart sank. He had a feeling he knew exactly where this conversation was going. *Fuck.* He decided to jump to the point. "Oh, do you mean Crush? Yeah, that bar is great. It's my local."

"Oh, is it? I thought I saw you there, but then realised I must be mistaken."

Here it comes.

"I was sure I was wrong because the person was with a *man!*" she whispered the last word as if it was scandalous.

He should've expected this. He ran through his options. Tell her the truth, tell her she was mistaken about who he was with or pretend it was someone else. The last one wouldn't fly because she knew it was him, that's why she approached him. He could tell her she was mistaken but when he thought back to that night, he realised they had been publicly affectionate, so that wouldn't work either. He had only one option, but he didn't know if he was ready to come clean. If he told Claudia now, it would be around the school by lunchtime.

Did he want everyone to know he was gay, or would he prefer to keep it quiet? He thought back to the time he had spent with Max this past week. Once he'd figured out his attraction, he'd been fine with it. His friends were still his friends. The only people he hadn't told were his children, but that would be a phone call he'd be making this afternoon.

He realised he couldn't do anything but admit it, and he was surprisingly okay with it.

He smiled into his coffee. "Yeah, that was me."

Claudia's eyes widened comically, and Trent almost burst out laughing. "Oh, oh. I didn't realise you swung that way. I mean, um, that's great. How long have you been together?"

"Not long, it's a fairly new thing." He wasn't going to give her too much information.

"Oh, that's...great," she repeated.

He smiled as he took another sip. He had no doubt that he would have several visits throughout the day from colleagues wanting to see the "new" Trent.

Eight hours later, Trent was exhausted. He'd pretty much had visits from every member of staff that had been working—as he'd expected. Each one had come with a stupidly see-through excuse for why they needed to speak to him, and once they had, it had turned to questions about his break. It had gotten so bad that he'd gone out to his car at lunchtime to make sure he had peace and quiet for a while. He knew it would die down soon, but at the moment, he was newsworthy.

Getting into his car, he blew out a breath and looked at his phone. He saw he had three messages, all from Max. The first was just a goofy smile emoji, the second asked how his first day of school went, and the third made his heart beat faster, *I miss you x.*

God, I miss you too. He didn't know what to reply; he still wasn't sure if it was fair to make Max put up with the issues he had with Trish. He couldn't believe she had walked in on them almost...he stopped.

"What the fuck!" he said out loud. "How the hell did she get in?" He thought back through what happened yesterday. He and Max had been cosying up on the sofa, and the next thing Trish was in the apartment.

He lifted his phone again, selecting a number, hoping she would answer like last time.

"Hey, Dad." Jocelyn said.

"Hi, sweetheart. How are you?" Trent closed his eyes at the sound of her voice. He didn't know what her timetable was and could only assume when he'd called at previous times, she'd been in class.

"Good. I'm really enjoying the classes."

"Brilliant. I knew you'd do well. You know I'm here if you need anything. Okay?"

"Yeah, I know." She paused. "Sorry I've not been in contact much."

"It's okay. I understand uni comes first now. You're really busy." He let her off the hook. He didn't know why she'd pulled back from him, but he wasn't going to bring it up. He was just glad she answered the phone.

"No, Dad, family comes first. Or, at least, it should."

"It's okay. Don't worry." He changed the subject before he started to cry. He missed both his kids; he'd not seen them for about three months now. "I wanted to ask you something. Do you still have the key to my apartment that I gave you?"

"Yeah, of course. Why?"

"Where do you keep it?" He ignored her question for the moment.

"It's on my keyring here."

"Can you double check you still have it please, sweetie?"

"Okay." He heard her rustling around, then a jangle of keys. "Yeah, it's here. What's going on, Dad?"

He blew out a breath. He hadn't thought it would be Jocelyn's keys, although that doesn't rule out Trish having made a copy of it.

"Dad?"

"Sorry. Your mother let herself into my apartment yesterday, and I'm trying to figure out how she did it."

"Why did she do that?" Jocelyn sounded angry. "That's not her place!"

"I don't know why. That's what I'm going to figure out."

"I have no idea why she'd do that. I know she complains about you whenever I go over there, so I've stopped going as often."

"I'm sorry you have to deal with that. I don't know what's going on with her lately."

"She has a lot of…men over, so Harper tells me. And she keeps getting more beauty treatments. I don't know why she can't just leave it alone."

"I know, Jocelyn. But you must remember she has a lot of expectations on her shoulders from your grandparents. She was never able to shake their teachings no matter what I tried to tell her." He wasn't going to take a leaf out of Trish's books and start badmouthing her to his kids. All that would do is put them in the middle.

"Oh, I just remembered she left me a voicemail last night. She was ranting about you cheating on her with her old decorator or something. I wasn't really paying attention to it to be honest."

Trent decided he needed to be honest because he knew Trish wouldn't keep quiet. "I do have something else to tell you."

"What's up?"

Trent was blown away by how much they were talking today. Usually, Jocelyn said the basics, and then had to run. "Do you have time to chat with your old man for a bit longer?"

"Yeah, I have a free period now, so I have about half an hour before I need to head off."

"Okay." He blew out a breath. "I realised over the past week or so that I...have feelings for a friend of mine."

"All right. Who is she?"

"She is a he." He held his breath.

"Okay. Oh, I see." She didn't say anything for a minute.

"Is that okay?"

She burst out laughing. Trent was sitting in his car, still in the school parking lot, and his daughter was laughing at him. He closed his eyes, thinking it sounded like music. It had been too long since they had had this.

"And why are you laughing at me, young girl?" he mock growled.

"Sorry. Sorry. It just crossed my mind that Mum made you gay!" She burst out laughing again, and Trent joined her.

"Not quite," he said when he got his breath back, wiping the tears from his eyes. "I didn't even realise I was until I spent some time with Max last week."

"Do you mean Sean's Max?" she asked.

"Yeah. How did you know?"

"I've met him at Asher's before when I've been babysitting. He seems nice."

"Yeah. I forgot you'd met him already." He went on to tell her a little bit more about him, leaving out the gory details, of course.

"He sounds amazing, Dad. I'd love to meet him properly."

"Really?"

"Yeah, really." He heard her blow out a breath. "I've missed this."

"Me, too, sweetheart." He sniffed. "Would you like to come around for dinner one evening this week?"

"Sure. Hold on…" He heard her rustling again. "I can do tomorrow or Thursday this week if that's any good?"

"It is for me, but let me check with Max, and I'll get back to you."

"Great."

"Thanks, Jocelyn."

"You're welcome."

"One more thing, and I'll let you go."

She chuckled. "Okay."

"Can you send me your timetable, so I know when's the best time to ring you?"

"Sure."

"Thanks. Love you, sweetheart."

"Love you, too, Dad. Bye."

"Bye."

Trent sat for a while longer, enjoying the knowledge that bridges seemed to have been built with Jocelyn. Maybe one day, they'll get to the conversation about why she was so distant these past few years.

He needed to speak to Harper but decided to call Max first and see if he was free for dinner with Jocelyn.

"Hey, you," came Max's voice when he answered.

"Hey. Sorry, I hadn't replied to your messages, you would not believe the day I've had."

"That's okay. Are you all right?" Max sounded concerned. "Do you want me to bring some dinner over tonight?"

Trent didn't want Max paying for food all the time, but tonight he relented. "That would be amazing. I have a few things to talk to you about."

Max laughed. "That sounds ominous, not sure if I want to come over now."

It was Trent's turn to laugh. "No, everything's fine, I promise."

"Okay, I'll take your word for it. Chinese sound good?"

"Fantastic, thanks."

"Okay, I'll be over in an hour or so."

"See you then."

Trent rung off and turned his engine on. He'd ring Harper when he got home.

After a shower, Trent sat on the sofa and called Harper. He was not looking forward to this conversation. Harper was still living at home with Trish, and so far, every time he'd spoken to Harper, she was angry and quoting what he believed was Trish's thoughts, not her own.

"Dad," she answered.

He was surprised. He thought she'd make it go to voicemail. "Hey, sweetheart. How are you doing?"

"I'm fine. What do you want?"

Trent sighed. "I need to ask if you still had the key I gave you to my apartment?"

"Of course I do. Why?"

"Are you sure you have it, and you haven't lost it?"

"It's in my drawer in my room. Why, Dad?"

Trent closed his eyes, thinking he understood where Trish got access to his apartment. He wondered how many times she had let herself in, in the past.

"I just wanted to make sure you still had it and knew you could use it whenever you needed to. That's all." He wasn't going to explain the truth, not when she lived with Trish.

"Yeah, I know. Is that all?"

"No, I wondered if you wanted to come over for dinner this week?" He didn't hold out much hope.

"Sorry, I'm busy."

He shook his head. "I'd really like it if you could come over. There's someone I'd like you to meet."

She was silent. "Like who?"

"A close friend."

"You mean a new girlfriend."

"Not quite."

"Just spit it out, Dad."

"Fine, a new boyfriend." He waited for her to blow up at him, but it never came. "Harper, you still there?"

He heard what sounded like a sniffle. "Yeah," came the quiet reply.

"Are you okay, sweetheart?"

"Yeah."

He thought maybe she was crying, but it was unlike her. "Are you sure?"

"Yeah, I'm sure. When do you want me to come over for dinner?"

Trent sucked in a breath, shocked at the about turn in her. What made her change her mind? "I'm not sure which day yet. It will either be tomorrow or Thursday. Can I message you later?"

"Sure. I've got to go."

"Okay, sweetheart. I'll speak to you later."

"Bye, Dad."

He couldn't believe she'd agreed to come, at least for the moment. He told himself not to get his hopes up until she was actually at his door.

A knock sounded. Max was a sight for sore eyes, and Trent enfolded him in his arms, holding him tightly. He never expected to get so close so quickly.

"I could get used to coming back to that every day," Max said.

"Sorry, been a long day."

"I'm not complaining." Max pulled back and cupped Trent's face. He closed the distance and kissed him chastely. Then pulled back and lifted the bag. "I come bearing gifts."

The smell of the food hit Trent, his stomach growling in response. Max laughed. "Someone's hungry."

They dished up the dinner and took it to the sofa to eat, tuning the TV into some gardening programme for background noise.

"So, what did you want to talk about?" Max asked.

Trent turned sideways so he could look at Max without twisting. "I came out at school today."

Max coughed; something must have gone down the wrong hole. Trent reached for Max's drink and passed it over.

Once he'd stopped choking, he croaked out, "What!?"

"You heard me. Someone at school had seen us out on Saturday, so I decided to own it. I came out to that person knowing that it would go around the school in no time."

"Why?"

"Three reasons. Firstly, there was no denying it was me on Saturday. Secondly, knowing this person, it would spread to school soon anyway, and thirdly, I don't want to hide." He whispered the last part, looking down at his plate.

"Wow."

"That's not all either."

"There's more?" Max stared at him, shock written all over his face.

"I came out to Jocelyn and Harper too."

"Jesus, Trent, you don't do things by halves, do you?" Max sat back against the arm of the sofa, having copied Trent's position.

He laughed. "No reason to. Plus, Jocelyn asked to meet you. Are you free tomorrow or Thursday for dinner?"

Max stared at him, then smiled. "Either is fine."

"Tomorrow then."

Max blew out a breath. "Unbelievable."

"What is?"

"How well you're taking it."

"Yeah, I've no idea. Maybe I'm just getting too old to mess around now."

"You're not old!"

"I'm twelve years older than you, Max. I'm nearly forty."

"I know, and I don't care." Max put his plate down, reached over to take Trent's plate and climbed on his lap. "You're mine," he whispered when his face was close.

He nodded. "And you're mine." A statement, not a question. He grabbed the back of Max's neck and pulled him down for a kiss. Pulling away, he kept Max where he was but reached for his phone. "Hold on a second." He sent a message to Jocelyn and Harper telling them to be there tomorrow at six. Then he focused back on Max.

Later that evening, they warmed the food up again.

CHAPTER THIRTEEN

MAX

When Max arrived at Trent's apartment at five-forty-five the next evening, before he even got in the door, he could smell the dinner Trent had obviously been cooking.

"Wow, that's smells delicious," Max commented as Trent opened the door for him.

"Nah, nothing special. Cottage pie is all. I just know it used to be my kid's favourites, so thought I'd soften them up a bit." Trent laughed.

"I don't know if that's a good thing or a bad thing."

"What?" Trent returned to the cooker, put oven gloves on and placed the dish into the oven. Max watched his ass as he bent, getting distracted from Trent's question. "Max?"

"Huh?" He refocused on Trent, seeing he was smirking at him.

"See something you like?"

"Shut up." He threw a towel at him, laughing.

"So, what's either a good thing or a bad thing?" Trent came over and wrapped his arms around Max's waist.

"That the kids might need softening up." Max was a little apprehensive about meeting the two girls, but he tried not to show it.

"They'll be fine. Harper might struggle a little, but Jocelyn will be all right and will help bring Harper into the fold. We've nothing to worry about."

"Okay." He kissed Trent, unable to resist his mouth being so close. It got a little out of hand until a throat clearing made them jump. Max swung around, wiping his mouth.

There in the doorway stood Trent's two kids, staring at them with differing expressions.

"Hey, come on in." Trent brushed past him, walking over to them and enveloping one in a hug. The other stepped back and closed the front door. Trent let go of the first one and walked to the second. She didn't go in for a hug but allowed Trent to kiss her cheek. "Come meet Max."

Max took a breath and walked further out of the kitchen area. "Hi, nice to meet you both."

Trent gestured to each in turn. "This is Jocelyn, and this is Harper. Girls, this is Max."

"Hey, Max," said Jocelyn, smiling.

"Hey," said Harper, nodding her head slowly.

"Can I get you some drinks?" Trent asked the girls.

"I've got wine...yes, Harper, you can have a little if you'd like to...water, juice, coke and milk."

"And I brought some beer," added Max, walking over to the bag he'd brought with him.

"A beer would be good," Harper asked hesitantly, looking at her dad.

Trent nodded. "Just one though, please."

"Thanks." Harper took the offered bottle from Max.

"Jocelyn?"

"Coke, please."

Harper snorted. "Might've known."

Jocelyn threw a dark look at her. "I'll have wine later when I start eating, Harper, otherwise I'll get sick. All right?"

"You drink whatever you want, Jocelyn. Ignore Harper."

"As always," Harper responded so quietly Max might've he'd misheard.

Trent fetched Jocelyn's drink, bringing Max some wine at the same time.

"Thanks."

"So, dinner is going to be..." Trent looked at the clock, "...about another fifteen minutes. Do you want to sit on the sofa or at the table?"

"Let's sit at the table, then we're all together," Jocelyn suggested, walking that way. Everyone followed, Harper, naturally, choosing to sit next to her sister. It had already been set for dinner so there was less to do later. It was amazing to see the similarities between the three of them when they were in close proximity. Both girls had a Mediterranean look to them, but it was Trent's features Max could see on their faces. All had long, straight noses, deep set eyes and perfect cheek-bones. Their mouths were slightly different: Trent had a larger bottom lip, Jocelyn had more of a pout and Harper seemed to have a natural smile, regardless of her demeanour. Their teeth, though, were identical.

"Okay, let's get all the awkwardness out of our system, so we can get to enjoying the evening. Jocelyn, Harper, shoot. What do you want to ask?"

Jocelyn smiled. "When did you start seeing each other?"

Trent relaxed back in his chair. "Officially, last Thursday. Unofficially," he looked over at Max, smiling, "I think we were tiptoeing around each other for a couple of weeks at least."

"Longer for me," Max admitted. Trent's eyebrows rose, and Max blushed, wishing he'd kept quiet. "About three or four months. Maybe longer."

"Seriously? And how did I not know this?" Trent asked, mirth in his eyes.

"I can keep a secret when I need to."

"Uh-huh."

"Does everyone know?" Harper asked, looking down at the table.

"If you mean your mother, then yes, she does. And my school and Logan and Asher. I'm not hiding from anyone."

"How can you go from being straight to being gay?" Harper asked sharply.

"It's not a case of being straight or gay. At least not to me. I've not been attracted to any other guys that I'm aware of, except for Max. I'm leaving a label out of this, Harper. I was attracted to your mother when I was younger, and now, I'm attracted to Max. I'm not trying to pin a label on what I am. You call me whatever you want if you feel the need to explain my preferences. I'm just going with I like Max." Trent took his hand and squeezed.

They were quiet for a moment until Trent changed the subject slightly and told them about his experience at work the previous day. Max had not heard all of it and soon they were laughing about the outrageous excuses his colleagues had come up with, just to chat to him about his new-found boyfriend. The timer had gone off in the middle of his explanation, so Max had waved him down and went to get the food out of the oven. He brought the dish to the table and rested it on the hotplate, fetching utensils for everyone to help themselves.

"Thanks, Max," Trent said.

"No problem," Max leaned down and kissed him, not thinking about his daughters' reactions until afterwards. He looked over at them, seeing Jocelyn with a smile and Harper with a look of confusion.

Once Trent had finished his story, Jocelyn asked Max about his job.

"He's an interior designer," Harper answered for him. Max looked over at her in shock. "You redecorated our house last year. I remember you."

Max nodded, surprised she had put two and two together. "Yeah, I did. I didn't realise the connection until the other day," he admitted.

"Have you done many jobs?" Jocelyn continued her questioning.

"Yes. I've been designing for about two years roughly now. I have a good client base and recommendations, so have plenty of work coming in. At present, I'm booked up for the next three months."

"Really?" Trent asked.

Max nodded. "I've obviously had to take a few weeks off, with what happened last week but, yeah."

"What happened last week?" Harper asked.

Max looked at Trent, wanting his input as to how to handle that question.

"Max got beaten up outside a club. He was in the hospital for a day or so, then came to stay with me. It was how we got to know each other," Trent explained.

"Are you okay now?" Jocelyn asked, looking at him in concern.

"Yeah, I'm okay, just a little bruised still," he said, smiling. Max will give them their dues for not asking for more details.

"How old are you?" Harper asked, suddenly.

Max choked down the food he'd just put in his mouth. "I'm twenty-eight."

Jocelyn and Harper both laughed.

"You cradle robber, Dad!" Jocelyn laughed.

Trent lifted his napkin and threw it across the table at her. "Shut up, you."

"He's closer to my age than he is yours!" she continued, laughing her head off.

Max knew Trent didn't mind the joking. They'd had
that discussion last night about ages, and neither of
them cared.

Trent changed the subject. "Harper, how's college
going?"

She looked down at her plate, and Max saw her jaw
tighten. "Fine, thanks."

"Are you enjoying it?" Trent continued.

"Yeah. I love learning the languages, so yes, I am."

"That's great. You're really good at them too. What
about you, Jocelyn. How's uni?" Max let Trent lead the
conversation. He could tell, even if Trent hadn't previously explained the issues with their relationship, that
he was trying to get information out of them while they
were willing to give it.

"It's great. I'm getting to work with some nice
companies on my placements and although the course-
work is hard, I'm enjoying it."

"That's great news! Have you decided what you're
going to do at uni, Harper? I know you still have
another year left, but do you know?"

"It doesn't really matter, does it? I'm not going."

"What do you mean, you're not going? Why not?"
Trent put down his cutlery and leaned his elbows on the
table.

Max looked at Harper, seeing her face flush in what
looked like anger. *Uh-oh, this is not good.*

"It doesn't matter. I need to use the bathroom."

Harper walked away, and he heard her shut, but not slam, the bathroom door.

TRENT

"What is she going on about? Do you know?" Trent looked at Jocelyn.

"This is the first I've heard about it. She's wanted to be a translator for as long as I can remember. I have no idea why she wouldn't go."

"Okay. Keep eating, I'll be back." Trent stood from the table and walked down the hallway towards the bathroom. He stood outside the door waiting for Harper to exit. When she did, she jumped to see him waiting for her.

"What do you want?" she asked.

"I want to know why you're not going to uni?"

"You know why I can't go, Dad," she almost snarled at him.

He held his hands out. "If I knew, I wouldn't asking, would I?"

"Because we can't afford it!"

"What do you mean we can't afford it? Of course, we can. I've been paying into your account since you were a baby," he countered.

"Well, Mum says you've not been paying. That you've been spending the money on all your floozies. So

I can't go to uni." Harper stormed past him towards the main area.

"Hey, wait just a minute, young girl. First of all, I'm not seeing any floozies, I never have. Max is the first person I've become close to since I left your mother. Secondly, Harper, I promise you, I've been paying into that account. I have not missed a single month since you were born." Trent followed her, stopping her with a gentle hand on her arm.

"Well, then something's gone wrong because Mum says there's nothing there."

"Nothing of what?" Jocelyn asked.

"Harper says your mother has told her there's no money for her to go to uni. But I don't see how that can be true because I've been paying into both your accounts since you were children. There will be more than enough to pay for you to go to uni." Trent looked at Jocelyn. "You're still getting your money, aren't you?"

Jocelyn looked at her plate. "No," she whispered.

Trent's heart began to race. "What do you mean, no?"

"The payments stopped about four months ago." Still, she didn't look up.

"Why didn't you say anything?"

"Because I thought you couldn't afford to pay anymore. I didn't want to upset you."

Trent blew out a breath and gripped his hair, trying to understand what the hell was going on.

"How have you been managing?"

"I got a job."

"Flipping heck, Jocelyn. No wonder, you're struggling with the workload. I don't understand what's going on because I've been paying three hundred pounds a month into the account to pay for both your university fees. I can show you my accounts if you don't believe me."

Max got up from the table and came to stand next to him, wrapping his arms around his waist from behind and resting his chin on his shoulder. It helped calm him.

"Right, I will get to the bottom of this tomorrow. I'll go to the bank in the morning and see what's happened. Maybe they've frozen the account or something."

"I'm sorry, I yelled at you, Dad," Harper whispered.

Trent pulled out of Max's arms and wrapped his around Harper. For once, she let him. "Don't worry about it, Button. We'll get it sorted, one way or another." He kissed her forehead.

"Does anyone fancy ice cream?" Max asked, trying to diffuse the situation a little.

"Actually, I think Harper and I should call it a night," Jocelyn said quietly.

Trent nodded. "Okay, keep in touch though, all right. Not so long between phone calls from now on."

Harper nodded, keeping her face down. Jocelyn stood from the table and came to give him a hug. "I will, Dad. I promise."

"I'll let you know what the bank says after I've been to see them."

"Do you want us to come with you?" Jocelyn asked.

Trent considered for a moment. "Actually, that might be a good idea because the accounts have your names on as well, the bank may give me more information if you're there too. What time do you have classes?"

Jocelyn answered first, "I finish at two."

"I finish at three."

"Okay, so if I leave work slightly earlier, I'll pick you up from uni, Jocelyn, and then we can head over to fetch Harper."

"All right. Night, Dad. Night, Max." Jocelyn gave Max a hug before heading to the front door.

"Bye," Harper said, looking at them both but not moving towards them. She turned and followed her sister.

Once the door was shut behind them, Trent counted in his head the amount of time it was until they were more than likely in the lift.

Then he blew. "What the fuck is going on? How can there be no money in the account? That's why I've had hardly any money because I've been solely paying for my kids to go to university. Trish was paying the bills for the house, so I said I'd pay for uni. That way the kids still had a roof over their heads. There has to be some mistake." Trent paced backwards and forwards across his living room.

"Do you have online access to the accounts?" Max asked.

Trent shook his head. "Only my own accounts, which would only show that I've been paying. Not that they've been receiving. What if I've been paying into the wrong account all this time? I never thought to check! Fuck!"

Trent felt Max's presence a second before his arms came around him and held him tight. He needed it. He felt like he was about to explode into a million pieces.

"Let me take care of you tonight," Max whispered. Trent looked down at him and nodded once, jaw tense. He allowed Max to take him by the hands and lead him to the bedroom. Once there, Max kissed him. First, it was just pecks on his lips, cheeks, nose, eyelids until Trent took over. He grabbed Max's head between his hands and fused their lips together, their tongues battling as Trent felt Max grip his shirt. He felt his lips become bruised, but he didn't care. Trent needed this release. He couldn't keep it bottled up.

He tore his lips away, grabbing the hem of Max's shirt and pulling it roughly over his head, before doing the same to his own. Then he devoured Max again while they scrambled out of their clothes. Max's nails dug into his back, and they both tried to get as close as they could to each other. Trent began to walk forwards, pushing Max further towards the bed until Max stopped him.

"Use me," Max said, looking at him.

Trent frowned. "What?"

"Use my mouth. I want you to fuck my mouth." Max eyes were half-lidded as he spoke.

Trent didn't say anything as Max climbed onto the bed and laid on his back, hanging his head over the edge of the bed. Arousal shot through his body at the sight of Max all laid out for him, and he walked closer. When he was level with the bed, Max reached up and grabbed Trent's cock with no hesitation, sliding it straight into his mouth. Trent groaned with satisfaction, feeling the wet heat surrounding him.

Max licked around his cock a few times before taking him deep. Trent pulled back, not wanting to go too far, but Max grabbed Trent's ass with both his hands and pulled him closer. He could feel his cock sinking further into Max's mouth, making Max gag. Trent tried to pull back, but Max had a good grip on him. He watched as Max took his cock all the way until his nose touched his balls. Then Max let him pull back. Max gasped for air.

"Are you all right?" Trent asked, worried.

Max just smiled and pulled Trent back to him. He did the same again, pulling him all the way in, but this time, he swallowed around his cock when it was all the way in. Trent saw stars as he pulled out.

"Fuck, Max!"

"Use me," Max gasped.

Trent looked at him for a moment, then nodded tightly. Max smiled and opened his mouth. He pushed his cock into Max's mouth—his throat really—and pulled back. Again and again he did it, allowing Max breaths in between. He watched Max's throat, seeing his cock outlined there and reached down to rest his hand gently. When he next pushed in, he felt it. And that was it, he was gone. He increased his speed, trusting Max to tell him when he needed him to stop, which he did by pushing Trent's hips away. Trent rested one hand on the back of Max's head and one hand on his throat as he kept pumping his hips. He was mesmerised by the feel and look of his cock in Max's throat.

"Fuck, that's it, Max. Take it all. Take my cock in your throat. Fuck! That's so good." Trent was almost there when Max grabbed his ass and swallowed him again, not letting him retreat. Max kept sucking until Trent's control snapped. "Fuck! I'm coming! I'm coming!" He groaned hard, gently raking his nails across Max's pecs as his climax tore through him. He almost fell on Max but moved to the side at the last moment. "Holy fucking hell, Max!"

They lay there, breathing heavily for several minutes before Trent could get the energy to move his head and look at Max. Max had moved his head, so it was on the bed, but other than that was in the same position. Trent felt a lot more relaxed after that, but he needed to help Max out. His cock looked painful from where he laid. He turned on the bed so he was the same direction as Max and set about sucking hard at Max's skin, Trent knew he would leave a mark and couldn't quite begin to feel bad about it. Everyone would know Max was his after tonight.

Trent let go of Max's hair but began sucking and biting at his lips. His hands travelled the length of his torso until he met his cock and squeezed. Hearing Max groan and feeling the bite of his nails in his shoulders, made his arousal shoot through the ceiling once more.

He didn't think he'd be able to get hard again so quickly, but his body called the shots.

He bit his way down Max's chest and abs, making sure to avoid the still bruised areas and laid in between Max's bent legs, his head level with his cock, arms wrapped underneath and over his hips.

Trent looked up at Max, seeing the blissed-out look in his eyes, and keeping eye contact, he moved his left hand to make sure his cock stayed against his stomach, then he leaned down and licked between his balls, so slowly. He felt Max's stomach contract and smiled. Then he closed his eyes and set to work licking, biting, sucking his balls until Max was a bumbling mess below him. Other than his hand holding him in place, he never once touched his cock.

He began to retrace his path back up his body, biting with a bit more force when he saw the lovely red marks left from his downward journey. Max looked divine with bite marks and scratch marks and hickeys all over him. Trent thought he should feel sorry about that, but at the moment, he didn't. When he reached Max's nipples, he tortured them—there was no other word for it. By the time he'd finished, they were red and rock hard, just like both their cocks.

Trent pulled away a little and reached across for the bedside table. Grabbing a condom and lube, he sat back on his knees, keeping Max's legs wide beneath him.

"Tell me if you need more prep as I go, all right?" Trent gritted out, brain barely working, but enough to know this would be the first time he had properly prepared Max independently.

Max nodded, biting his bottom lip, and Trent couldn't help but lean back down and bite it for him.

Sitting up again, he lubed his fingers and reached for Max's hole. He rubbed it around the entrance pressing gently against him for a few seconds before letting one finger begin to penetrate him. Max arched against him, and Trent withdrew and entered over and over until his finger easily moved into Max's ass. Then he added a second finger, feeling Max tense up at the intrusion initially, then opening for them. It took a little longer for him to take two but when Max said, "Three!" Trent began pushing in a third.

Max groaned but not in pain, his hands gripping the covers below as his head shook back and forth and his hips undulated against Trent's fingers.

Once he was easily taking his three fingers, he gently withdrew them, opened and fitted the condom on his once-again erect cock, then lubed himself generously. That taken care of, he moved over Max, leaning down to take his mouth in another blistering kiss as his cock fitted nicely against his hole.

Trent reached one hand down and held his cock, breaking off the kiss to look at Max's face as he breached him. Max's mouth opened wide in a silent sound, and he pushed towards Trent as much as Trent pushed towards him. In no time, he was seated as far as he could go inside him. He paused for a moment and looked down at Max, waiting for his signal he was all right.

"Fuck me! For god's sake, fuck me!" Max shouted.

Trent's control broke, he withdrew his hips and slammed them back, holding his weight off Max so he got the best position. His body was covered in sweat after only a few short moments, but the noises coming out of Max's mouth were lust inducing. Max reached up and pulled him down on top of him, wrapping his legs around his back and hanging on for dear life. Trent rested his head in Max's neck as he pumped his hips as fast as he could, chasing their climaxes.

Max added to it by scratching the length of Trent's back, then digging his nails into Trent's ass.

"Fuck, fuck. Do that again," Trent gasped as arousal spiked his system.

Max complied, and Trent hit the point of no return, he repeatedly slammed into Max, encouraged by his sounds and words, "Fuck me. That's it, shove your cock in my ass. Jesus fucking Christ, yes. Ah, god, fuck, yes!" He felt the moment Max found his release, both with the clamping down on his cock and with the teeth Max bit into his shoulder. Trent obviously didn't mind because at that, he was done.

"Max! Fuck! I'm coming!" Trent's rhythm faltered, but he held himself deep inside Max as he came harder than he could remember coming, even since they'd been together.

As the release lessened its hold, Trent stayed on top

of Max, both breathing heavily. He was free from tension, free from stress and content.

After a few moments, he felt his cock begin to release from Max's ass, so he reached to grab the end of the condom before gently pulling out completely. Max hissed and tensed a little at the withdrawal, but then flopped back down. Trent threw the condom in the trash and grabbed a wet cloth, wiping his own stomach and cock before doing the same with Max, who only flinched a little when he first began.

"Thanks," Max croaked, arm over his eyes.

Trent threw the cloth in the direction of the wash basket and laid down next to him. "No problem."

Max rolled over and rested his head on Trent's chest and winding a leg to fit in between Trent's. "That was amazing."

Trent huffed out a laugh. "It was. Fuck, I've never come so hard."

"Time for sleep," Max said, yawning.

"Yep." Trent reached to pull the covers from underneath them so they could cover them instead, and they both snuggled in.

He honestly didn't think he'd sleep with everything going on, but he would try while Max was close to him. Even if he didn't, he would stay and hold him.

CHAPTER FOURTEEN

MAX

Max woke to an empty bed and dark room. He looked at the glowing digits of the clock, which said it was three in the morning. The other side of the bed felt cold, as did the pillow, so Max knew Trent had not been there for a while. He rolled to stand, aware of the aches and pains of their lovemaking last night. And it was lovemaking, even if Trent had been angry and had taken him hard, he had been careful and considerate too. Max was more than happy to have been able to give Trent the release he so obviously needed. It was just a shame he couldn't help in any other way.

He relieved himself in the bathroom, then fumbled around to find his briefs before walking to the living area. He saw Trent sat on the sofa, open beer on the coffee table, TV on but sound off. Walking towards him, he tried to make a little noise, so Trent could hear him coming. Rounding on him, he realised Trent was asleep sitting up. He smiled as he gazed at him, forehead creases smoothed, breath even, but he was going to have a crick in his neck if he'd been in that position for long.

Max knelt in front of him and smoothed his hands up Trent's thighs, trying to bring him out of sleep slowly. "Trent?" he whispered. "Trent? Wake up for me, sweetheart."

Trent made a snuffling sound before lifting his head and groaning, his hand immediately reaching for the back of his neck. Max winced, knowing exactly how that would be feeling.

"Oh, sweetheart. I bet that's sore." He straddled Trent's legs and used his hands to massage the back of Trent's neck and shoulders, hoping to alleviate some of the pain. Trent leaned his head against Max's chest and rested his hands on his thighs.

"Fuck, that hurt," he croaked, voice hoarse from sleep. "Thanks."

Max continued for a moment. "That any better?" he asked.

Trent moved his head from side to side. "Yeah, thanks." Then rested his head against the back of the sofa and looked at Max.

Max brought his head down and kissed him, softly and slowly, then pulled away. "How are you doing?"

Trent closed his eyes and shook his head. "I've no idea. My brain has gone on hiatus now."

"I know you want answers, Trent, but there is nothing you can do until this afternoon. Try and relax a little, eh?" Max pushed his groin against Trent's. "Do you want a distraction?"

Trent pressed his hips up while holding Max down with his hands. "As much as I would love it, I would be no good to you at the moment. I'm shattered."

"Come on, then, let's get you back to bed."

Max climbed off and pulled Trent up with his hands. Linking their fingers together, he walked Trent back to the bedroom, tucking them both back under the covers. He wrapped himself around him as much as he could, hoping to help him relax enough to sleep some more. Within minutes, Trent was asleep, but Max stayed awake long after, wishing he could help.

Trent's alarm clock woke them three hours later. Max, usually one to bounce out of bed as soon as the first chimes had begun, groaned groggily as he rolled off Trent's chest. If they hadn't both had to go to work, he would've thrown the clock out the window.

He rubbed his hands over his face, noticing the bed move as Trent got up.

"Do you want to share a shower?" Trent asked.

"Do you want to get to work on time?" Max joked.

"I suppose I better as I'm leaving early."

Trent stood and walked to the bathroom, and Max heard the shower start. He wasn't really going to let him shower by himself. He believed Trent needed another release to calm him. He followed a few minutes later, seeing Trent already in the shower with his head bowed under the spray. He climbed in behind him and slid his arms around to the front, ignoring his cock for the moment. He stroked and petted his chest, kissed his back, smiling in amusement as he saw the nail marks in his back.

"I've marked you up," Max said.

Trent turned and circled his arms around Max. "I did you too."

"You have? Where?" Max looked down at his chest, seeing a few red marks dotting his torso. "Looks good to me," he said, smiling.

"And here." Trent lifted a finger to run along his collarbone and the side of his neck. "Sorry, I kind of lost control. You might need to wear tops with collars for a while."

Max rolled his lips in and closed his eyes and arousal streamed through his system at the idea of being visually identifiable as belonging to someone. As belonging to Trent.

"Sorry." Trent pulled back, and Max realised he'd mistaken what Max was feeling.

He pulled him back. "Don't be sorry. It's hot. I was trying not to come at the idea that I'm claimed," he whispered.

Trent looked into his eyes for a moment, then nodded as if reaching a decision, then he lowered his head and kissed him. Max slid his hands in Trent's wet hair, deepening the kiss as much as he could. Then he slid his hands down his chest towards their erect cocks, gripping them both in one hand. With the water acting as a lubricant, he began to stroke them both, receiving and giving groans and moans but not rushing anything. It may make them late, but they both needed it.

After leisurely taking his time, he couldn't take any more and began tightening his grip and stroking faster. They stopped kissing and just breathed into each other's mouths until they came almost simultaneously over each other. Max let go of their cocks when his became too sensitive and picked up the soap. He began to wash Trent, who washed him in turn before they got out and dried off separately. Max knew they would be leaving later than they should, but he couldn't get it in him to care this morning.

They dressed quietly, making small talk, mainly with Max trying to distract Trent a little.

"I'm going to have to go. I'll grab a bagel or something from the café on the corner before I head to school." Trent leaned over and kissed Max before grabbing his bag and keys and headed to the door. There, he hesitated. "Would you come with me today?" he asked quietly without looking back.

Max's heart broke for him, and he fought to stay back and not go over. "Of course I will."

Although Max had heard last night, Trent told him the plan again, and then he left. Luckily, his house latched itself, otherwise, Max would've been stuck. He shook his head and smiled. He loved the fact Trent had so much trust in him. That brought him up short before he left. Fuck. He loved him. Though why he was surprised, he didn't know.

Max drove home to collect his things before heading out to his first appointment of the day. At nine-thirty, he had a slightly later start than Trent, but he was guaranteed to hit some traffic.

Arriving just before his time, he knocked on Mr Sanders door and waited for the elderly gentleman to answer.

"Good morning, young Max. How are you today?" Mr Sanders was a wonderfully enlightened and energetic man for his generation. He had a shock of white hair, perfectly combed and he dressed in his best every day of the week. He claimed his enlightenment came from having two gay grandsons and a bisexual son-in-law. Max had been surprised when he'd mentioned about his son-in-law because an acquaintance of his was in a similar situation but would never admit to being bisexual. He said it would cause too many issues as to why he was married to a woman and had two children. Max could see both sides of it, he supposed, but he admired Mr Sanders son-in-law for being honest and open about it all.

"I'm very good, Mr Sanders. How are you this fine morning?" Max entered and shut the door behind him, following Mr Sanders into his kitchen.

"Good, good." He looked over his shoulder at Max and smiled. "I can tell you're very good, Max. There's something that gives you away." He laughed and turned to make coffee as he always did.

Max unconsciously lifted a hand to the hickey he'd spotted in the bathroom before leaving home. It gave him a thrill every time he saw them, and he was certainly not hiding them from anyone. And if anyone had any issues with them, then they didn't have to hire him, did they? He knew Mr Sanders would have no issues, but some of his other clients might.

Mr Sanders set a coffee in front of Max and sat opposite him at the table. "So, have you redone the changes for me?"

"Yes, I have. I hope you'll like them. I've included a couple of little extra points as well that you might want to consider, but they can be removed if they don't work for you." Max spread out the papers and talked him through what they were looking at. Mr Sanders was holding a nineteen-fifties style reunion for his classmates and their partners in a couple of months, and he'd asked Max if he would like to take care of the interior design aspect. It wasn't what Max usually did because it would be only a temporary weekend-long design inside a huge banquet hall of a local hotel. But he'd been inspired by the stories and plans Mr Sanders already had in place and decided to have to go. They'd been working together for the last three months to make sure as many details as possible were correct to the decade he wanted.

Max had been elbow-deep in research for weeks and had loved every minute of it. So much so, that he considered adding another bow to his string and advertising for these types of jobs as well. That would need a lot more thought because, as he had told Trent last night, he was already booked solid for the next three months. If he did this, he may have to consider taking on a partner or something.

He spent the next hour and a half discussing the project before he had to leave for his next appointment. "I'll look into the colour scheme a little more and see if I can source some swatches to give us a better idea of how they'd look. I'm sure I can find something that will work well."

"Thank you, Max, as always. You're doing an amazing job." Mr Sanders patted him on the back. "Make sure you keep tight hold of him," he said, pointing to Max's neck. "You're glowing, my boy. Hold tight, and don't let go."

Max smiled. "I don't plan to let go, Mr Sanders."

"See you in a couple of weeks, Max."

"Bye." He turned to his car, smiling. He wished he had grandparents like Mr Sanders.

His next appointment was a consultation with a Miss Rosen, who wanted her lounge redesigned to a more minimalist look, much to Max's silent dismay. To top it all she wanted the monochromatic look. He spoke to her at length about her reasons for it, trying to explain his reasonings as to why he thought another look might work better. In the end, she was adamant, and he told her he would have to decline. She wasn't happy, but he had been able to give her the names of two other people he knew would help her out, which gave him some brownie points.

After that was another quick consultation with Mrs Ward about her kitchen refit. He couldn't do any wrong in her eyes apparently and she agreed with everything he said. It always worried him when clients did that because it was usually after he left that they thought about what he said and realised it wasn't what they wanted after all, then they had to start the process all over again. He told Mrs Ward, he would create a quote for her, and then get in touch once she'd had time for the designs to sink in and they would discuss them again. There was no way he was going to start the job without double checking first, otherwise, it would be twice the work for half the pay.

He managed to fit in a quick lunch by stopping at a deli for a takeaway chicken Caesar salad and a fruit pot, along with a coffee and a bottle of water before heading over to Miss Timms, or Alice as she had asked him to call her. He'd already done her kitchen, and she was happy with it, so he knew her style already. This time she wanted her lounge redesigning, and they were able to quickly decide on a lot of details. Alice already knew it would be a wait before it could be done, and she was more than happy with the delay.

Sitting in his car before heading off, he blew out a breath. This was roughly a usual day when it came to quotes and consultations. He usually made sure to have one day a week like this except if he had a long job. If a job took two weeks, then he'd have a day before it started and then a day as soon as it finished. That way people weren't waiting too long.

He glanced at the time and started the car, heading for the centre of town. Maybe he could grab drinks before the others arrived, he'd be early anyway.

TRENT

Trent finished work at one-thirty after explaining a little about what happened to his boss. He sat in his car, debating whether to call Trish or not and see what she knew about the accounts. As far as he knew, the only names on the accounts were his, Jocelyn and Harper's. He'd been the only one paying into it, so he hadn't seen the point in adding Trish's name. He decided to call and see what she said. He didn't think it would be her, but something niggled at him.

"Yes?" she answered, voice harsh. "What do you want?"

"I've been told there has been a problem with the university fees being paid. There's enough money in the accounts so I don't know what's happened. Have you received any paperwork or phone calls about it?" Trent wasn't going to tell her that he'd spoken to Harper and

Jocelyn about it, otherwise, she may just go ranting to them.

"I've no idea what you're talking about," she said snootily.

"The fees for university should be coming out of Jocelyn's uni account. You know, the one I've been paying into each month? The uni said there's been a problem receiving the fees. Have you heard anything?"

"No, I've heard nothing."

"Do you have any ideas what could have happened?"

"How should I know, Trent? I'm not involved in all that, am I? That's your job, not mine. If the money's not there, then you've obviously not been paying it, have you?"

Trent rolled his eyes, then paused. "Who said anything about the money not being there?"

Trish didn't say anything for a moment, making Trent's instinct flair. "Well...if the fees aren't being paid, then why else would it happen?" she finished hastily.

"Hmm, well I was only asking. I'm heading to the bank now to sort it out anyway."

"Oh, really? Okay, well...let me know...what happens."

"Okay," he said slowly. She'd certainly changed her tune. Now she wanted to know the outcome when, only minutes before, she said it wasn't her problem. He rung off after saying goodbye, a little more confused than before. He shook it off, then started the car.

Both his daughters had been waiting outside their respective uni and college when he'd pulled up for them. None had said very much other than the usual, "Hi, how are you?" as they had driven to the car park. Trent locked the car and walked towards the bank. His palms were sweating, and his clothes felt too tight for his body. He relaxed fractionally when he saw Max waiting for them outside the bank, holding a tray of drinks.

"What's he doing here?" Harper asked sharply.

"Harper!" admonished Jocelyn.

"This is family business," she snapped.

Trent couldn't deal with their sniping today, so for once he snapped back. "*I* need him here."

"It's okay, Dad. We know he's a part of the family now." Jocelyn linked her arm in his.

As they reached Max, Trent realised he needed something before they entered. "Max?" he croaked.

Max looked at him, then quickly passed the drinks to Jocelyn before enfolding Trent in his arms. "It's okay, sweetheart. Just breathe, okay. Just breathe. Everything will work out. Let's just find out what's happened first, and then we can deal with the fallout. All right, just breathe for me, sweetheart, okay." All the time Max talked, he'd been rubbing Trent's back and holding him tight, letting him rest his head in his neck.

He took a deep breath, then pulled back, looking at Max before kissing him chastely. "Thanks," he whispered. He looked over to his daughters to see Jocelyn with tears in her eyes and Harper appearing a little sorrier than before. "Let's go."

Trent led the way into the bank, heading to the reception desk to request a meeting with the bank manager. To begin with, the clerk said it wasn't possible today, at least until Trent had fired back, "Well, apparently my bank account has been emptied, so I want someone to talk to. Now!" After that, they had been seated and asked to wait while the manager finished with his previous client. They sat and drank their drinks before being called back to the manager's office some twenty minutes later.

When the bank manager saw how many people there were, he asked for another two chairs to be brought in. It was a tight squeeze, but they made it.

"How can I help you today, Mr Walker?" he said with false cheer.

"I've been paying into two accounts for the past almost twenty years to pay for my children's university fees. I was told yesterday that the payments had not been sent to the universities like I had requested them to be. I'd like to know why."

"Okay, Mr Walker. Let me just go through some security details. Are you okay to do that in front of present company, or would you prefer...?"

"It's fine," he interrupted.

"Okay." The manager, Mr Pickering, went through the questions without issue. "Right, let me see. Um, I can see the two accounts that you mentioned. Um, the payments wouldn't have gone through because there's no money in the accounts." He looked scared to be the bearer of that news.

Trent froze. "What do you mean, they're empty?"

Mr Pickering turned the screen around for Trent to see and there it was in black and white, zero balances on both accounts.

"Where the fuck is the money?" Trent bit out. "I've been paying one hundred and fifty pounds a month into each account for as long as I can remember. Where is it because I sure as hell haven't withdrawn it?"

Mr Pickering turned the screen back to him and clicked and typed a bit more. "According to this, withdrawals have been made steadily for the last year, varying in amount and times of the withdrawals. I don't know what else to tell you, Mr Walker. The accounts are empty."

"No one else has access to the accounts. Only me and my daughters when they reach eighteen. No one…" he paused. No way. It couldn't be.

"Trent?" Max's voice broke his thoughts. "Are you okay?"

Trent looked at him, not really seeing him. He turned back to the manager. "Can you see who made the withdrawals? Or which account it went to?" he asked, fearing the answer.

Mr Pickering cleared his throat, looking decidedly less comfortable by the minute. He clicked a few more buttons. "A Mrs Trish Walker." His eyes narrowed marginally. "She is also registered as one of the people able to access the money."

"Fucking hell!"

"Mr Pickering, could you give us a moment please?" Trent heard Max ask.

He couldn't believe Trish had done this. She knew what it meant for the kids to go to university. They'd decided when they'd first had Jocelyn that their kids would have to opportunity to go if they wanted to and had made sure they could afford to put something away each month for them.

"Trent, are you okay?" Max asked, crouching in front of him.

Trent shook his head. "There must have been about forty thousand pounds in that account, Max," he whispered. "Forty thousand." Trent slumped in his seat, his brain unable to process anything else.

"Shit," Max said.

"Oh, god, Dad." Harper came over to him and flung herself to her knees next to him. "I'm so sorry I said it was you. Mum said it was, and I believed her. She'd been saying loads of things about you lately, and I'd gotten so cross that you didn't seem to care about me that I started believing everything. I'm so sorry." She burst into tears, and Trent picked her up and cradled her in his arms.

"It's okay, Button. It's okay. No harm done. We'll sort it out, okay." He stroked her hair, allowing her time to calm. He glanced over at Jocelyn, seeing tears running down her face. "You okay, Juice?" He used his nicknames for them both, hoping to make them feel more grounded.

"I can't believe she'd do that to us," Jocelyn whispered brokenly. Max stood and went to her, wrapping his arm around her shoulders. She turned into him and cried.

Once the kids had calmed enough, Trent set Harper in the chair next to him and called for Mr Pickering. When he entered, Trent told him to freeze the account, even though there was no money in it. "No one is to touch that account in any way, do you hear? And revoke all access except mine."

"I can't do that, Mr Walker. Mrs Walker has to be present for that to happen."

"Revoke all access except mine," he repeated. "The police will be getting involved." Jocelyn and Harper gasped. Trent looked at them both. "I'll explain later."

"Okay, all access revoked except yours, Mr Walker."

"Thank you. We'll be leaving now." They all stood and exited the room, then the bank.

Trent made it as far as the alley next to it before having to break away from the group. He rested against the wall and broke down. A few seconds later, Max was there, arms around him, talking though Trent couldn't hear a thing.

He had no idea how long they'd been there when his tears had finally dried up. As his awareness returned, he realised he was cradled in Max's lap as they sat on the floor of the alley.

"Sorry about that," he croaked.

"Don't be sorry. You needed that."

"Where's Jocelyn and Harper?" he asked, realising they weren't with them.

"They've gone to a bakery down the street. We'll catch up with them in a bit," Max said matter-of-factly.

Trent heaved a sigh. "I'd like to say I can't believe she'd do it, but all these little things have been adding up in my head."

"Like what?"

"Breast enhancements, botox, new clothes, the house redesign. It all needed money. She obviously didn't get enough through her PA job for it all." He shook his head. "A year! She's been stealing money from our kids for a whole year, Max! How can a parent do that to their child?"

He felt like he was getting his second wind, so stood up, helping Max when he admitted his legs had fallen asleep while Trent had been sat on them. They walked slowly to the bakery.

"I need to go and confront her," Trent said into the silence.

"Are you sure that's a good idea? Would it not be better to speak to the police?" said Max.

"No, I don't think they'd be able to do anything anyway because her name was on the account, although how it was, I don't know." He couldn't remember ever signing anything to add her to it. When Jocelyn had been born and they'd had the conversation about it, they had agreed that he would pay into their university accounts and she would pay the rent, then they'd split the other bills. That way, they still had their own money left over for anything they wanted. It was why he'd never thought to put her name on it—because she never paid into it. He'd had to reduce the payments once they'd divorced because he couldn't afford to pay that and his rent otherwise, but he'd still paid into it.

"Could you speak to your brother? He might have more information for you." Trent noticed Max sounded worried, understandably. Trent didn't want to confront her, but he didn't think he'd get answers any other way.

"Yeah, I might call him later. But I need to go and see her. See what she says about it." He blew out a breath. "I can't believe she's done it. I would never have said that she'd have the balls to do something like this."

"People surprise you when you least expect them to," Max responded.

They arrived at the bakery and saw Jocelyn and Harper sat in a window seat inside. They entered and Trent went to sit down while Max ordered a couple of drinks.

"Hey. How are you both?" Trent asked carefully. He knew how he felt about this all, but it would've come as more of a shock to his daughters.

"Confused, mostly. Shocked. Why would she do this?" Jocelyn frowned.

"Because she's greedy," Harper answered without any emotion clouding her voice. It worried him. Harper was the most emotional of all of them. She kept everything inside her and let very little out. "I had wondered why she was home at weird times of the day." She looked down at her hands and fiddled with her fingers. "Years ago, I remember her working long hours, but lately, she's been home at similar times to me. You know how my schedule is not full days, right?" Trent nodded. "Well, she's been home at eleven in the morning, one and two in the afternoon over the last few months. I can't even remember when it started. I never thought anything of her behaviour. I knew she'd always been…difficult." She looked up at Trent. "Why didn't I realise something was wrong?"

He reached across the table to hold her hands in his. "Because you have your own life, and it's not your job to be her caretaker or parent. You concentrated on yourself, which is as it should be. If anyone should have noticed, it's me." He squeezed her hands before letting go and leaning back when Max arrived with their drinks.

"Hey, how are you doing, girls?" Max asked.

Trent loved the fact that Max had taken to the girls so quickly. He watched as he talked to them, seeing Harper shift a little closer and her face begin to clear. Jocelyn was her usual friendly self. He was so glad they got on well. He sat, listening to their conversation turn from the situation at hand to college and university, and he knew Max was trying to distract them. His heart turned over as he looked at Max. Max caught his eye, smiled hesitantly, then went back to the conversation. How had Trent wasted so much time without him. A couple of weeks ago, he would never have thought he'd be in a relationship, let alone one with a man. But surprisingly, he was fine about it all. He didn't have any hang-ups about being gay or bi, or whatever. He supposed it had something to do with his friends being gay and so open about it.

When this was all over, he was going to sit down and talk to Max about their future. Because as far as he was concerned, he was all in.

CHAPTER FIFTEEN

MAX

Max was glad when Trent took over the conversation. He had no idea what he was doing; he was just trying to distract the girls a bit while Trent seemed to have withdrawn inside his head.

"Shall we head out?" Trent asked, standing.

"Are you sure you want to do it this way?" Max asked, finishing the last bit of coffee. He honestly thought Trent was making a mistake and needed to at least speak to his brother first. But it was Trent's choice.

"Yes, I think it's best. I'll call Samuel on the way though and let him know what's going on."

Max blew out a relieved sigh as he stood. "Thanks."

Trent reached for him, and he went into his arms without fighting. "I know you're worried. You don't have to come. It might be better if you didn't—"

"I'm coming. I'm not letting you do this alone. You

don't need to." Max was firm with his words. He'd be more worried if he wasn't there, to be honest.

"Okay. Let's go then." Trent let him go but linked their fingers together before leading the way out of the bakery.

They were parked in different areas, so Max said goodbye and headed to his own car. They were heading straight for the lion's den, so he knew he wouldn't be far behind them. He'd remembered the house from when he'd worked on it, every time he drove past, he'd shiver.

Throughout the drive, all he could think about were the worst-case scenarios. He just hoped like hell she didn't own a gun.

When he pulled up, the others were already there and waiting on the pavement. He quickly joined them. Trent pulled him to the side where the girls couldn't hear.

"I've been talking to Harper, and she thinks Trish is going to be here. Do you want to stay outside?" Trent asked Max.

"No. I'm coming in with you. If it makes things worse when we're in there, then I'll consider leaving. But to begin with, I'm there." Although he was worried sick, he wouldn't leave them to face it alone.

"Okay, in which case, can I ask that you keep an eye on Harper, please? I'm not too worried about Jocelyn, but Harper could easily be swayed and pulled back in with Trish's words."

"Sure, no problem."

"If things get bad, get out, then call Samuel—both girls have the number—then call the police. I have no idea how she's going to react, but you leave me there and get the girls out. Do you understand?" Trent was firm and kept eye contact, making Max realise he was completely serious about the leaving him part.

He blew out a breath. "I will do everything in my power to keep those kids safe."

Trent nodded once, then kissed him. "Thanks." He walked back. "Let's go."

"Wait. What did Samuel say when you called?"

Trent shook his head. "I had to leave a voicemail. He must be in court or something."

They walked up the path to the house, and Harper let herself in, calling for her mum. "Mum! You home?" Max noticed there was only a faint tremble to the words as he closed the door behind them.

No one answered from without the house, so they began to look around.

"Mum?" Jocelyn shouted.

They searched the whole house, only realising something was wrong when they reached the main bedroom, drawers were open haphazardly, clothes littered the floor, wardrobe doors were half open.

"It looks like she's gone," Trent murmured, studying the room and ensuite. "Toiletries are gone, some clothes are gone. It looks like she knew we were coming." Trent sounded as confused as Max felt.

How would she have known they were on their way to see her? They'd not told anyone except each other and none of them had been apart since the decision to confront her. Except Max, but he knew *he* hadn't rung her. It must've been *his* call that had tipped her off.

Trent began to go down the hallway. "Harper? Check your bedroom, see if anything is missing. Little things, like keys or money or cards or anything you wouldn't have had on you."

Max noticed tears streaming down Harper's face but before he could go to her, Jocelyn was with her, guiding her to the bedroom. This must be excruciating for them. Their own mother had not only stolen their money but had also, it seemed, skipped town.

He followed Trent down the stairs and into the lounge. It was just as he remembered except a little more lived in. He watched as Trent scanned the bookshelves, table, chairs, then went into the kitchen to do the same thing, finally the office. There, they found a drawer slightly open, which when fully opened showed some receipts.

Trent sat in the office chair, then began to sift through the receipts. "What the fuck?" He studied them harder, then slumped back in the chair again. Max took the receipts from him. He didn't understand why they'd upset Trent. The receipts were for pawn shops showing a watch, cufflinks, a pocket watch, a few necklaces and a ring. "What's the matter, Trent? These are just from pawn shops."

Trent laughed without humour. "Some of those things listed were things I had go missing. I bet if I checked, I'd be missing a few more things too."

"How did Trish get them?"

"Probably the same way she entered the house that night we were together. She must have got a key from somewhere. It includes my dad's watch. It was a family heirloom. I was waiting for one of the kids to get married, then I'd pass it on."

"So, she let herself into your house and stealing your things to sell to pawn shops? Why did she need all this money? Even with everything you told me earlier, this still amounts to a lot of money for what she seems to have had."

Trent rubbed his hands over his face vigorously. "I have no idea, Max. This is getting more fucked up by the minute."

Just then, Jocelyn and Harper came in. "My key to your house is missing, as is some jewellery and my wallet. The one I had my extra money in," Harper said, barely keeping herself together.

Trent stood and went to her, wrapping her up as she fell apart. "Shhh, it's okay, sweetheart. We'll sort it all out."

Max indicated for Jocelyn to go with him, and they headed for the kitchen. "We need to write a list of everything that seems to have gone missing from what Trent and Harper have said so far and from what you know." He saw a notepad on the fridge and pulled it down. Grabbing a pen, he sat at the table with Jocelyn and began the list. By the time Trent and Harper had joined them, the list covered nearly a full page.

"If you add in anything else you know is missing, we'll be able to give it to whoever needs it," Max said.

"Thanks, Max. I think we need to call the police in now. As much as I don't want to do this, I think we need to. Trish has gone too far. I'm so sorry girls, but I think this is the best route."

Jocelyn and Harper nodded but didn't say anything. Trent stood, indicating for Max to come with him. At the doorway to the lounge, Trent said, "Could you please stay with them while I call Samuel and the police? Could you maybe order some takeaway or something, even if they don't want to eat, they might when it gets here."

"Of course I will." He wrapped his arms around Trent. "How are you holding up?"

"By a string, to be honest. It just seems so unlike her. And yet, everything so far points to her. I don't get it. She never used to be bothered about beauty and money when we were married, it was more about status. Anyway, the police will figure it out, I'm sure."

Max felt powerless to help him in any way, so he just kissed him. Just a small kiss to let him know he was there for him. For as long as Trent wanted him.

Five hours later, they were all flagging, but it was over. Samuel had turned up before the police had and made sure everything was documented should things need to be taken further. Samuel had said he thought they had a good case against Trish, if they found her, which was going to be the crux of the issue.

Trish had, apparently, skipped town with the last of the university money. Hence the taillights.

Max couldn't believe what had been coming out in the woodwork. Little things here and there that individually no one would have thought about, but together they painted a different story. Things like her being home at different hours of the day, she'd quit her job as a PA two years prior and had nothing to support her or Harper, except for Trent, who for obvious reasons, couldn't pay for everything she needed, let alone wanted.

He was beat. It was nearing midnight, and they all needed sleep. The police had left about half an hour ago, and Samuel was still there talking with Trent about options. Jocelyn and Harper were dead on their feet, he could tell just by looking at them.

They'd all be better staying there, but he knew there'd be issues with that, so he made a phone call.

Twenty minutes later, an acquaintance turned up. He was a locksmith, and Max had him change every single outside door, including the garage. The man was halfway through the final lock when Trent came in.

"What's going on?"

Max turned, blushing. "I hope you don't think it was presumptuous, but I've had the locks changed. I thought you might want to stay here, but Harper might be worried about Trish coming back. This way, she doesn't have to worry about anyone turning up who shouldn't. And you don't have t—" He stopped talking when Trent's lips hit his own, making him stumble back a few steps before he regained his balance.

When Trent finally pulled away, Max asked breathlessly, "What was that for?"

"For being here. For knowing what I need. For helping." Trent kissed him again. "For being you."

Max buried himself in Trent's neck, holding him tight. "I love you."

Trent pulled back and clasped Max's head in his hands. "What?"

He took a breath. "I said, I love you. I know it's only been a couple of weeks, but I've been attracted to you for months. I never thought we'd ever have a chance. Thank you." He saw tears in Trent's eyes and wasn't sure what they meant.

As the tears overflowed, Trent leaned his head against Max's. "I love you, too. Fuck me, but I do."

Max kissed him, tasting the salt on his face. He couldn't believe it. This was so not the time to be doing this.

TRENT

As he held Max in his arms, he replayed what just happened. Max had said he loved him. And even more,

Trent had said it back. He was a bit shocked by how all right he was about it all. But he didn't care. At that moment in time, it was all his.

He couldn't believe Max had been so observant to know that being in the house would be difficult for them and for him to take the initiative and change the locks meant more to Trent than Max could ever realise. Max had been thinking about his kids and doing what he could to keep them safe. Trent couldn't ask for more.

They eventually said goodbye to everyone who was leaving and secured the new locks. Jocelyn and Harper went straight up to bed after hugging them both. Trent was glad they had taken a shine to Max, especially as he would be around a lot. At least Trent hoped he would.

He flopped down on the sofa and let out a huge sigh. Max dropped beside him and curled into his side.

"That was one long ass day," Max said with a yawn.

"That it was."

The next thing he knew, the sun shone through the open curtains. It took him a minute to realise where he was before he went to get up. Realising Max was half on top of him, he moved slightly to slide out from beneath him, then staggered upright, feeling aches and pain in places he wished he didn't. He was getting too old to be sleeping on a sofa. He heard sounds coming from the kitchen so headed that way, needing a drink of water.

He found Harper cooking breakfast, and Jocelyn laying the table. It was a bit of a shock to find Harper cooking; he had never seen her cook before or heard that she had the inclination to do it.

"That smells good. What'cha cooking, Button?"

"Papa!" Harper laughed.

"What?" Trent loved the sound of laughter. It was a bright start to his day, after all the crap they were thrown yesterday. And he wouldn't bring notice to it, but for the first time in a long time, she had called him Papa. When she first started learning Italian, she swapped from Dad to Papa overnight, and it stuck for the longest time. She stopped after the divorce. It was great to hear it again.

"It's only bacon, sausage and eggs. Nothing spectacular. I thought you might be hungry." She blushed.

"I'm always hungry. And thanks. Do I have time for the bathroom?"

She laughed again. "Of course."

He turned after winking at Jocelyn and headed for the upstairs bathroom. He did his business, found a couple of spare toothbrushes under the sink and brushed his teeth. Then splashed his face with cold water. He would need to go home today to pick up some clothes and things ready for staying here. He certainly wasn't leaving Harper alone.

Heading back to the kitchen, he heard more laughter, recognising Max's voice. As he entered, he saw Max sat at the table, talking to Harper and Jocelyn with a mug in front of him.

"How come I didn't get coffee when I came in here?" Trent pouted.

"You didn't ask. The first words Max said this morning were a whispered 'do we have coffee?' I think he needed some to become human again." Harper ducked the towel Max threw towards her. "Hey, mind the oven! *Sei un idiota!*" She laughed as she called him an idiot.

"Hey, hang on. If you're going to curse at me, do it in English so I can understand!" Max complained, looking to Trent for help.

"You're on your own. I've put up with this for years!" He laughed as he sat next to him.

"Thanks," he said with a pout. Trent leaned over and kissed him chastely, several times.

"Good morning," he said quietly.

"Morning, handsome," Max whispered.

"All right, you two. Enough canoodling. Time for breakfast." Jocelyn placed plates in front of them both. It looked delicious.

"Thanks, Harper, Jocelyn. This looks great," Max said.

"Yeah, thanks."

"It's okay."

They ate breakfast with companionable conversation and for a short time after. Then Harper turned to Trent.

"Papa?"

"Yes, sweetheart."

"Could I come and live at your apartment instead of here?" She looked down at her hands, fiddling with her fingers, which she did when she was nervous.

Trent was quiet for a moment. "Of course, you can. I thought you'd want to stay here because of everything you have, but if you don't want to, you don't have to."

"I want to live there," she whispered.

"Oh, Button, of course, you can. We can sort it out today, no problem at all." He hugged her close. In a way, he was glad she had chosen to live at his house. He would've quite happily stayed here for her, but this didn't feel like home anymore, and he certainly couldn't afford the bills on it. But if she had wanted to stay, he would've figured it out somehow.

"Thanks, Papa."

That decided, Harper spoke to Jocelyn and asked for her help to pack her things up. Neither were going to college or uni that day, and Trent had decided to call in sick too. No way would he be able to concentrate with everything that's going on.

"I'm going to have to head out," Max said quietly after the girls had left the kitchen.

Trent was a little disappointed, but he knew how busy Max was especially with taking some time off for his injuries. He also knew Max was filling his days with consultations and expanding his diary as much as possible before he was able to do more strenuous work, hopefully, next week.

"That's okay. Get yourself to work. I'll text you later."

Max leaned forward and wrapped his arms around Trent's neck. "Don't do anything I wouldn't do."

"That doesn't leave a lot, Max," Trent said in a serious voice.

Max hit his shoulder, then kissed him slowly. Trent slid a hand into Max's hair and the other to his ass and gripped tight with both, enjoying the moan Max gave him. Their kiss deepened, tongues sliding along each other's. After several minutes, they pulled apart, leaning their foreheads together, gasping for breath.

"I love you," Max whispered into his mouth.

Trent kissed him again, slowly this time. "I love you."

"See you later? Shall I come to yours? Unless you want to come to mine for dinner? With Harper of course, and Jocelyn if they want to."

"I'll ask them and see what they want to do, then let you know if that's okay?"

"'Course." Max kissed him again, then picked up his stuff and left with a wave and a shout goodbye to the girls.

Trent needed to make sure he held tight to Max. He was a keeper, that was for sure.

CHAPTER SIXTEEN

MAX

He drove home to pick up some more paperwork. He had been requested for a large job on behalf of a very wealthy couple. They wanted their whole house redecorating, a top to bottom refurbishment job, which was a substantial fee for Max, so he hadn't wanted to turn it away. He'd already booked them in for a month later and it was a job that would take probably four to six weeks, if not longer.

As he climbed his stairs to his office, he felt his ribs pull a little. They were the only part of his incident that still pained him, and even then, it was only occasionally. All his other bruises had faded, but he made sure he would finish this week out with nothing too strenuous. Well, if you could call sex with Trent not strenuous. He laughed, realising that was probably the reason his ribs were protesting this morning, rather than aftereffects of his injuries.

He spent the next two hours listening to the couple bickering about the different aspects they wanted in each of the rooms and the prices each item should cost. Max was no longer surprised that they wanted everything that was the most expensive, even if the items didn't even go with their theme. They believed if it was expensive, then they should have it. Max had tried to offer them cheaper and better alternatives, but they hadn't wanted to know. Max had learned through his two years designing that if he didn't do as the client asked then they would blame him for any minor issues that came up. Whereas, if he did as they requested, and they didn't like it, they didn't have a leg to stand on. He could then charge extra for having it redone as he had originally offered. Sneaky but necessary.

When Max finally left them to their twelve-hundred-pound bottle of wine, his stomach growled at him. It was lunchtime. He drove to Pop's, which was near to where his next appointment was and grabbed the menu.

"Hey, Max, what canna get ya? Your usual?" Maria asked. She was a lovely Scottish woman with gorgeous red hair and was the daughter of the owner, who everyone called Pop; no one knew his real name. He was Pop to everyone, young and old. Maria had been here for much longer than Max had been coming.

"Yes, please, Maria. How are things with you?" Max asked.

"Oh, usual as always. Pop's beginning to slow down though, so we're looking to take on a new chef to help out a bit." Max could see the worry in her eyes and wondered if Pop was doing okay, health-wise.

"I'm sorry to hear that. Let me know if I can help at all, all right?"

"You boys are always helpin' out when we need it, no need to be doin' more now," she said. "But thanks, anyhow. I'll get ya order put in. I'll be back in a jiffy."

Max smiled as he watched her go behind the counter and do her job. He didn't know what would happen if something happened to Pop. Maybe Maria would continue, he didn't know. It would be a shame if she didn't. Pop's had been a fixture in Cambridge for so long, he knew a lot of people would be upset about it.

Grabbing his mobile, he decided to call Trent to see how he was holding up with everything. He hated having to leave him this morning after everything that had happened yesterday, but he couldn't cancel his consultations on such short notice.

"Hey, you," Trent said when he answered.

"Hey. How are you doing?"

"Yeah, I'm all right. I'm just helping Harper pack up the last bits and pieces she wants to take with her, then we'll be heading home."

"That's good. Are you sure you're okay?" Max was worried Trent was pushing himself too far, but he knew he'd do anything for his kids, no matter what anyone said.

He heard Trent blow out a breath. "Yeah, I'm doing okay. Trying not to think about it too much, to be honest. Every time I do, I get angry all over again, and there's nothing that can be done about it. Might as well try and move on best I can."

"Make sure you ring me if you need me, all right. I only have this next appointment, which will take about an hour tops, then I'm just catching up with paperwork and stuff." Maria brought his coffee over, placed it in front of him and held up ten fingers, which he took to mean his food would be about ten minutes. He nodded and mouthed, "Thank you."

"I know, thanks. I'm sure I'll see you later, anyway, won't I?" Max heard a note of uncertainty in Trent's voice and quickly tried to remedy that.

"I'll be there with bells on," he declared.

"Good, though that might get a little noisy later on." Trent's voice had lowered in volume, probably so Harper didn't hear.

"I can take them off then, don't you worry." He laughed. "So, is Harper taking over the whole bedroom?"

"And probably the living room too." Trent chuckled. "Doesn't matter. She can bring whatever she feels she needs to, as far as I'm concerned."

"I know, I'm only teasing. How is she holding up?"

"Not great. She's never been one to show too much emotion, she'd prefer to keep it inside, but even she has been crying on and off throughout the day."

"Has Jocelyn been over?"

"No, Jocelyn decided to go to uni this morning because she had work to hand in, but she'll probably be at home later on."

Maria brought his food over. "Thanks, Maria."

"Are you at Pop's by any chance?"

Max laughed. "I might be. Who's asking?"

Trent's laughter warmed his heart as it flowed through the phone into his ear. "Well, I best go. Harper's shouting me. Enjoy your lunch, Max. I'll see you later."

"Okay, I love you." Max rolled his lips in trying to keep from smiling like a lovestruck teenager.

"Love you too. See you soon."

They hung up, and Max began on his cheeseburger and chips. He couldn't wait to see Trent later.

Max pulled up at his next appointment. The house was a small, detached property in a good area, and from the looks of the garden, it was well kept. He grabbed his folder and laptop and knocked on the door. Mr and Mrs Lowell were a middle-aged couple who didn't want to spend excessively but still wanted their house to look neat and tidy. Max could understand that. He talked them through the options available to redecorate their hallway. He enjoyed this type of job because the clients knew what they wanted and what they liked so could make decisions easier. The appointment didn't last long, and Max was on his way home to make some phone calls and source swatches, antiques and wallpaper.

It was only as he parked up and saw Trent's car that he realised he'd driven to Trent's apartment instead of his own house. He debated carrying on to his place, then thought about Trent and realised he wanted to see him. He shut off his car, grabbed his paperwork—he wouldn't leave confidential information on his front seat—and his bag and headed up in the lift, after saying hello to the security staff.

As the lift ascended, he thought about how much his life had changed in the short time since the opening of Crush's Garden Bar. He never believed he'd be in a relationship with Trent; he always thought he would have to watch him from afar.

He was a little concerned about how well Trent had taken to being gay though, and he kept waiting for Trent to freak out and change his mind. Max didn't know if that was his own insecurities playing with his mind or whether it was a real issue he should be concerned about. Mistress Staci had told him to trust his instincts, but he couldn't quite figure out what they were telling him. He shook his head, he just needed to let it play out however it happened, and if Trent ended it, then Max would have to deal with it.

Exiting the lift, he walked to Trent's door and knocked. Harper opened the door and, after a brief hesitation, smiled at him. "Hey, Max."

"Afternoon, Harper. How are you doing?" He leaned in slowly to kiss her cheek, waiting to see if she'd pull away before he got to her, but surprisingly, she let him.

"I'm all right. I didn't quite realise how much stuff I

had," she said with a laugh, "so it's taking longer than planned to get my room sorted."

Max took his coat and shoes off and hung up his bag before resting his folder on the table, so he'd remember to take it with him later. "A girl your age should have loads of things. It's a rite of passage, isn't it?" They laughed. "Do you need any help with anything?" He knew she'd say no, but his manners dictated he ask anyway.

Harper bit her lip. "Actually…" she scrunched up her nose. "Nah, it's okay. I'll get it done."

"No, what were you going to ask?"

"I wondered if you'd help me decide where everything goes?" she said, quietly, looking at the floor.

Max was surprised at the change in Harper, but maybe he shouldn't be. She'd been brought up by Trent *and* Trish, and it was only the last few years that she'd been subjected to only Trish. And she'd had a huge blow to her confidence. He was glad she was trying to build bridges, just as he was.

"I'd love to. It's part of my job, after all."

Harper looked up at him and smiled. "Thanks, Max. And…I'm sorry for being so unkind before."

"Consider it forgotten." He put his arm around her shoulders and walked her back to her room.

They found Trent in there, trying to move some boxes. He glanced up and smiled when he saw them. "Two of my favourite people." He put the box down and came over to them. He kissed Harper on the cheek, then turned to Max. "Hey."

"Hey, yourself." Max felt dumbstruck every time he saw Trent. He was gorgeous. Trent came at him and pressed their lips together. He felt Harper pull away.

"Uh, you guys, not around the innocents, okay?" Harper laughed and danced away as Max and Trent tried to grab her.

"As if you've never kissed someone." Max chuckled when Harper went red, and Trent narrowed his eyes. *Uh-oh.* "Changing the subject. What needs doing Harper?"

Seeing relief and gratitude in her eyes, Harper explained what she had. There were boxes that needed emptying, currently on Jocelyn's bed, and then there were some pieces of furniture, which had already been put together. Max could see that it wasn't going to work in the current design.

"Hold on." He went to get his laptop from his bag. Going back into the room, he brought up his usual design program and set to work with creating the basic layout. A few minutes later, he called them over. "Right, I'm going to design what I see, and then you can have a look and see what you think to it and make changes if you need to, all right?" he asked Harper.

Harper looked at Trent. "Is that okay, Papa?"

Trent smiled at his daughter. "Absolutely. It's your room now. Just remember that Jocelyn needs to sleep here too when she visits." He gave Harper "the look" that every parent knows how to give their children.

She smiled. "Yes, Papa."

Max got to work designing, making sure he included

all the furniture that was currently in the room, and Trent and Harper began sorting through the boxes to see what she'd brought. They couldn't do much proper unpacking until Max had finished.

Twenty minutes later, Max called them over again. "Okay, let me know what you think." He spun the laptop around so they could both see it.

"Woah!" Harper's eyebrows went into her hairline and her mouth dropped open.

"Great job. It looks brilliant. What do you think, Harper?" Trent asked.

They both jumped when Harper started crying.

"If you don't like it…" Max was at a loss. He had no idea why she was crying. He watched as Trent enfolded her in his arms, making soothing noises to her.

When she calmed, she wiped her face with her hand, looked at Max and whispered, "I love it." She took another deep breath. "No one has ever asked me what I wanted, except if it was for birthday or Christmas. Even…" She looked at Trent and bit her lip—like father like daughter. "Even when you divorced Mum. You didn't ask what I wanted. I wanted to live with you." She looked down at her hands.

Max's heart broke. He looked at Trent and saw the same reflected in his eyes. "Oh, sweetheart," Trent said, "I am so sorry. I honestly thought I was doing the best for you because she would be able to give you a lot more than I would've been able to. I'm sorry I didn't ask what you wanted. I thought you'd say you wanted to stay with your mother, but I see now even if that was your answer, I should've asked."

"It's okay, it wasn't so bad. She was hardly there to be honest."

"That doesn't make it any better, Harper. If I'd known what was going on, I would've sorted it sooner. I'm so sorry for everything that's happened."

"It's not your fault, Papa. It's *her* fault." She glanced over at Max, then back to her father. "I'm so glad you have Max now. He is way better than Mum."

It was Max's turn to get teary, but he refrained from letting them fall, at least most of them. He smiled across at them both. "I'm glad to have your Dad. He means a lot to me. And so do you and Jocelyn. Even though I don't know you well yet, I hope we can get better acquainted."

Harper got up and gave Max a hug. "I'd love that." She pulled back and looked back at the laptop. "And I love this. Thank you."

"Okay then, let's get to work." Max jumped up from his perch and rested the laptop down. "First things first, let's move the big stuff."

Over the next hour, Trent and Max humped and dumped the furniture to where Max had advised on his designs. It took a bit of manoeuvring because they had to work around the boxes that were on Jocelyn's bed, but once they'd got the majority in the right places, they were able to move those boxes, and then move Jocelyn's bed. It all fitted perfectly and gave the girls more room.

Trent went to the lounge to call for pizza for dinner when they'd finished. Max and Harper got drinks ready for everyone, and Harper had received a phone call from Jocelyn saying she was on her way. They were chatting and laughing when Max's phone rang. It was an unknown number.

"Hello?"

"Good evening, Mr Hughes. This is a courtesy phone call to let you know that your assailant has been found and dealt with. You will have no issues with him from this moment forward. Enjoy the rest of your evening." Then the phone went dead.

Max looked at his phone, then pocketed it. He knew who it was who'd called. He also knew he wouldn't be able to tell anyone it was them; it was how they worked. They looked after their members and took violence seriously. How was he going to explain it to Trent?

"Are you all right?" Trent's voice cut through his thoughts.

Max looked at him. "Yeah. I'm fine."

"You sure? You look a little…I don't know, unsure?"

Max glanced across at Harper, who was doing a good job of pretending not to listen. Max dropped his voice to a whisper. "Can I talk to you about it later?"

Trent frowned at him but nodded. "All right."

"Thanks." Max leaned forward and kissed Trent, but they were interrupted by the doorbell. Trent pulled back with a tortured groan. "Always the same." Max laughed.

Dinner was a lot lighter than it had been the last

time they attempted it. There was laughter and smiles, which made up for the small uncertain glances Trent kept giving him. He knew once Jocelyn had gone back to the dorms and Harper had settled in bed, he would have to give Trent something to work with. He just wasn't sure what.

TRENT

"Okay, talk to me. You've been out of sorts all evening, even if you put on a good face for the girls." Trent wanted to know what had got his boyfriend twisted up. It was ever since that phone call.

Max sighed. "Can we get in bed first?"

Trent nodded, and they began to disrobe separately, then they climbed naked under the covers, and Max laid his head on Trent's chest.

"You're worrying me, Max."

"Sorry. I just don't know how to explain what I need to." He blew out a breath. "All right. The phone call was telling me that the person who beat me up has been caught."

"That's brilliant news! Why wouldn't you want to tell me that? Is there going to be a court date or anything or haven't they told you yet?"

"That's what my issue is. It's not the police that have dealt with him. It's AN."

"What do you mean AN? Why are they dealing with it and not the police?" Trent was confused.

Max sat up facing Trent. "Remember how I said I can't tell you much because of confidentiality and everything?" Trent nodded. "Well, this is the same thing. If a member doesn't adhere to the rules and guidelines, there are consequences."

Trent's stomach dropped, he really didn't like the sound of AN. "What kind of consequences?" he asked.

Max shrugged. "I honestly don't know. Only thing I do know is that membership is permanently revoked for violence."

"Why can't you tell me more?"

"I've told you before that it is part of the rules. Only members are allowed to know more information."

"What about boyfriends of members? Surely they have a right to know where their partners are?"

"I don't know, Trent. Possibly most couples join together. I really don't know."

"Can you ask them?" Trent wanted more information.

"I can try." Max reached for his phone.

"You're going to call them now?" Trent looked at the clock, it was ten o'clock.

"The phones are answered twenty-four hours a day."

He watched Max dial and hold the phone to his ear. "Hi, I'd like to ask a question…Yes, it is…four, one, seven, two, nine…All right, am I able to tell my boyfriend more about AN? He's concerned about some things…Yes…Of course…Thank you."

He saw Max close his eyes at the same time as he turned his phone off, and he knew the answer would be no.

"They won't allow any information to be divulged to a non-member. I've already given you more than I should have. I'm sorry, Trent."

"It's okay. It's not your fault. I'm not happy about it, but it's fine."

Trent laid back on the bed, one arm behind his head, looking at the ceiling. Max laid down next to him but not touching. Trent drew him closer, so Max was back in his previous position on his chest.

"I'm really sorry."

"Honestly, don't worry about it. Can I ask you to do one thing for me though?"

"What's that?" Trent could hear the trepidation in his voice.

"If you visit a club, write the name in a sealed envelope and put it somewhere I'll know to look in case something happens. Then I'll be able to find you." It had been a worry of Trent's ever since Max's beating. If no one knew where he was, how could they know where to look if something went wrong? "I won't look unless I have to." And he wouldn't, as much as it killed him, he wouldn't.

Max lifted onto his elbows, looking at Trent strangely. "Why would I need to go to a club again?"

"Well, I know I can't give you everything you need, so I assumed..."

"You assumed I'd go to someone else?" Max sounded hurt by that.

"Well, yes. I know it's what you need sometimes, and although I don't like the idea, I'd prefer you to get what you need that you can't get from me."

"I don't know whether to be comforted by that statement or upset."

"Why?" Trent was confused now.

"Because you're basically giving me permission to fuck someone else!" Max's voice went hard. "If you don't want me, then you need to be clear now, Trent. I'm not in this for shits and giggles, you know."

"Fuck, no, that's not what I meant. Shit, I can't explain properly. Max, I love you. There is no doubt in my mind that I love you. But I know you need things I can't give you, like BDSM. I wouldn't know where to start with it, other than ordering you around, and I know that's not what it's about. I don't want you to miss out on those things, so if I have to share you with the likes of Frederick," he tried to keep his voice even, "then I will do whatever is best for you."

Max was silent for a minute, just staring at him. Then he smiled and snuggled into his chest again. "You silly man. Whatever is best for me? That is you. You are best for me. Everything else is background noise. Forget about the clubs; I won't be going to them anymore."

Trent was shocked. "But what about your needs."

"I can work with what we do. Maybe I can show you

a few things, but if you don't like them, then it doesn't matter."

"But it's part of who you are," Trent argued.

"It is, but I can deal with it. I can't deal with being with a person that's not you. The clubs stop. End of."

They were quiet for a moment before Trent felt Max kiss his chest, then move and tongue around his nipple. "Someone's feeling horny."

"I always am around you," Max replied, moving to his other nipple.

"We need to keep the noise down this time…fuck!" Trent said through gritted teeth.

"We can certainly try, can't we?" Max joked as he used the tip of his tongue to flick repeatedly against the tip of his nipple, making Trent feel it in his cock.

Trent grabbed hold of Max's head and pulled him up to kiss, instantly frantic to get closer to the man he loved. As their lips met, he wrapped his arms around Max, holding him close. Their talk had left him a little rattled, and he wasn't so sure that Max could just switch off his needs, even though he said he'd be fine. Trent didn't want half of Max, he wanted the whole of Max.

Max swung a leg over Trent's body to straddle him, then ground their cocks together. With how tight Trent held him, Max didn't have much room to move so Trent let go a little, though didn't leave his lips. He gentled the kiss, thrusting and withdrawing his tongue, tangling them together, then pressing their lips together once more. Eventually, they came up for air, but Trent didn't want to stop, so cradling Max's face in one hand, he trailed kisses up Max's jaw, down his neck and across his shoulder, leaving little bites along the way.

He felt Max reach for something—a condom and the lube probably—but he kept touching and kissing him. One hand smoothed down Max's back to his cheeks, feeling the sweat beginning to bead on his skin, squeezing and raking his fingernails across the surface and making Max thrust forward.

"Fuck, Trent. You feel so good." Max kept up his thrusting rhythm, sliding their cocks alongside each other, smashing them between their bodies. "Lube...take me."

Trent got harder with the whispered plea, and he grabbed the lube, flicked it open and put some on his fingers. He'd had to let go of Max's head to do it, and Max took the opportunity to return the favour, biting and licking his way across Trent's body. Max groaned against his skin when he smeared the lube around Max's hole, pressing gently against it. Max must have bored down because a finger slipped in easily, and Max's groan increased, Trent hearing it even pressed against Trent's chest as he was.

It wasn't as easy to prepare him from this position, but Trent loved the idea of Max riding them to completion, so he wasn't going to change a thing. He'd just be extra careful to make sure he didn't hurt him when he finally entered him.

Thrusting the finger in and out, Trent allowed Max time before adding a second, to which Max bit down on

Trent's pec and thrust his hips forwards again. Shortly after, Max fucked himself back onto Trent's fingers, their cocks slipping nicely together.

Adding a third finger, increased Max's thrusting and quiet chanting. "Fuck, Trent, please fuck me, please. I need you. Fuck me. God!"

Having mercy, to Max and himself, he reached between them to his cock, ripped open the condom and slid it on. Slicking it up, he sat Max upright to get a better position. "Jesus Christ, Max, you look decadent like that." Max was glassy eyed, flushed, messy-haired and breathing hard—the picture of sex.

"Please. Please, Trent."

He couldn't deny that, so he held his cock steady against Max's ass and held his hip with his other hand. Max slowly lowered himself until he was sat against Trent's hips, and Trent's eyes rolled into the back of his head.

"Fucking hell, that feels good." Max swivelled his hips in a circle, making him go cross-eyed. "Ah, god!" He tried to be quiet, but he couldn't help it; it felt amazing. "Fuck yourself on me, Max. Ride me. Now," he demanded when Max didn't move fast enough.

Trent felt Max's posture straighten, then placing his hands on Trent's chest, began to lift and fall on Trent's cock, whimpering each time. The vision of Max on top of him and his cock disappearing in Max's body had Trent nearing his climax quickly. He didn't want to go fast though. "Slow down. That's it. Make it last for us. We're not coming for a while yet." He didn't know where this was coming from, but Trent liked the idea of making them wait for the orgasms.

He placed one hand on Max's upper back and one on his ass cheek and pulled him forward until he was laid against him. He moved him so Max could still fuck himself, but it was shallower and would hopefully take longer. Never normally into prolonging orgasm, Trent found a new respect for those that were. It was not easy slowing things down when his body demanded satisfaction. Several times, he felt Max begin to move faster and Trent followed until he realised then took a breath and slowed them down again.

"Ah, god. I don't know how much longer I can last, Trent." Max's voice was gritty.

"Let's try a slight change." Trent pulled out from Max with a wince and a groan, then placed Max on his side facing away from him. He curled around his back, lining himself up again and slid straight back in. "Holy shit." It just about killed him, but he kept still until the urge to thrust abated a little.

"Fucking hell, Trent. Let me come!" Max almost snarled.

"Not until I say so, sub," Trent whispered into Max's ear as he slid his arm under Max's neck. He wouldn't have normally brought the word into their bedroom, but it felt right. And watching Max's reaction proved it felt right to him too.

"Yes, Sir," Max hesitantly replied.

"Good." Trent felt pleasure race through his system at Max's words, nothing to do with the pleasure streaming through his body from the way Max's body hugged his cock. He withdrew a little and slid back in, repeating the motion as slowly as he could. He reached forward to encircle Max's cock with his hand, feeling precome leaking from his tip. "Such a good sub."

Max linked his fingers with the hand that was under his neck, the other hand gripping the sheets below them. There wasn't much room for him to manoeuvre anywhere, so Trent did all the work this time. He was getting to the end of his control, so he bit at Max's shoulder in warning, then turned Max onto his stomach all the while still inside him.

"Time for me to ride now. Come on, Max, you can take it." Trent rested his hands on the bed just under Max's armpits, straddled his legs and began sliding in and out, slowly to begin with, then getting faster. The tightness of Max's ass rubbed him in all the right places and with Max thrusting back as well, Trent assumed Max was riding the sheet below him too. "Nearly there, Max. It feels almost too good to stop." Trent threw his head back and groaned at the ceiling, trying to keep it quiet, but he knew he failed.

"Fuck, fuck, Trent. I don't think I can keep going. Let me come. Please let me come. Fuck, please!" Max was almost wailing at this point.

Trent was there, so he said, "Come, Max, come now." He began spilling inside of Max with his final word and felt Max's body clamping down on his, extending his climax further. He stayed resting inside of Max as the aftershocks went through them both, breathing heavily. He grabbed the base of the condom and withdrew carefully, wincing with sensitivity, then flopped onto his back. He noticed Max hadn't moved.

"You okay," he asked, resting his hand on Max's back.

"Uh-huh," Max replied.

"Do you want a shower?"

Max just groaned in response, which Trent took to mean no, but they probably should. Trent blew out a breath, then stood, disposing of the condom in the bin beside the bed. Looking at the clock, Trent realised that was almost a marathon for them, no wonder they were both wiped out. He laughed. "Come on, Max. Let's get cleaned up."

There was no answer, so he went around the bed and saw Max was fast asleep. Trent smiled. He'd leave him to sleep, but he needed to move him so he could get a clean sheet on the bed. He remembered being able to change the sheets below the kids while they were still sleeping when they were younger and wondered whether he could do the same with Max. He decided to try.

Fetching clean sheets, he flicked the current ones off the corners before situating the new sheet on two corners of one side. He slid the sheet underneath the current one, pulling gently to fit the opposite corners in place. With some of that movement, Max had rolled over, leaving only a little of the old sheet underneath him. Trent carefully pulled it out before covering Max with the duvet.

Pleased with the result, he threw the sheet in the washing basket and walked to the bathroom for a shower. Although he was tired from their lovemaking, he wasn't tired enough to sleep yet. Maybe after a hot shower he would be.

Getting cleaned up was quicker when it was only him in there, and he was back in the bedroom in no time, still not tired though. He put on some pyjama trousers and went to get a drink. Looking across the darkened room as he drank his water, he saw his laptop and had an idea.

He refilled his glass and went over to the sofa, opening his laptop and turning it on. He kept thinking about AN. It can't be so bad, otherwise, the police would be trying to take it down, and he'd heard nothing about it on the news or from Logan. When the laptop had loaded, he opened the internet browser and searched for AN. It brought up some random things that had nothing to do with BDSM or clubs, so he tried refining his search. It took a few attempts but eventually he found the same logo that had been on Max's phone the other week: a white 'A' and a red 'N' on a black filigree background.

He clicked the logo, and it expanded to fill his screen before fading into the top right corner, leaving behind a black background and the word "Anonymity." A white button appeared beneath the word telling him to "click for membership details." He knew this was what Max had signed up for, but he was still unsure. He had hoped there would be a bit more information before the sign-up section.

He didn't hate what he did with Max, and although Trent felt like he wasn't really into the BDSM scene, maybe he could learn to be, for Max's sake. Or maybe he might end up liking it. Or maybe he'd end up hating it. He had no idea. But he had to try. He clicked the button, deciding, regardless of the result, he would at least try it out.

After signing up, paying the fee, which made him wince a bit and reading the terms and conditions, he understood what Max was trying to tell him about *not* being able to tell him anything. The rules and guidelines were very strict about it, and he supposed he understood the need for it. He wouldn't mention anything to Max about becoming a member just in case he was refused. And it would also give him the chance to get up the courage. He blew out a breath. Hopefully, this would add to their relationship, not break it.

CHAPTER SEVENTEEN

MAX

Max woke before Trent for a change and decided to get a start on breakfast. He didn't have much to do that day, he had no consultations booked in but had originally planned to get his paperwork up to date. From their discussions yesterday, Max believed Trent and Harper were going back to their respective daytime duties, therefore Max was going to do the same.

He grilled the sausages and bacon when Harper came in. "Good morning, Harper."

"Morning."

"Now, are you a morning person or do I need to shut up and stay away?" he asked only half-jokingly.

Harper laughed. "I'm a morning person. You're safe. Although could I please have a coffee?"

It was Max's turn to laugh as he poured her a cup. "It's not brilliant. I need to try and get Trent away from this awful stuff and onto something decent." He pulled a face when he passed it to her.

"It is really bad, but at least it's hot."

"That's very true. Still, new coffee is needed desperately."

"It will be added to the shopping list, don't worry. I know you both hate it, so I'll change it." Trent's voice made Harper jump, then laugh.

"Buongiorno, Papa."

"Good morning, Button." He laughed at the face she pulled. "You'll always be my Button no matter how old you are." He kissed her cheek, then headed over to Max. "Good morning, love," he whispered as he kissed Max.

Max smiled against his lips. "Good morning, sweetheart."

Trent grabbed a coffee, then sat at the table with Harper while Max finished off the cooking, after waving away help. He almost dropped the eggs when he heard Harper's next comment.

"You don't have to keep quiet because I'm staying here, you know."

Max looked over his shoulder at Trent, seeing his face scrunched in confusion, and Max bit his lip to keep from laughing at his innocence. He caught Harper's eyes, and she smiled. He shook his head and returned to his cooking.

"What do you mean?"

"When you have sex, you don't need to keep quiet. I know all about the birds and the bees." Harper said it so matter-of-factly that Max snorted before he could help himself.

When there was no answer, Max looked again and saw Trent staring at Harper with his mouth open wide.

"I think he's trying to catch flies, Max," she said smugly.

"I think you've shocked him, Harper," he replied in the same tone, still looking at Trent.

"How did you…? What…? Why…?" Trent blew out a breath and closed his eyes. "I didn't want you to be uncomfortable," he said finally.

"I'm not." She looked down at her fingers. "I'm content. It may sound stupid but when I hear you, I feel happier because I know you are happy, and I know you're in love. And it makes me feel loved in return. Which I know sounds stupid—"

"No, it doesn't," Max said, turning off the grill and coming to the table. He crouched down next to Harper's chair. "It doesn't sound stupid at all. You've been in a house where there doesn't seem to have been much love since your dad left. It can't have been easy for you. Even if it came about in an awful way, I'm so glad you found your way back to your dad."

"Thanks, Max."

"Trent, don't be so shocked. She's sixteen for god's sake." He laughed as he ran his hand along Trent's back as he walked back to the kitchen. He plated the food and placed them in front of the people who were coming to mean so much to him.

"Harper, I wanted to tell you that you don't need

to worry about university. If you would like to go, then you will go, I will make sure of it," Trent announced.

"But it costs—" she began.

"No. Don't worry about the money. I will sort it," Trent interrupted.

"We," Max interjected. "We will sort it."

Trent looked over at him with gratitude and leaned forward to kiss him. "Thank you."

Max saw Harper swallow hard and knew she held back her emotions. "You deserve it, Harper."

"The problem is…it might be more expensive than normal," she said, then quickly added, "but I can change my plans. It's not a problem. Don't worry."

"Harper. Take a breath. Talk to us. Tell us what you want to do and let us decide if it can be done or not, all right?" Trent said softly.

She did. "I want to go to university in Italy. They do a two-year course, which integrates you into using the language quicker, and I would get to see Italy as well. I was told being submerged in the language is the easiest way to learn it fluently. I'd like to do that if it's possible."

"Okay, we'll look into it. Give us what details you have about it, and we'll do the rest."

"It's okay if I can't go though, all right. If it's too expensive, then I'll find a course in England."

"I will let you know if that's the case, all right? Stop worrying. We'll make it work somehow."

"Grazie, Papa." She turned to Max. "Grazie, Max."

Then she smirked and said, "I'm going to have to find an Italian name for you, Max."

"Good luck with that." He laughed.

After spending so much time at Trent's house, Max finally went home for more than a breeze through. Inevitably, a knock sounded at the door not half an hour later. He walked to the door, knowing exactly who it would be.

"Good morning, Max. Where is your boyfriend today?"

"Good morning, Mavis. How are you?" Max opened the door wider so she could enter.

"Good, good, thank you for asking. So, where is your man?"

Max laughed. "He's at work, Mavis. He's a primary school teacher, so he has to teach all the kids about interfering old busybodies, like you." He sounded harsh, but he knew she wouldn't take offence.

"Well, it's busybodies like me who get things done around here," she threw back.

He laughed again. "Quite right, quite right indeed. What can I do for you anyway, or were you just coming to see if my better half was here?"

"I've not seen you for a while, Max dear. I was worried about you," she answered softly. "I saw a man creeping around looking at your house the other day.

He didn't go inside, he just looked around the outside, then he wandered off again. I thought maybe you'd had some trouble."

Max walked into the kitchen, debating what to tell her. She might be a busybody, but he didn't want anything to hurt her. It might be better to tell her some of it so she could be vigilant. He sat down with her and a pot of coffee and spilled the beans about his beating and Trent and the man being dealt with. Obviously, he left out the AN bit.

"Bloody hell, Max. Why is this the first I heard about it? Why didn't that man of yours tell me?"

"Because he had no idea who you were, Mavis! I hadn't told him about you yet. As far as he was concerned, you were a nosy neighbour, and that was it. It was only when he came back and told me about you that I told him who you were."

"Well, someone had to keep an eye on you, Max. You were heading for trouble with all that 'dating' you were doing." She used finger quotes to emphasise her point.

"I'm fine, Mavis. Everything's fine now, all right?"

She smiled. "It is, isn't it? Oooh, I'm so excited. Do you have a date for the wedding?"

Max choked on his coffee. "What wedding?"

"Yours, you silly boy. Surely, you'll be getting married soon?" She narrowed her eyes.

Max expected the thought of marriage to freak him out, but it didn't. With all the problems with his parents and their marriage being a sham, he thought he'd detest the idea of signing away his independence. But the thought of having Trent as his and his alone was blinding. He would love nothing more than to marry Trent. Just not yet. It was a bit soon.

"If we are still together in a few months, maybe there will be a wedding in the future, but not yet, Mavis. We've only been together a week!"

"Doesn't matter how long you've been together so long as you're happy," Mavis said with a knowing glint in her eye. "And you, my boy, are ecstatic."

Max laughed. "Yes, I am, Mavis. Yes, I am."

TRENT

Trent had just put his bag on the table after finishing work when there was a knock at his door. He opened it to find the two police officers from the day of the bank incident.

"Good afternoon, Mr Walker. May we come in?" Trent couldn't remember the officers' names.

"Of course. Would you like a drink?" he asked, manners on autopilot.

"No, thank you. Hopefully, we won't take up too much of your time."

"Okay, take a seat. How can I help you?" he asked. He hoped they had more information about Trish.

"So, we've investigated further into the missing

money and your missing ex-wife. We have a bit more information to share with you and gather your thoughts on if that's okay?"

"Sure."

"After looking into the accounts at the bank and the information they provided along with some CCTV footage, we were able to find out that your ex-wife had an accomplice. She's been in a relationship with a bank cashier for the last fourteen months. From what we gather, the cashier had been siphoning money out of your children's accounts and into your ex-wife's account over the entire period they were together. Initially, the money was small amounts until they suddenly began getting larger. We have no information as to what the funds were spent on after they had been transferred, but we do know that the final transfer happened as you were waiting in the bank on Tuesday afternoon."

"The cashier transferred the money while I was actually there?" Trent couldn't believe the gall of the guy.

"Yes, he had been working the desk when you arrived and through the CCTV, we could see he saw you, went onto his computer, used his phone, which he shouldn't have had on him to begin with, and then he left the bank. And hasn't returned."

"He's gone with her?"

"That's what we assume at the moment."

"Do you know where they are?"

"Not, at present, no."

"How did you find out about him?"

"A couple of things. When we looked at tracing the transfers, there was a thumbprint of someone trying to hide what they were doing. They were good, but not as good as the people we employ. Therefore, we were able to see which computers the transfers were made from and at what times. This led us back to the cashier, even though he tried to make it look like it was all your ex-wife's fault. We were also able to obtain your ex-wife's telephone records. It showed a phone call from a mobile at the same time the cashier made one, and it was confirmed it was his number."

Trent blew out a breath. "Do you know who the guy is?"

The police officers looked at each other. "Yes, we do. He is the youngest son of the owner of the bank. He's twenty-one."

Trent laughed. "Jesus Christ, Trish, what the hell are you doing? He's twenty-one years younger than she is!" He shook his head. "Doesn't really surprise me, though."

"We wanted to ask if there was anywhere you can think of that she may go to or visit?"

"Um, she is close to her parents, and I wouldn't put it past them to hide her because in their eyes, she can do no wrong. Other than that, she loves Spain. We used to go to the Costa Dorada with the kids. No idea where else."

"Thank you, that will give us somewhere to look."

"Do you think you'll find them?"

"I'll be honest with you, Mr Walker. I think we will find them. Eventually. I wouldn't hold my breath on it being too soon though. What I would suggest is contacting the bank; they should be able to refund you the money since it was the fault of an employee. My advice? Go on with your lives. We'll be in touch when we have more information or questions."

"Thank you for coming, officers."

He showed them out the door just as Max came up the hallway.

"Hey, everything okay?" Max asked as he watched the police officer's leave.

"Yeah, they just came with more information." Trent proceeded to explain what the police had just told him while he made coffee—new stuff he'd just bought.

"Wow, so not great news then."

"Well, you see, I think it is." Trent laughed at Max's shocked face. "Not the bit about the missing money, that's a pain in my ass, but the rest...yeah."

"Care to explain?"

"Trish isn't in our lives anymore. Yeah, there's a chance she'll come back and get caught, and we'll have to deal with the court case and everything. But she's not here now. She's not interfering in our lives. She's not messing around with my daughters. She's gone. We can carry on with our lives as we see fit, without having her barging in every minute of the day. We can be happy. Sorry, happier. And to top it all, the police think the bank would refund the money because an employee was involved." Trent sat next to Max. "What more can I ask for?"

"I have something for you," Max said, his smile huge.

"What's that?" he replied.

"Come with me." Max stood and walked into the bedroom with Trent following behind, checking out his ass. "Shut the door."

"What have you got me?" Trent asked. He didn't like Max buying him things, but he wouldn't be mean and throw it in his face. Max began to undress, and Trent raised his eyebrows. "Do you have a special gift for me?" he said as he stared at Max.

"Uh-huh." When Max finished undressing, he went over to the window and rested his hands against it, looking back over his shoulder at Trent. "Fuck me."

"Who's the boss here?" Trent replied.

"I am, this time," Max said, voice low and brooking no argument.

A shiver went down Trent's spine with those words and the thought of Max telling him what to do. "Okay, what do I do?" he whispered.

"Get undressed and fetch the lube and a condom, then stand behind me, not touching."

Trent did as he was told as fast as he could; he didn't want to leave Max waiting. As he reached for the lube, he saw his hands were shaking. Anticipation sung through his veins. He walked to stand behind Max as he'd been told to.

"Good. Now use just your fingers to prepare me. I

don't want any other part of your body to touch me at all, just your fingers." Max leaned down slightly and arched his back so Trent had better access.

"Fucking hell," Trent whispered.

"What was that?" Max whipped back at him.

"Sorry."

"That's okay, I hadn't explained you needed to be silent. Next time you talk without permission, you will be denied an orgasm."

Trent clenched his jaw against the arousal flooding his system but didn't say a word. He flicked the lid off the lube and slicked his fingers before rubbing it around Max's hole. He'd only done this a few times now, but each time was easier than the last, he was getting more confident.

"Fuck, that's good," Max said when Trent breached his ring.

Each time Trent added a finger, Max praised him for his good work, making Trent relax further. After readying him with three fingers, Max thrust back against him, pushing him back a step to stop him from touching Max.

"Oh, god, Trent. I don't want you to stop. Fuck!" Max rested his head against the window, and Trent heard him take a breath. "Okay, remove your fingers."

Trent did.

"Put the condom on your cock and slick it up." Max looked over his shoulder at him, maybe to make sure he obeyed his commands. "A little more, perfect, now slide it all over so you're nice and slippery for me. Good."

Max paused, and Trent looked at him. As soon as they locked eyes, Max spoke. "Hold my upper arms only. Now fuck me."

Trent swallowed at the order, more turned on that he thought he'd be. He gripped Max's biceps with one hand and used his other to position himself before sinking into Max's body. He placed his other hand on Max's other arm. It gave him leverage to pull and push and fuck him. It wasn't easy though, making sure he didn't grab him in other places, and therefore, he was able to push his arousal back a bit. At least until Max started moving.

"Right. Stand still holding my arms."

Trent blew out a breath, trying not to say a word. Max began pushing back onto Trent's cock, then moving off, then back on again. It was slow motions, but the vision of Max fucking him was overwhelming.

"Fuck, Trent. Let go of my arms." As Trent let go, Max leaned further forward, getting purchase on the windowsill to brace himself and fuck back faster. Trent braced himself as best he could with nothing to hold onto. The feel and visual of Max's ass sliding up and down his cock, of his cock disappearing into his body was his undoing. He knew the rules though, he hadn't been told to come, so he had to fight it back. Trent's breathing became erratic, he tried thinking of different things, and he began to sweat with holding back the need to come.

"I'm there, Trent, I'm there. Grab my hips and come for me. Come now!"

Trent wasn't sure what noise he made when he grabbed Max's hips and came, but he was almost certain he had not said a word as he'd been told to, but he couldn't be one hundred percent sure.

"Jesus Christ, Trent. You're going to kill me." Max rested his head on the arms that were braced on the windowsill, breathing heavily. Trent smiled as he saw the window was a little fogged up. There was still a little light in the sky, but no one could see them, other than the neighbours across the way, and Trent found he didn't care. He pulled out from Max, holding the end of the condom and disposed of it in the bin right next to them but stayed where he was, other than that.

Max glanced over his shoulder and smiled at Trent. "You can speak freely now."

"Thank fuck! Holy hell, Max. I don't know about me killing you, but you sure know how to make me feel my age." Trent helped Max stand, steadying him when he was upright. He turned him and wrapped his arms around him before bending his head for a kiss. "I love you, Max Hughes."

Max came for another kiss, deeper than the last, before pulling away. "I love you, Trent Walker."

"Papa? I'm home!" Harper called.

"Good timing," Max whispered, laughing.

"I'll be there in a minute!" Trent called back.

"Take your time! This is the second time I've been back! But I'm starving so I'm not staying away any longer!" Harper's laughter echoed through the apartment along with Trent and Max's groans and curses.

The following day after having contacted the bank, Trent sat in the bank manager's office staring at him in shock. "You're offering me how much?"

The manager cleared his throat. "In light of all the problems and the fact it was an employee at fault, we are offering to replace the money that was in the account before the withdrawals began, and also provide you with compensation of the same amount for the troubles you have had." Trent looked at Max in shock, seeing a similar expression on his face, then turned back to the bank manager when he continued, "That would mean we would transfer eighty-seven thousand pounds into the account of your choice."

Trent shook his head, unable to believe it. Maybe he would be able to get Max to update his apartment now. He looked at Max again, smiling.

ELEVEN WEEKS LATER

MAX

"I'm not sure this is a good idea," Max said to Frederick, who had called him to come help with a new sub he had.

"You don't have to touch him or be a part of it, except to help me see what he needs," Frederick replied.

Max was torn. Frederick had never asked for his help before, and he was reluctant to refuse, but he had also told Trent he would never go to a club again. "I need to speak with Trent. Can I call you back in a minute?"

"Sure, make it quick."

Max rang off and called Trent.

"Hey, you."

"Hey."

"Everything okay? You sound upset."

"Frederick has been on the phone asking if I could help him with his new sub. I know I told you I would never go to a club again, but Frederick has never asked for my help before. I don't—"

"Max. I trust you. The past few weeks, you have told me when you needed something, and we've worked around it together. If you want to go and help Frederick, go."

"I promise I won't take part in it, only as an advisor."

"Max. Stop worrying. It's fine. Do what you need to."

"Are you sure?"

"Yes! Go. Help Frederick break his sub in or whatever. I'll see you later."

"Thank you. Love you."

"Love you back."

Max called Frederick back straight away, confirming he'd be there and checking the name of the club. He grabbed a few bits he might need and dressed in his leather pants. He wanted to make sure he gave the air of a Dom tonight, so no one tried to mess with him.

He called a taxi as his car was in the garage overnight, and within half an hour he was at Sinned. He gained entry with his thumbprint as always and headed to the bar; they would know where Frederick was. The bartender pointed him to room three, and he made his way to the back of the club. He saw Frederick standing outside the room with the door very slightly ajar.

"Hey, glad you're here."

"No problem. What do you need help with?"

"Okay, this sub is new to the scene. He has a little

experience on the light side of things but wants to try things a little…darker."

"All right. What do you need me for?"

"Let's go see." Frederick walked in the door and held it open for Max.

He saw the sub lying naked, save for a harness, on his back on a bondage table, arms and ankles strapped to the side, knees bent and strapped in place exposing him, blindfold covering his eyes. The sub bit their lip, and he stared. *No way.* "What the hell?" He turned to Frederick. "What's going on?"

Frederick smirked. "He asked for help, so here I am. Helping." He walked over to the sub and whispered something in his ear, receiving a nod in return, then walked back to Max. "Enjoy. Oh, his safeword is Trish." Frederick let himself out the room and closed the door behind him.

Max turned to stare at the vision in front of him. The vision of Trent laid out for his pleasure. It was more than he'd ever imagined. Hang on, how was he even allowed in here? He wasn't a member. Never mind, question that later.

"Are you going to come over any time soon because the silence is starting to freak me out a little." Trent's voice was quiet, but Max could hear the tremor in it. They had done some things at home, little things to educate Trent in the whole lifestyle, so Max knew a little of what Trent liked and didn't like. He had a few ideas of what he'd like to try here, where there were more toys to use.

He shook his head, holding back a chuckle, then smiled and put his Dom hat on. "I'm here." He walked over to the table, leaning down beside him. "Are you sure about this, Trent? You don't have to do this for me," he whispered.

"I'm doing it for both of us."

"All right. I'm going to do one thing first." Max leaned over and kissed Trent with everything he had in him. "Thank you."

"Thank me later." Trent chuckled.

"Right, the rules. You may call me Sir. You only speak when I say you can, moans and groans are fine, but words are not. I want you to use red, yellow and green when I ask. Green means that everything is fine, and we can continue. Yellow means you are unsure. Red means you don't like it. I know your safeword, so if you really don't like what's being done, use it and the scene will finish immediately. I will not be telling you what I am going to do but use the colours or your safeword if you wish; these words can be spoken freely at any time." Max's voice had taken on his usual Dom voice, and it filled him with a sense of pride that he could do this with Trent. He hoped Trent would like what he was thinking of doing. "Do you understand the rules?" This would be Trent's first test.

Trent nodded. Max smiled as he passed the test. "All right then. Let's begin." He saw the tell-tale tension seep back into Trent's body at those words, but Max hoped he could relax him again soon.

He walked over to the cupboard and selected a soft

tailed flogger, used more as a tease than for pain, although it was possible. Max turned and walked back to the bed, laying the flogger next to Trent before reaching out to touch his ankles. The first contact made Trent jump before he settled again. Max slid his hands up and down his legs repeatedly, getting closer and closer to his cock, but never actually touching it. Max's hands roamed higher across his abdomen and chest, avoiding his nipples. He kept his touch featherlight to increase the sensation, raising goosebumps along the way.

Max touched every inch of skin he could reach save for the two areas he knew Trent would want him most. Then he picked up the flogger. He held it above Trent's stomach only letting the smallest amount touch him, making him flinch again, and let it smooth across his skin the same way his hands did. This time though, he didn't avoid those areas. Every time it touched his nipples, Trent would arch up into it. When it slid across his cock, it would jerk as if reaching for more.

Tortured groans came from Trent's throat as Max increased the pressure from the flogger. Not teasing as much now but bringing a lot more sensation to his body. He rested the whole of it against Trent's cock, allowing him the freedom to thrust against it, knowing it would do nothing but heighten his arousal.

Throughout, he kept an eye on Trent's face, reading the biting of his lips as to whether he was all right or not. At one point, Trent turned his head and mouthed his bicep, probably trying to keep in his words. He loved to hear Trent's vocals usually, but he didn't want to break the silence just yet.

He grabbed some of the tails of the flogger, and then wrapped his hand around Trent's cock, not allowing him the full impact of his hands. He stroked up and down with them, seeing Trent move his hips in time and kept it up for a few minutes. Then he let go, to Trent's groans of denial, dropped the flogger and grabbed his cock again. At the first touch, Trent's cock jumped and leaked some precome, which Max used to slick his way. Every time he raised his hand to the top, he twisted, rubbing against the sensitive underside. Then he held still and used his thumb to rub against the nerves continually until Trent was thrusting against him erratically.

He let go.

Trent's groans followed him as he left the bed and opened a drawer, finding a small vibrator. He returned to his previous position and took hold of Trent's cock again. He began his torture once more, repeating what he'd done previously. This time though, when he had Trent flexing against his hand, he switched on the vibrator, making Trent's body still and ran it up the inside of his thigh, so he could get used to the sensation. He didn't stop there. He moved the vibrator higher, to the crease between his thighs and balls, then slowly across his balls, making Trent tremble. Then he smiled as he got to the base of his cock. Trent's vocal pitch was increasing although he hadn't heard words yet, he was pretty sure he would when he did this.

He held the vibrator against Trent's cock and slowly ran it up the underside until he reached the nerves, where he held it for a moment to the increase of Trent's moans, and then slid it down again. He did it again, holding it against the nerves for a little longer this time. Trent's body trembled hard, though Max was unsure whether he was trying to get closer or further away. It didn't matter because he couldn't go anywhere, strapped as he was.

Max repeated this over and over again, each time holding it on the underside of his hood for longer until precome trickled out of his cock at a constant rate, and his body was tensed so hard, Max thought he'd break. Max lifted the vibrator off to a tortured groan. He was impressed by Trent's refusal to talk; he was usually difficult to keep quiet.

"You're doing well," Max allowed. He knew exactly what he was going to do next. They had played top and bottom over the past few weeks, and Max knew that Trent enjoyed switching as much as he did. It had taken Trent a little while to get used to being fucked, so Max really wanted to drag out this climax. He wanted to make it last all night, but he didn't think *he'd* last that long. He walked over to the side of the room, which held the larger toys, and quietly wheeled over a favourite of his: a fucking machine. He went back to the drawers and chose a dildo about the same size as Max himself, then attached it to the machine.

Standing next to Trent again, he began to stroke his cock, which although hadn't lost all his hardness, needed a little tender loving care. Trent flinched as soon as Max touched him, probably not expecting the touch as Max hadn't said a word. He reached forward to one of Trent's nipples and pinched it, making him arch against the bindings. Max twisted his fingers a little, and Trent bit his lip as he jerked in place. He flipped open the bottle of lube that waited next to where they were and drizzled some over Trent's hole. Trent jumped again, groaning slightly with Max's hand movements.

Max rubbed the lube around his hole, pressing gently to begin the process of preparing him. By the time Trent was taking three of Max's fingers, Trent moaned with every breath and bit his lip or arm. Max removed his fingers from Trent's ass and opened the lube again, covering the dildo with plenty enough to make its entry easier. Then he pulled it closer.

"I have a present for you," Max crooned as he let go of Trent's cock, much to his denial. He checked the settings before placing it where it needed to be. He pushed it close enough that it began to breach Trent's hole, even though Trent clenched. "It's all right, relax for me, let it in."

Max saw and heard Trent take a deep breath and let it out slowly before his hole relaxed and the dildo slipped in further. Trent's groan echoed through the room. He let the dildo shallowly fuck Trent to relax him further, then when he did, pushed it further. Once it was able to go all the way, he pulled it back and positioned it properly.

"A little bit of noise now," he warned him and

switched it on. It was a gentle hum and squeak as the dildo began to move. Max adjusted it a little to make the most impact and watched as Trent took the dildo repeatedly. He had set it for alternate rhythms so Trent wouldn't get used to one sensation, it would continually change in sequence. "Good, sub, you are taking that so good." He watched for a little longer to make sure it was correct and wasn't going to hurt Trent, then moved to his previous position at the side. He ran a finger along the underside of Trent's cock, making him tense his muscles and groan more. Max smiled. It sounded like Trent was enjoying this.

He reached for the flogger again, dragging it softly over Trent's inner thighs, then higher over his balls and cock, making Trent contort his lower body. He continued higher across his stomach, his nipples, his throat. Max knew from experience the softness of the flogger would highly sensitise Trent's skin. He drew the flogger back down, lifting it off when he reached his nipples, then quickly flicked his wrist to hit them with the ends of it. Trent bowed off the table as far as he could, moans falling out of his mouth continually. Max repeated the action, then dragged the flogger down his skin again towards his groin. Lifting the flogger off Trent, he flicked it towards his balls and cock, making Trent jump, then Max soothed his skin again with the softness.

Trent's breaths were coming faster and faster as the dildo increased its speed. Max had never seen something so beautiful as how Trent looked at that moment in time. His skin had a sheen of sweat, his chest a flush of red, his ribs protruding with his heavy breathing, his mouth open or biting his lip, his toes curled, his fists clenched. He was magnificent.

He was also nearly there. Max grasped the base of Trent's cock hard to make sure he didn't come. Once he was sure Trent wouldn't, he removed the dildo, eliciting another tortured groan from Trent. Another day he would see Trent climax with just the dildo, but today Max needed it to be him. Trent had given him such a gift in this, he wanted to share it with Trent.

He whispered his words so as not to startle Trent. "I'm going to unstrap you." He still couldn't believe Trent had not said a word.

He undid the straps, then helped Trent move to the bed, he was still blindfolded. Max positioned Trent so his body was on its side with his bottom leg straight and his top leg bent and resting on the bed, opening Trent up to his perusal.

"So beautiful," he said as he smoothed his hand over Trent's cheeks, hole and taint. "My turn." He couldn't keep the Dom voice completely.

Max reached for the lube and slicked his cock and Trent's hole, even though there was still plenty from the dildo. They had been checked at a clinic and cleared for over four weeks now, and he was so glad he didn't have to use a condom anymore. He didn't need to prepare Trent any further, so he moved in behind him and began his slide into heaven.

TRENT

He had been right on the edge of orgasm when Max had removed the vibrator. In the few minutes after, he had managed to calm a little, but then with the dildo as well, he had been on the brink again.

He had been working up to this night for weeks, ever since he received the approval of membership for AN seven weeks ago. He'd gone onto the app and started searching for Frederick, knowing he wasn't going to be able to pull it off himself. Luckily, Frederick had his photo attached, and Trent managed to find him after a few days of searching. In his first message to him, Trent had explained who he was and what he wanted, expecting Frederick to refuse him. But he hadn't, and eventually, they had come up with this scenario. There was no way Trent would've been able to set himself up like this *and* get Max here without something being given away, so he'd enlisted Frederick's help, no matter how embarrassing it was having another man see him naked and blindfolded. He'd given Frederick a lot of trust, and Frederick had not let him down. He'd have to thank him properly later.

He gritted his teeth as pleasure streamed through his body as Max's cock slid inside him. Some of the pleasure came from, he was sure, the fact he wore a blindfold and couldn't see what was happening. He could only feel it. His cock was still rock hard after its earlier treatment.

He felt Max withdraw completely, and Trent's body followed when it felt empty, receiving a hand smoothing his cheeks. Max moved again, straddling Trent's one straight leg, moving the other higher up the bed.

"Ready for me? Speak freely from now on," Max said.

"Fuck, yes. Please!" Trent said, voice hoarse from the groaning noises he'd been making.

Max's cock made the smallest motions, in and out, for what seemed like forever until he was finally seated completely. Trent groaned at the full feeling, wishing he could see Max's face. Max withdrew slowly, but not as slow as before, until Trent felt the fullness recede before pushing in again. The sensation of Max's cock rubbing against his insides made his cock jerk. He could remember how it felt when he did the same thing to Max.

He felt Max move position again, leaning forward and resting one hand behind Trent's back and one on the bed underneath the knee of his bent leg.

"Bit faster now," Max said, voice like gravel. "Fuck, you feel good. I won't last long."

He withdrew and thrust in, his cock raking Trent's insides. "Fuck! Oh, god, Max. Sir." He quickly amended his words, hoping Max wouldn't stop what he was doing to reprimand him.

Max said nothing just increased his speed again. Trent couldn't believe they had waited so long for this.

Why had he not suggested it earlier. It was fucking amazing. The whole scenario had been beyond his wildest imagination. He thought BDSM was all about pain until Max came and enlightened him. Even when Max had explained, he had still been unsure, but now he wished he'd taken the plunge earlier.

"I'm not going to last. Fuck, Trent. Look at me." With those words, the blindfold was ripped from his eyes and dimmed light streamed in. It took a minute for his eyes to adjust, but then his gaze didn't leave Max's. Max looked wrecked. He had a sheen of sweat on his body, and the tension in his body was immense. "I'm gonna come. Fuck!"

Max sped up more, changed his angle slightly, and Trent almost jumped off the bed. "Fuck! Fuck! I'm coming!" Trent shouted as Max hit his prostate, and his body locked down for his release.

Without even needing to touch his cock, he began spurting his load onto the bed below, shouting Max's name. He felt Max follow him, releasing into Trent's ass, then dropping down onto him, breathing heavily.

Trent could feel nothing but the aftershocks through his body. Max lifted off him, pulling out carefully, making Trent wince. He was going to be sore later, but he didn't care. He was glad he could move again though. Or at least he would be glad when he had fully functioning limbs.

He opened his eyes when he felt movement and lifted an arm for Max to snuggle into his chest. Even if he was Trent's Dom at this moment, there was no better place than feeling Max rest his head on his chest.

"Thank you," Max whispered.

"You're very welcome," Trent replied. "Let me know when we can do this again." He paused then added, "At least, once I'm not so sore." He laughed.

Max chuckled. "Sorry, you will be for a bit, but we'll get a bath when we get home. That will help."

"Thanks." They laid in silence for a few minutes before Max spoke.

"Um, how did you get into this place?" Max asked.

Trent wondered whether Max would ask that. "Well…a few weeks ago, I looked into AN to try and find more information. I couldn't, so I decided to join." He wasn't sure if Max would be angry at the whole truth.

"And what?"

"My approval came through seven weeks ago," Trent said quietly.

"Why didn't you tell me?"

"I have been trying to get the courage to do this for us. I searched for Frederick so he could help me arrange this surprise for you. I knew…I knew you'd be reluctant to let me do this if I told you about it beforehand."

Max was quiet for a moment. "You're right. I just don't want you to push yourself to do this if it's not what you want," he said finally.

"I needed to see what it was about. And if you couldn't tell, I think I enjoyed myself." Trent laughed.

He wrapped his arms tighter around Max, not

wanting to move anytime soon. He'd thought that BDSM wasn't for him. He was glad to have been wrong about that. He would be happy to experiment a little more. He was sure Max would steer him in the right direction.

<hr>

FIVE MONTHS LATER

TRENT

"What do you mean, you've never seen that film? How could you? It is an epic Halloween film. Yes, okay, it's animated, but you should know it's good just because of who made it!" Trent shook his head in disbelief as he walked to the door to answer the knock. They had originally been discussing costumes for the Halloween party they'd been invited to next month before it dissolved into what the best film was.

"They have her," were the first words out of Samuel's mouth as he burst through the open door. Trent couldn't remember seeing him as excited as this before.

"What? Who?"

"Trish! And George. They have them. They're in custody right now."

Trent just stared. He didn't know what to say. They had waited for so long to hear the words that he'd given up hope they would. He felt arms come around his waist and knew Max was there, helping. He had a mix of emotions running through him: he was relieved that she would be made to pay for what she'd done to their kids; he was pissed off that she was back to mess with his life again; he was worried about how Harper and Jocelyn would take the news; he was scared she wouldn't get charged.

"Come on, Trent. Let's sit for a moment," Max led him to the sofa and sat him down, then sat next to him.

"I never thought she'd be found in all honesty. I thought she'd just disappear from our lives and never be heard from again," he whispered.

Samuel came to sit in front of him on the coffee table. "She won't be coming anywhere near you or the kids, Trent. I won't allow it. The police won't allow it. We have enough evidence to send her to prison for at least a couple of years. George too. You'll only have to see her at the court hearing, no other time." He paused. "I will say though that the kids will have the option to speak to her if they want to. But they don't have to, it's their choice."

Trent rested his head in his hands and blew out a breath. He felt Max rest his head on his shoulder and wrap his arms around his waist and back again.

"Everything will be fine, Trent. She can't hurt us now."

Max was right. They'd been through enough these past few months. Harper had adjusted to living with Trent and had just started her final year at college.

Jocelyn was into her third year of her degree; she had stopped working at the job because Trent had insisted she concentrate on her degree instead.

They were all finally living the lives they wanted to live, living it the way they were supposed to be living. Even if he had an unplanned addition to his life, in the form of Max, he wouldn't have it any other way. People still asked him what he identified as, and he'd finally set on bisexual because it was the easiest route to explaining about Trish and Max. It didn't sit right with him, and he leaned more towards the gay label. But it didn't matter to him what he was labelled as, he loved Max and that was that.

He sat up. "What's the plan now? Where do we go from here?"

"Well, the police and I have all the information we need to go for immediate trial but whether they will allow it is another matter. I need to speak with a few more people to find out what's going to happen from here out. I just thought I'd come and tell you so you knew, rather than hear it on the grapevine." Samuel leaned forward, rested his hand on Trent's shoulder and squeezed.

"Thanks, Sammy. I appreciate it."

"Don't worry, Trent. She'll definitely be going down. I'm just not sure for how long." Trent nodded. "I'm going to head out and get started on chasing down the people I need to. I'll keep you posted with the information I get. Hopefully, we can get a quick trial so it's over and done with." Samuel stood after squeezing his shoulder once more.

Trent felt Max stand and heard him and Samuel talking before the front door closed. His mind had gone on hiatus now, he didn't know what to do.

"Hey, you," Max said, quietly. "How are you holding up?"

Trent thought about the question for a moment. "I don't really know what to think. Although Samuel said she's in custody because I've not seen her, it seems as if it's not real. Does that even make sense? I don't want it to mess up our lives. I wish so badly she'd just stayed gone. Not because I don't want her to pay for what she did, but because it's messing us all up again."

Max knelt on the floor in front of him. "Nothing is going to mess us up, Trent. I promise. There is only good that can come from her being arrested. We can finally close the door on the 'what if's.' We now know there is an end in sight. Once this is finished, we can finally put it behind us. I know you've put on a brave face all these months, but I know it was always in the back of your mind. Now, we can finish it. Together."

Trent looked at Max, saw the determination in his eyes and took strength from that. Nothing could tear them apart. At least he hoped nothing could. "I'm sorry for rebuffing you," he said suddenly.

Max looked at him confused. "Rebuffing me? When?"

"The first time you kissed me. I remember being so

confused and conflicted. But I pushed you away and hurt your feelings. I'm sorry."

Max smiled. "Well, it all worked out for the best, didn't it?"

Trent smiled back and leaned in for a kiss.

It had taken two weeks before they could have a trial, which was fast in the scheme of things, but not to Trent. Samuel had worked his magic and managed to keep Trish and George detained without bail, saying they were a flight risk as evidenced by their previous taillights. The trial hadn't lasted that long, only about three hours, but it had felt like a lifetime during the process.

Max had insisted on being there, making things a little easier on Trent, especially as Jocelyn and Harper had been there too. Neither of his daughters had wanted to see Trish before the trial, even though Trish had requested a visit. He didn't blame them. His friends and family had been there to support him: Carter, Luke and Ava had his back, his mother sat quietly next to them, Sean, Asher, Zak, Ethan and Logan had all been there as well. Eric had been on set and sent his apologies.

His mother had been a pillar of strength. Ever since he told her he was gay four months ago, she had been on the phone constantly checking he was doing okay and making sure no one was "giving him grief"—her own words. She hadn't been surprised at his declaration and when he'd asked why, she just said that he had always liked boys more than girls, even from an early age, so she had never been worried until he chose Trish. All the time he'd been with her, his mother had worried. She didn't have that feeling about Max, she said. He was a godsend. Trent agreed.

Samuel had declared Trish an unrepentant mother, who had caused her children emotional distress, instability and a certain degree of neglect. Harper's statement was read out in court, detailing the things she'd had to deal with: cooking her own food, washing her own things, buying food for the house, cleaning. Trent had been devastated when he'd heard it, looking at Harper in distress when he'd found out this had been happening since just after he'd left. Harper had been eleven, and she hadn't said a word to him about it. He planned on discussing it with her later, not to upset her by telling her she should have told him, but to apologise for not seeing it happening.

Jocelyn's statement was also read out. She was able to explain the more intimate side of her mother's life. She knew about the men Trish had brought home over the years, she knew about the affairs with married men and other stuff as well.

George Pickering had received a reduced sentence because he had provided additional evidence against Trish. According to George, Trish had been swapping out Trent's B12 prescribed tablets for her own anxiety medication. Trent had worried about proving this because his medication had been used and his prescription refilled several times over the last few months. Samuel had explained that. He'd told the court that when he'd seen Trent after their phone call and hospital visit, he'd been concerned about his demeanour, it hadn't seemed right to him. They'd taken the medication to the hospital with them, but Samuel had confiscated the bottle on the way home and had Trent refill a new prescription.

Samuel had been able to get the bottle tested, and once it had been, the police had confirmed the results: Trish's fingerprints were all over the bottle and the capsules inside. This had been the cause of Trent's headaches, nightmares and jitteriness. Unfortunately, the results had arrived after Trish had already fled. As for the missing items, well, that was explained when Trent had found the receipts in her desk and when police had watched CCTV evidence. She had been entering Trent's house, stealing his belongings and pawning them off for the money.

To say it was eye-opening was an understatement.

It made Trent realise how out of touch he'd become in his own life since he'd divorced Trish. And from that moment, he vowed to be better. He knew exactly what he wanted from his life now.

As they left the courthouse into the fresh air, he took a deep breath and pulled Max to a stop.

"You okay?" Max asked, ever the worrier.

Trent nodded. "I love you. This court case has made

me realise just how much I love you. It's made me realise how much you support me, how much you make my life better, how much you keep me young," he said with a grin. "You have been with me every step of the way through this fiasco, through my awakening, through getting to know my children again. You have made my world a better place. You've made me want to live life to the best of my ability. With you by my side, and I cannot thank you enough."

He knelt on one knee, keeping eye contact with Max, seeing his eyes widen and hearing gasps around them. He reached into his pocket for the ring he had been keeping on him for the last two months, waiting for the right time.

"We've never been a couple to take things slowly, ever since the first moment. I don't see why this should be any different. I know how I feel, I know what I want. It's you. With me, beside me, before me, after me, any which way I can have you. I love you with all that I am and all that I'll ever be. Max Hughes, will you marry me?"

Trent saw tears running down Max's face as he croaked out, "Yes."

He smiled and slid the ring on Max's finger to the applause all around them. He stood and kissed Max softly, wiping away the tears with his thumbs. "I love you."

"I love you," Max replied, wetly, holding Trent tight.

FOUR MONTHS LATER

MAX

He couldn't believe how much had changed in the past year. He had known Trent for a little under two years but everything between them started one year ago today. It was only fitting that they married on the same day.

He was getting married. Max bit his lip as he smiled. They were not having a huge wedding, just a small registry office one with a few family and friends, then they'd go back to Crush for the reception, thanks to Tom; he had insisted on closing Crush for the afternoon so they could celebrate in peace.

Max messed with his tie again, straightened his jacket and altered his collar. He was eager to get moving but waited for Jocelyn to say he could leave the room. Jocelyn and Harper had received their engagement well and had taken it upon themselves to work with Tom and Ginny for the reception. Max and Trent had left them to it, happily. As far as they were concerned, the reception was more for their friends and family to mingle. They both just wanted the wedding done so they can officially call themselves married.

He had sent invitations to all his family and almost everyone had confirmed they would be there. He hadn't expected his parents to come, especially as the invites had been clear that he was marrying a guy, and they didn't disappoint when their refusal was received.

A knock rang out and Jocelyn poked her head around the door. "Time to giddyup!" She laughed. Max rolled his eyes and shook his head. "What?" She looked at him innocently. Jocelyn had decided to take care of Max this morning, and Harper was with Trent.

"Sometimes I wonder about your age," he replied smirking.

"Not much younger than you, stepdaddy!" she joked.

Max stopped. It was stupid but he just realised what marrying Trent meant. He was gaining two daughters. Two daughters.

"Sorry, Max. I won't joke about it again." Jocelyn sounded upset.

He walked to her and hugged her tight. "Don't be sorry." He let her go and looked at her. "I'm stupid. I've just realised, I'm gaining two daughters." He smiled at her. "I have two daughters." He hugged her again, then pulled back, seeing tears running down her face. "Oh, sweetheart, you're ruining your makeup." He went and searched for a tissue.

"So worth it," he heard her say. He walked back to her with tissues, trying to help clean her face. "It's okay, I'll go check it in a minute."

"I love you, Juice. As much as I love your father." He hugged her again despite her laughter at his using her nickname and felt her wrap her arms around him tightly.

"I love you, too, Daddy."

"God, now you're making me cry!" He pulled back, wiping his eyes.

Ginny pushed through the door, eyes wet too. "It's time."

Max sniffed, wiped his face and straightened his jacket for the tenth time. "I'm ready."

They had agreed to not see each other before the wedding but with a little twist. They had spent the night together but had parted ways at eight this morning. It was now nearing one and Max wanted nothing more than to see Trent. He was bundled into the wedding car Tom had insisted on paying for and sped off.

After arriving, he was taken to a small room to wait, and Jocelyn said she was going to go see her dad, and then she'd be back. He was alone with his thoughts and memories again. At least until there was a knock at the door. "Come in." He looked up and saw Harper standing hesitantly in the doorway. "Come here, Button." He pulled her into his arms and hugged her tight.

"Ti amo, babbo," she replied. *I love you, Daddy.*

He swallowed hard at hearing her call him Daddy. "Ti amo, figlia," he replied, wetly. *I love you, daughter.* She pulled back in surprise. Max shrugged. "I've been learning a few words. I thought it might help you." Now, it was her turn to tear up. "Stop! I can't have you and Jocelyn looking like I've made you cry!" He laughed.

"Thank you for making my dad so happy."

"You don't need to thank me. He's made me just as happy. You all have."

They hugged again, and then Ginny was back saying it was time to go. Harper quickly ducked out to go back to her father, and Jocelyn came running down the hall as they were heading to the registry office. She linked her arm through Max's, and they waited for the door to open. Janie was stood in front of them ready for her flower girl duties, and Max quickly leaned down to kiss her cheek.

Max's breath caught when the doors finally did open, and he saw Trent standing at the front of the short aisle. He smiled at the most gorgeous man on the planet. The music began, and he walked the last few steps as an unwed man.

Max and Trent stood at the entrance to Crush, welcoming everyone as they entered, hugs and handshakes all around. When he saw Charlotte enter, he enveloped her in a hug, which she reciprocated. They clung to each other for a while before Max pulled back. "Thank you for coming," he said sincerely. When he'd sent the invite to her, he really hadn't been sure whether she would come or not.

"How could I miss my baby brother getting married?" she said with a tremulous smile. "I'm sorry Mark isn't here." She didn't need to say more. Her husband was a good man, but he took Max's parents' side on the whole "gay" thing.

"It's fine. You're here, which is more important. Thank you." He hugged her again, then introduced her to Trent. "Charlotte, this is my husband, Trent. Trent, my sister Charlotte."

"Nice to meet you, Charlotte."

"You, too, Trent. Congratulations."

"Thanks."

"I'll see you both later." She walked off straight to the bar.

"Maxy!" He turned at his nickname and braced himself when he saw Livvy running towards him. He caught her up in a hug, almost toppling when she wrapped her legs around him too.

"Jesus, Livvy! Give a man some notice." He laughed.

She jumped down again. "Why? You've never dropped me yet!" She turned to Trent. "You must be my new brother." She grabbed Trent and hugged him, whispering something in his ear. Trent nodded and smiled at her.

"Nice to meet you, Olivia. And thank you for the painting you sent. It's amazing."

She waved her hand. "Bleurgh! Livvy, please. I'm not stuck up like 'those people at home,'" she effected a posh voice with her final words. "And you're welcome."

They all laughed. "I love you, little sis," Max said.

"Love you too. Now where are my nieces?"

Trent chuckled. "You are going to get on so well with my daughters. They're over there." He pointed to the head table.

They welcomed more and more people until Crush was almost bursting. One final person shocked Max because he'd never received an answer.

"Kieren!"

"Hey, Max. Long time, no see." Kieren held his hand out for a shake, but Max pulled him in for a hug.

"Jesus, I didn't think you'd come."

"I wasn't sure if I would be able to make it, so I didn't want to say yes or no and disappoint you."

"You wouldn't have. I would've saved a seat regardless. Wow. I'm so glad you're here. Trent, this is Kieren. Kieren, Trent."

"I've heard a lot about you," Trent said, shaking Kieren's hand. Max expected jealousy, but he couldn't see any in Trent's posture.

"You, too, though I've been out of touch a bit over the last few months. Congratulations."

"Thanks." Trent looked over his shoulder. "You're the last, so let me go sort out a seat for you."

"No, don't—"

"It's non-negotiable. I'll be back in a minute." Trent wandered off, and Max watched, smiling.

"You're happy."

Max turned to Kieren. "I am."

"Is he good for you?" The inflection in his tone made it clear what "good" Kieren referred to.

"Very."

Kieren nodded.

Trent returned. "I've sat you with Max's sister Charlotte if that's okay? There was a seat next to her for her husband, who didn't come."

"Great, thank you."

They watched as Kieren went off to find his seat. As Max looked around the room, he wrapped his arm around Trent's waist. All their friends and family together under one roof. What more could he ask for?

Two hours later, it was hard not to notice the interaction between Charlotte and Kieren. Max was unsure what it was, but they seemed to know each other already, and they were having what seemed to be a heated discussion.

"Are you okay?" Trent asked him, making him tear his eyes away.

"Yeah." He looked back at Charlotte just in time to see Kieren take her hand under the table. He frowned. He'd have to speak with Charlotte later.

"Time for the speeches," Tom called. Max smiled as Logan stood up to start the ball rolling.

Logan cleared his throat. "I remember when..." and they were regaled with the mishaps and mayhem of several of Trent's past indiscretions, much to his embarrassment and humour. Zak and Sean had stood up for him jointly since they understood about Sean's panic attacks and enjoyed embarrassing him too.

Then Janie had stood up next to Tom and had been handed the microphone. "Uncle Trent, Uncle Max, you're the best, and I have something for you." She gave the microphone back to Tom and received something in return. She walked towards them as quickly as she could without running, then stood in front of their table, holding out a red heart. Max's eyes teared up at the sight of the red heart decorated with their names, identical to the ones that were already pinned up on the noticeboard beside the bar. Charlie and Josh had been the first to receive a heart, then Tom and Ginny had added to it. As couples found their true love, hearts were added. And now, it was their turn.

This was turning out to be the best day ever.

BONUS CHAPTER

He walked down the street late at night, nothing but the infrequent streetlights leading his way, not even the moon. He was pissed off. He couldn't believe that asshole had got him banned from the clubs. Now how was he going to get his kicks?

"Fucking asshole," he said, huffing a breath. He had to find somewhere he could go. He hadn't found anywhere else where he could get what he needed: hardcore fucking with a large amount of pain, for the sub of course, not him.

He heard a car coming and moved to the side of the path, knowing, with the rain they'd had, that any car would splash water onto the pavement. He could do without walking home wet. He shook his head, where the fuck was he going to go.

The car, or van he realised as it came past him, stopped, and the back doors opened quickly. He stopped, thinking they needed directions or something, but two men jumped out and grabbed hold of him.

"What the fuck—" was all he managed before the air was removed from his lungs with a well-timed punch. Doubled over, he was unable to resist when he was dragged towards the back of the van. He was thrown in and the last thing he saw before a hood was placed over his head was a man silhouetted by a streetlight, lighting a cigarette, then exhaling the smoke.

"This would never have happened had you just abided by the rules and guidelines of the contract. Get ready to learn to consequences. Take him away." Then he heard, "Go!" as the doors slammed shut, and he felt the vibration of the van moving down the road.

Would you like to read more about Crush? Grab Book 4 now: Deep Down

Sign up to my newsletter to get the free Crush prequel short story, Love Conquers.

If you have a moment, would you write a review for Primary Seduction please? Reviews help other readers decide whether they would like to read the book, and therefore, are also important for authors.

ACKNOWLEDGMENTS

Emma Brown
Wendy Stone
Courtney Green
for all your help, this book wouldn't be the same
without you

To my readers
I thank you from the bottom of my heart for taking a
chance on reading my books

Thank you x

I am Elouise East but feel free to call me Elli. I write sweet and steamy connections in gay romance. I also touch on taboo stories under the name Elouise R East.

Books that tell the stories where friendship and family are the focal point - be it blood family or chosen - is very important to me. That's why I include a variety of personalities, talents, ages, situations and abilities as I believe a story needs, or a character needs. I want my characters to be real, to be relatable, to be free to have whatever views they tell me they have. And trust me, most of the time, I do not have *any* say in the matter!

My characters come to life on the page for me as well as my readers. Their stories unfold in front of me, and I have very little input into how they want to be shown. Just like real life, the lives of my characters change with every choice, every interaction and every conversation. And I wouldn't have it any other way.

I write books that are emotionally realistic, even if liberties are taken with other aspects of my stories. I don't know any other way to write. It comes from deep inside.

Who am I? A single parent to two children who make life worth living. An avid reader who still devours every book she can get her hands on. A student of learning about any subject that takes her fancy. An author of books she would read herself. And a romantic at heart who loves anything cheesy.

Who's in?

Stalk me here... ;-)
Website
Newsletter
All links

Soothe Me, Daddy

Spoil Me, Daddy

DARK & DIVERGENT

A Biker Make Three

Forbidden Temptation

Too Many Secrets

CHARMED

Treehouse Whispers

Rhythm Inside (Heard it in a Love Song Anthology)